S0-BNH-786

REBEL ON HORSEBACK

Also by Maxine Neely Davenport:
Saturday Matinee
Murder Times Two

Santa Fe 2017

REBEL ON HORSEBACK

Maxine Neely Davenport

Maxine Neely Davenport

Lance Publishing
Santa Fe, NM

Rebel on Horseback
A Novel

By Maxine Neely Davenport

First Edition

Printed in the United States

Published by: Lance Publishing
                  1205 Maclovia Street
                  Santa Fe, New Mexico 87505

Copyright ©2014 by Maxine Neely Davenport

All rights reserved. No part of this publication may be reproduced, distributed, or transmitted in any form or by any means, including photocopying, recording, or other electronic or mechanical methods, without the prior written permission of the publisher, except in the case of brief quotations embodied in critical reviews and certain other noncommercial uses permitted by copyright law. Permission requests should be mailed to the publisher.

Rebel on Horseback is a work of fiction. Names, characters, places, and incidents are products of the author's imagination and are not to be construed as real. Any resemblance to actual events, organizations, or persons living or dead is entirely coincidental.

ISBN: 978-0-9892431-1-7

1. Fiction.   2. Contemporary Women.   3. Western.

Cover art and interior layout by MediaNeighbours.com

This book is dedicated to my family.

Contents

The Migrants

On the south bank of the Rio Grande, where it winds between El Paso, Texas, and Juárez, Mexico, nine people crouched in a makeshift hut and waited for rain clouds to cover the full moon illuminating their location. Their excitement was tempered by fears they could die crossing the river into the United States, or they could be captured by the Border Patrol and returned to their native homes, only to begin the dangerous trip again. They waited in the village of shacks that served as temporary shelters for Latin Americans traveling north with dreams of finding jobs across the border.

Ramón Chavez bent forward, pretending to be absorbed in *All the Pretty Horses*, a dog-eared novel. Wire-framed glasses and a scruffy beard added to the disheveled appearance he'd adopted to hide his identity. With unkempt hair, faded jeans, and an extra-large T-shirt, he hoped to look and act like one of the locals determined to start a new life in America. He wore hiking boots that had seen better days. A baseball cap hid his forehead and shadowed his dark eyes as they shifted from the book to sneak quick inspections of his companions. The room stank of sweat from bodies held captive for several hours, waiting for their *coyote* guide to signal they could move on. Ramón ducked and covered his nostrils to filter the odors as he peered through long, thick eyelashes, making a mental note of each migrant's appearance, body language, and conversation.

He had positioned himself as a leader when he ordered one of the men to move away from a young mother who cringed as the man rubbed against her body. Ramón pushed between them, forming a barrier to protect the woman and realized, too late, this action might make him the target of a wolf pack forming within the group. If that happened, it would compromise his undercover work for the US Immigration and Naturalization Service. In training, he had learned that migrants now used the protection of informal gangs, called wolf packs, to improve their chances of a safe passage into the States and employment in a country that no longer welcomed them. He anticipated that an alpha leader would emerge by the time the *coyote* beckoned them to the river, and the others would be willing followers.

So far, the leader had been Pablo Mendoza. He sat near the door, nervous, distracted by a restless child in his arms. He suspected the young man knew little about the men he had recruited for this escape or that he was aware of how vulnerable these groups had become since Congress stepped up efforts to stop the border crossings. The INS had invested in better training, better detection equipment, and better-trained agents to crush the gangs—some with Mafia ties—who were establishing stash houses in remote areas of the United States, from which they transported the undocumented workers to farms and ranches across America. Ramón felt confident Pablo Mendoza was not aware that one of the newer undercover agents was buried within his group.

At the moment, Ramón had other worries. He wrestled with the complication he'd created by protecting the woman. Like the migrants, he could not make it as a loner, and he had very little time to rectify his course. His best bet was to make friends with Pablo, who unknowingly might lead him to the Mafia connection.

Pablo lifted the small child to his left shoulder and shook his right arm to restore the blood flow. Recognizing an opportunity, Ramón reached out to take the little girl, and Pablo willingly handed her over.

"Gracias. La niña es Rosita, mi sobrina." Pablo looked toward María. "Su madre es María, mi hermana."

Ramón nodded. "Me llamo Ramón," he replied and settled the sleeping child in his arms, holding his book with a free hand so he could continue pretending to read. He pulled the bill of his baseball cap lower, making himself less noticeable to the pack, allowing a better view of the child's uncle.

Pablo glanced at his watch. In exchange for free passage to America for María and Rosita, he had promised to recruit migrant workers for Raphael Cruz. The *coyote* should have been here by now. His reputation as one of the most successful guides in the business assured Pablo that if anyone could get them safely to the United States, Rafael could. However, every minute counted. Why the delay?

His eyes bore into this Ramón, who had offered to hold the sleeping child. The man seemed honest, with no ulterior motives, but Pablo had learned to trust no one. Prior to this trip, Pablo had been in the States for three years with a legitimate green card, but he worried that his return to Mexico could cost him his job in America; if he were caught crossing the Rio Grande with illegal immigrants, he would lose his card. He should have acted sooner to get María and her child across the border. His body felt heavy, as if it were filled with a weight that would drag him under water if he tried to cross the Rio Grande a second time. He imagined sinking in the river or being unable to run when they landed. He also worried that Rosita was too thin and pale to make the trip across the desert if they failed to connect with the van. Her restless whimpers frightened him. Glowering at his sister, he ordered her to stop weeping. María wiped her eyes and his heart softened. Her beauty made her even more vulnerable. He hated the men who didn't bother to hide their lust as they stared at her. He knew if he were captured, María and the child would be worse off than when they lived in Mexico. His eyes shifted back to Ramón. Perhaps this man would be willing to protect his sister if Pablo were captured. But something in the stranger's demeanor bothered him. He, alone, was reading a book. He had gone to school, maybe worked in an office. Truth is, Pablo thought, an educated man would be better for María, if it came to that. He looked at his watch. Clouds or no clouds, they must cross the Rio Grande tonight.

On the opposite side of the river, his Ford Expedition hidden in tall brush and cacti, an American Border Patrol agent sat manning a scanner, which caught the images of moving objects crossing the river or of immigrants running the first few hundred yards into the desert. Sometimes it pictured only the motion of tree limbs waving in the wind. The agent's shoulders tensed, and he stretched to ease the pain. Damn the wetbacks who made his life miserable and damn his supervisor for assigning him duty on the July 4th weekend. The job should have been given to one of the agents with less seniority. He moaned as gas pains shot through his gut. The tamales he'd picked up from a street cart on the way to work were putting his bowels on red alert. Clutching his belly, he notified headquarters he had to take a break and jumped out of the Expedition without waiting for their acknowledgment. He hurried around a cactus plant several yards from his vehicle and squatted.

Across the river, Rafael's scout monitored the border agent's message. Smiling, he lifted his cell phone to inform Rafael that all was clear to cross the river.

Rafael slipped down the street to the tin hut and opened the door. "¡Vámonos!" he whispered. The tallest man among the immigrants hurried forward and waved his friends to follow him. Three men pushed forward to be first in line. Ramón sighed; the wolf pack had formed behind the alpha leader.

Rosita woke and reached for her mother. Without speaking, Ramón exchanged the child for María's backpack and water jug. Carrying her heavy load with his own, he followed them to the river's edge. The boat wobbled alarmingly as the parties crowded aboard. Rafael pushed the boat into the stream and jumped in. He maneuvered the craft to avoid inner tubes and rubber boats carrying other desperate men and women. As they reached the far shore, the immigrants tumbled over each other, following Rafael up a well-worn trail toward a van waiting to transport them from Texas through New Mexico to Colorado.

Far away they could see fireworks brighten the sky over El Paso, as Texans began early celebrations of Independence Day.

2

The Bears

In northern New Mexico, a cool breeze diluted the heat reflecting off Brazos Mesa as Cara Morgan guided her horse up a narrow, rocky trail. Behind her, Clay Thompson followed, riding the Appaloosa he boarded on the Morgan ranch. Reluctantly she had agreed to take her father's place as Clay's fishing companion this Sunday morning, and they were on their way to a lake on the other side of the bluff. He stopped as Cara pulled aside to inspect a pile of steaming bear scat, dropped moments before in the dusty trail. She pointed through the trees toward the top of the mountain. "Looks like a sow and her cubs. Their tracks go up that way."

Clay pulled his horse aside. "Tell 'em to stay on the east side. I don't want to fight with a momma bear over the fish I catch."

Cara lifted her eyebrows. "That's assuming you catch one."

Clay pushed the Stetson off his forehead and gave her a quizzical look.

Ignoring him, Cara turned her horse to look at the valley below. "Nice view of the ranch house from here." Halfway up the mountain trail, one could look down on the headquarters commanding fifty acres of housing, barns, corrals, and fenced pastures in the lower valley. The log house her father built for his bride in 1968 faced east, set back fifty feet from the road, overlooking a broad meadow leading to the narrow Junction Creek, where water rolled over sculpted rocks that had fallen eons ago when the peaks formed. Far below, out of sight, a waterfall tumbled hundreds of feet into a natural pool, then hurried on for miles to join the Brazos River, which fed gardens, hay fields, and orchards on its way to the Chama River and finally on to the Rio Grande and the Gulf of Mexico. Heavy snows had fallen during the winter, and now in July, white patches still draped over the tip of the peak like a crocheted edging, slowly melting into lacy patterns. In addition to the ninety-five thousand acres encompassing the ranch, their corrientes—low-cost cattle rounded up and shipped from Mexico—grazed on another five hundred acres of leased government land extending north to Colorado.

The narrow trail Cara and Clay followed led over the mesa and served as the passage for the fall cattle drive to winter pastures. It cut along the edge of massive red rock on their left, leading around and over the mesa, where it dropped to meadows and a spring-fed lake on the south, surrounded by ponderosa pine, Douglas fir, and quaking aspen. Below the trail on their right, enough soil clung to the mountainside to support the growth of thick junipers and rabbitbrush for hundreds of feet down to Junction Creek. Cara lifted her binoculars to search the barnyards for Tony, the ranch manager. He would be checking on a prize registered Highland heifer, due to have dropped a calf last night, or perhaps he was welcoming the vanload of migrant workers scheduled to bale hay this week. If they had arrived, the van probably was hidden in the large barn near the corral or had been driven up the mountain road to the employee's camp near the lake.

Tony was nowhere to be seen, and Cara lowered the binoculars, wondering if she should have stayed home to oversee this employee operation. She worried about hiring undocumented Mexicans or Guatemalans coming through Texas rather than from the orchards of California. However, such gambling was part of her job. While Tony followed her father's scrupulous practice of hiring only documented workers, he never challenged Cara's instructions to ignore the law when they were desperate for employees—as long as the INS continued to look the other way. Until recently, there had been little danger the Service would clamp down on the ranchers' widespread practice, but she had read in the paper last week that Congress planned to pass tougher legislation to cover the loopholes. She now worried the INS would begin spot-checking the ranches for undocumented workers, because it was rumored that ranchers were providing drop-off sites from which the workers were being dispersed to other states. Those sites had been dubbed "stash houses," and most were dealing in illegal drugs as well as undocumented workers. According to the paper, Quail Creek, Colorado, had become a hub for the dispersal of migrant workers, and the village of Chama, New Mexico, only fifteen miles west of the Los Lobos Ranch, lay on a direct path from Juárez to Colorado, making it a handy stopover for loaded vans traveling north. Ranchers were being warned that new legislation would target employers who flouted the laws.

Cara realized something had to give. In her mind, she separated the ranchers like herself, who offered employment to undocumented workers to bale hay or ride fences, from the criminals who transported migrants and drugs. However, the government position seemed to be that one crime was as bad as the other. Soon ranchers would be at risk if they hired these men under any circumstance. Cara feared that without these seasonal employees, the ranchers' cattle business would die.

A second problem—the rustling of cattle—had emerged in the past few months. Los Lobos needed to hire more laborers in the summer to harvest the hay and soybeans, plus additional *vaqueros* to inspect the fences by horseback or in jeeps. She found it impossible to reason with her father concerning this issue. She had gotten the upper hand in hiring this newest group of workers mainly because their last hiring discussion ended abruptly when her father had complained of pains in his chest. Cara called her brother Howard, a cardiologist in Denver, who insisted their father come there for a complete medical checkup. Protesting that he was strong as a horse, her father boarded an airplane to Denver, grumbling that he would miss his regular Sunday of riding and fishing with Clay, which he suspected would be better for him than a plane ride to Denver.

With that thought, Cara glanced sideways and saw Clay, slouched in his saddle, leaning one arm on his saddle horn, watching her instead of the scene she had pointed to below. He was damned good looking, sitting there like a sexy, brash movie star, with that self-assurance some men seem to be born with. His lightly tanned complexion blushed in the heat of day, and a blond cowlick waved outward when he pushed back his Stetson. His blue eyes were dark with questions. She flushed under his surveillance, embarrassed that he'd caught her sizing him up. Heaven knew she'd had plenty of chances to admire this young tenant living in their servants' quarters over the garage, but it was unlike her to pay attention to any man, certainly not one obviously much younger. She was thirty-six; she bet he was ten years younger. He had become her father's friend, and she had been careful to avoid contact. Her chosen isolation on the ranch had left her with no desire for masculine company beyond her father, their ranch manager Tony, and the revolving work force. She had determined years ago to keep secret the scars she wore, where her breasts should have been. Those physical and psychological scars were private, and she had been successful in keeping them hidden. Reveling in the personal freedom her attitude afforded, she envisioned sharing her old age with her father, single but happy in her solitude.

Hiding behind binoculars, she surveyed the mountainside for the bears, but they were nowhere in sight. "Let's go." She lowered the glasses, tightened the reins, and kicked Buck's flank, expecting him to resume the climb. Instead, he backed into the bear scat on the edge of the trail. Spooked, he danced away, one hind hoof slipping on the soft soil at the edge of the trail. His right hip dropped as he slid downward. Cara quickly leaned forward along his neck and spurred him to solid ground. He snorted in relief and shook his body to regain equilibrium. Cara hung the binoculars over the saddle horn as if nothing had happened.

Clay whistled between his teeth. He didn't know his riding companion well enough to judge whether she merely teased or truly enjoyed cutting him down to size with the remark about his fishing. However, her quick-thinking maneuver to avoid sliding down the canyon toward the roaring creek impressed him. The trail was dangerous, and he doubted he could have recovered under the circumstances. He'd never seen her ride before, even though he'd moved into the garage apartment three months ago, after Dave Morgan suggested he use it while he waited for his wife's divorce papers to track through the district court system. Living on the ranch allowed him to be near the horses he boarded there, and he could get to his construction and lumber business in twenty minutes. He'd jumped at the chance to get out of town, away from the stress of his custody battle.

On the weekends, Dave and Clay shared a mutual love for fishing and had begun a Sunday morning ritual of breakfast on the ranch house portal before riding up to the lake. During all that time, Clay had seen only brief glimpses of Cara as she worked on the ranch. Dave brushed aside her absence from breakfast as if it were normal.

She was quite a sight—tall in the saddle, strong boned and muscled from heavy work. It was hard to determine whether her deep tan came from the sun or a Hispanic or Indian bloodline. Perhaps a combination. Her lips were full and needed no makeup to draw a viewer's attention. But her eyes told more about her personality than other features. They were almost black, dusky, reflecting a brittle glint that seemed to spike through whatever they viewed. A guy wouldn't want to tell fibs in the presence of such a lie detector. Her radiant smile and jocular horselaugh reminded him of her father. Her heavy, dark hair hanging below the rolled brim of her straw hat must have come from her mother's side of the family. He'd seen her before with a long braid down her back, but never with it swinging free to the rhythm of her horse's stride.

So this is the daughter Dave is so proud of! The reasons are obvious. She's even more beautiful, independent, and capable than her father described. Why, then, was her father so worried about her future? His concern didn't jibe with her outward appearance of wellbeing and composure. He called her a rebel, with a psychological makeup that came from her mother's family—a real fighter—and he bragged that Pancho Villa was a distant cousin of his deceased wife. Clay tried to see Cara from her father's point of view. Dave had complained that, although she was as good a rancher as any son could be, "She damn well refuses to marry and give me a grandchild to keep this place going after we both die."

Those words echoed in Clay's mind as he watched the rebel daughter confidently proceed up the mountain. It did seem strange that she hadn't married, but nowadays many women were choosing career over family. While he would never have said it to Dave, he'd wondered from the man's description of Cara's solitary lifestyle whether she might prefer women companions. He squinted, in deep thought, then shook his head. Everything about her signaled she fit comfortably into the company of men. Clay had not slept with a woman since his marriage started falling apart, over a year ago. He hadn't been interested. Today, he wondered what sleeping with Cara would be like.

He shifted in his saddle, sat up straight, and chided himself for his thoughts. He was Dave's friend and confidant. He had no business daydreaming about the man's daughter, who was, after all, several years older than he and heir apparent to one of the largest ranches in the state. He would be considered a gold-digger if he made his interest in her known, and that thought offended him.

Wind whipped up the canyon and Cara pushed her hat tighter as they neared the ridge. The trail narrowed, bounded on the high side by layers of rusty-red rock separated by stripes of light ash and butter-colored rock with dull green uranium ore and gray shale. On the right side of the trail, Cara scanned below for stray cattle that might be hiding in the rabbitbrush, pinion, cedar, and scrub oak growing to the creek's edge. She grimaced as her thoughts returned to her dad. Always working—that's how he described her, but it was a habit hard to break.

She continued to search past the thicket to the creek, which formed a clear ribbon of water with white ripples highlighting the smooth round rocks on the creek bed. In scattered places, the rocks created natural dams that held the water in pools until it spilled over and rushed down past the ranch headquarters. On the path, the horses' hooves dug into the soft dirt, their metal shoes clinking on an occasional rock uncovered by snow melt or spring rains. As they neared the top of the ridge, the trees began to thin and grass flourished in the meadow. Magenta-topped locoweeds, lavender phlox, paintbrush, and wild iris spotted the plateau. Late showers had fed the grassland, creating a carpet over the soil surrounding the rocks and chokecherry trees. Moths hovered over the creamy white flowers on the yucca plants, depositing eggs.

At the top of the trail, the horses shook their heads, loosening the straps on their bridles, and trotted downhill across the meadow to the lake. Dropping their muzzles, they sucked noisily, lifting their heads at last to snort water from their nostrils.

On the side of the mountain above them, a black bear lumbered to a resting place, grunting and sniffing, her head swinging high to catch the breeze that carried the odor of fish. Ignoring the whimpering cubs following behind, she ambled onto pancake rocks that towered above a deep-green bowl of grassland and water. The fragrance she followed rose from a camp sprawled on the left side of the lake below. She flopped to her thin haunches and waited for the cubs. The sow shook her head and growled, urging the cubs to hurry. Motion across the water drew her attention, and she squinted to focus on riders dismounting on the shore of an inlet hidden from the camp.

Far beneath the bear's gaze, Clay took both sets of bridle reins in one hand and touched Cara's elbow as she slid to the ground. She almost laughed. No one had helped her dismount from a horse since she was a child. It was like having a man open a door for her. Everyone knew she opened her own doors. She'd grown up working beside men who expected her to carry her own weight. She'd had to throw a seventy-pound bale of hay or get out of the way to let a man do it, and she wasn't about to allow that. There weren't many jobs on the ranch she couldn't do as well as a man.

After staking their horses to graze in the meadow, the two walked south along the water's edge, loaded with fishing gear. Without speaking, they stopped and cast lines into the clear lake that reflected cumulus clouds and blue sky like paint on a canvas. Cara relaxed, almost forgetting the migrant problem and her father's hospitalization.

At the foot of the mountain, unaware they were being watched from above, migrant laborers reveled in their day off from work. Lying on pallets they'd carried from the nearby cabins, the employees napped or played cards. Metal clanged against metal as men competed in a game of horseshoes. The aroma from the grills triggered saliva, relieving dusty throats. Loud joking and laughter followed them as they walked to the lake to splash water over their faces. The icy bath made them gasp. The water was not at all like the warm, muddy Rio Grande they had crossed to get into the States.

The workers stopped their games as a van drove into the compound and newcomers piled out, limping, stiff from a long ride from the Texas border. Some collapsed on the grass, kissing the earth. Pablo carried Rosita to a cabin doorstep, motioned for María to take charge of her, then hurried back to the van. He and the four men in the wolf pack sped away. Ramón and three of the migrants stood near the cabins, watching the van bounce down the rocky trail.

The employees rushed over to welcome their compadres to their quarters and to learn the latest news from the homeland. Luisa, a longtime resident of the camp, dropped the wooden spoon she was using to stir the wash pot full of beans and hurried over to the mother and child. A small dog followed, barking at all the excitement. Rosita struggled out of her mother's arms and chased the puppy behind the cabins while María went with Luisa to store her possessions near a bunk. The men hurried to the tables, wolfing down their first hot meal in days. Ramón dropped his backpack inside one of the cabins, concerned that Pablo had slipped back into the van and left without explanation. His connection to the *coyote* had disappeared. As an undercover agent, he was on his own.

From the pancake rocks, the bear spun her head away from the riders to listen for the cubs. Satisfied they were near, her nose lifted and she moaned a message as she sniffed the strong aroma coming from the camp below. The bear cubs tumbled to a stop beside their mother and she growled to quiet them, but their ears perked at the sounds of the child's laughter and the barking coming from the meadow behind the cabins. Excited, they headed down the trail toward the puppy and Rosita, as she grabbed the stick and threw it again. Ignoring their departure, the sow swung her snout toward the smell of fish. Joining the child and puppy, the cubs rushed forward to snatch the stick.

Delighted to see the bears, Rosita clapped her hands and ran to pick up one of the fuzzy pets. Under his weight, she tumbled over and the two of them rolled on the grass. The cub's small claws dug into the girl's face and she froze, her eyes wide with alarm. Her screams roused the puppy to growl at the cubs, who yipped, boxing and biting in their rough play.

As the humans hurried toward the noise in the meadow, the mother bear loped to the campfire, searching for the fish. She stood alone, unnoticed, sniffing near the abandoned grill. She backed away from the heat of the fire and dug her nose into the garbage pail where fish heads lay, mouths open, eyes glazed like marbles. Her mouth full, she lifted her head to catch the frightened squeal of one of the cubs. Chewing as she ran, she galloped toward the noise. The crowd shrieked and scattered when she arrived on the scene. She slapped one of the cubs away and grabbed the dog by the nape of the neck, flinging him aside, roaring at the cubs, who retreated toward the forest. She then charged toward the screaming humans, who fanned out like a covey of birds. The cubs barked at the excitement, took small steps back toward the commotion, then stopped to watch. The sow wheeled, clamped her jaws on the child's arm, and dragged her toward the waiting cubs.

The campground exploded with noise and turmoil as the migrants threw rocks and sticks at the bear. One stone hit her in the head and she crouched, releasing the child. A rifle shot blasted through the air, and the mother bear stumbled and fell, rising and limping a few more steps. Another bullet hit her, and she lay down with a soft moan. Two other shots discharged above the migrants' screams, and the cubs dropped like toys flung to the floor.

The boom of the rifle ricocheted over the trees where Cara and Clay sat in the shade, eating lunch. Pale green aspen leaves above their heads rattled like loose change. The pair turned, staring toward the noise.

Cara reached for her hat and stood to get a better look in that direction.

"It's too early for hunting season," Clay said. "Why are they shooting?"

"We don't allow hunting around the camp, anyway. It's too dangerous." Cara's voice was harsh. Chills raced over her body as three more blasts sounded, and a babble of male voices smothered a woman's screams.

Cara's first thought was that she needed her father. He'd know what to do. "It's coming from the migrant camp. Somebody's in trouble." She ran to untie her horse. In a single, fluid motion she mounted and pulled the horse's head toward the south end of the lake.

"Hey, wait a minute," Clay yelled. "I'll go with you."

"Come on!" she called and pressed her knees into the horse's ribs, urging him to a gallop.

Cara arrived at the camp, her heart beating against the rifle now cradled on her arm. She followed the sound of the woman's screams but could see nothing through the crowd. She rode to the edge of the group and spoke to a vaquero she recognized.

"José, ¿qué pasa?" she called.

Before José could answer, other workers screamed, "¡Un oso negro! ¡Un oso negro!" They pointed to the woods where men gathered around the body of the bear. The camp supervisor stood nearby, holding a rifle.

Cara relaxed. The migrants weren't shooting at each other. She dropped her rifle back into the scabbard, jumped from the saddle, and pushed her way through the crowd. Migrants moved aside to let her near the child, whose eyes were rolled back in their sockets. A teenage girl knelt beside her, rocking back and forth, screaming with each breath. Blood covered her arms and smeared across her face. Cara's breathing quickened.

"¡Ay, Dios mío!" Spanish words slipped from her lips at the sight of bloody gashes on the child's face. She would have scars. Cara unconsciously brushed her hands across her chest.

A tall man, who had taken charge, was making headway, slowing the bleeding from the child's arm. Cara had never seen this man, nor others in the crowd, including the mother and child. Unbidden, she wondered if they could avoid the hospital, where questions would arise about the lack of proper identity papers.

In Spanish, the man in charge ordered the screaming mother to hush, and she turned to the comforting arms of Luisa. Cara eased back into the crowd and took full measure of the scene. This man did not blend into the crowd around him like the perfect piece of a puzzle. He obviously was a new arrival. His coloring was the same, but his uncallused hands were not hardened by manual labor. He wore a scraggly beard only days old. His black hair hung in long unwashed strings pulled back with a band, topped with a baseball cap similar to the other migrants.

The child cried out, and the man leaned forward and kissed her forehead, murmuring her name and Spanish words to comfort her. His movement released his hold on the artery and blood spilled over his hand. His head wrenched up and he shouted to a woman standing behind the mother.

"Déme su fondo." The woman hesitated, then pulled up her skirt and stepped out of her slip. She held it out to Cara, turning her face away from the men who looked away or examined their feet.

"Tear it into strips," the man ordered in English. "We need a tourniquet." His English was as precise as his Spanish—another anomaly. Cara grabbed the garment and ripped it into long, wide sections.

"Press here." He nodded to a spot under the child's arm. Cara pressed her hand on the artery while the man wound the cloth around the child's arm and chest. The bleeding slowed. He tied a bandage over the child's shoulder and another under her chin and over her head, to cover the claw marks on her face.

We have to get her to the hospital right away, Cara thought. Her life is worth more than the damn ranch. "We need a telephone," Cara said, wondering how she could have forgotten her own. The man frowned but didn't speak. She leaned toward him, yelling to be sure he heard. "We have to get her to the hospital!"

He faced her as if confounded by her presence. His eyes were so brown they were black, piercing, and sparks glinted behind his dirtied eyeglasses. He yanked the eyewear off and folded them into his shirt pocket.

Cara nodded toward the child. "Are you her father?" He paused, and without looking up, shook his head.

Cara switched her attention to the crowd. Someone must have answers. As if to hide what they knew, their eyes shifted from Cara's stare. Relief flooded over her when she saw Clay riding into the camp. He swung from his horse as it skidded to a stop. "What happened?"

"Looks like a bear attacked this child. She's bleeding badly. We need an ambulance." Her voice was strong but her hands were shaking.

He dug into his saddlebag. "I'll call Mountain Rescue."

As he punched in the numbers, Ramón interrupted. "Can an ambulance get up the trail?"

"They can make it."

"Call Tony too," Cara said. "We'll need the truck for passengers."

Clay nodded and walked away from the crowd as Cara rejoined the circle around the child. "What else can we do?" she asked the man in charge.

Still not speaking to Cara directly, he loosened and retied the tourniquet and began massaging one of the child's feet. Cara took the other but felt inadequate, frustrated, not knowing what she was doing, trying to mimic the gentleness of his strokes.

Clay spoke over Cara's shoulder. "They're on their way. Tony will guide them up. How's she doing?"

"Going into shock, I'm afraid," the man said. "How long will it take them to get here?"

"Tony will have to wait for the rescue van, and it'll take fifteen minutes from the ranch. Maybe half an hour."

The Hispanic looked at the child and spoke to one of the employees. "Trae un cobija." The man ran to the cabin and returned with a woolen shawl, which the man tucked around the child.

Ignoring Cara, he spoke to Clay. "The mother has no visa or green card. There may be problems at the hospital."

Clay looked at Cara.

"We'll deal with that when we get there," Cara said, irritated but not surprised the man refused to engage in conversation with her. Could it be he didn't know she was one of the ranch owners? Perhaps he did and was observing the accepted ritual of not looking directly at his superior. She told herself to ignore his arrogance. She had more serious problems. For one thing, she realized she should have taken charge of monitoring the immigrants' healthcare, despite her father's insistence that he could deal better with county officials concerning migrant issues. They hadn't dreamed he would be unavailable in an emergency like this.

She stared again at the Hispanic, who continued to tend to the child. Who the heck was he? Something about him seemed familiar, though she was sure she'd never met him. He was not someone you'd forget. His handling of this emergency, along with his language skills, indicated he was well educated. Where had he gotten his expertise in wrapping tourniquets? How did he know the mother had no green card? Was his own card in good order?

"Will you go to the hospital with her?" Cara asked. "They'll need someone who speaks English."

He hesitated and looked at the woman who comforted María. "No. Perhaps this woman can." He glanced toward the road as if anxious for the emergency vehicle to arrive. Cara shrugged as he whispered something to Luisa. She nodded and he hurried away, disappearing behind one of the cabins.

Cara stared after him, shaking her head. She felt hot blood flushing her cheeks. The man could have dealt with the hospital staff better than Luisa, who'd had no interaction with county officials. "I'll go myself," she said and strode toward the road where Clay waited impatiently for Tony and the Mountain Rescue vehicle to arrive.

Clay put his arm around her shoulder. "I picked up your fishing gear. Your catch is in the saddlebag. I'll take the horses down to the stable and see you later at the hospital."

She nodded and watched as Clay mounted his horse and led Buck toward the jeep trail. Across the meadow, the men worked furiously to slaughter the bears. They sliced through the bears' bellies, top to bottom, pulling the guts into wash tubs. The pale flesh stood out against the dark green of the forest, surreal, like a Renaissance painting of hunters after the kill.

Sure that the sheriff would be involved before long, Cara worried about the suspicions he might harbor when he found new workers on the ranch with subtle differences in dress, unshaven, trying to hide behind the regulars or the cabins. Oh, if only her father were here! He had successfully limited law enforcement access to the campsite by occasionally taking the sheriff fishing at the lake. That option was not available to Cara.

As the workers completed their work, Tony appeared, dust whirling around the pickup. The mountain rescue medical van pulled in behind him and he pointed to where the child lay. The medics hurried to her side carrying a gurney, but Tony shifted his attention to the migrants working at the edge of the forest.

"Well, I'll be damned," he said.

Hanging from the branches of a tree were the skinned bodies of the sow and two small cubs. Tony hurried toward the cabins. Cara turned and watched as he spoke to the workers, then disappeared behind the cabin where the new man had gone. Her anger returned. What was Tony doing joining the slaughtering party when he should have been assisting the rescuers? She waited in the truck until he reappeared and climbed behind the wheel without speaking.

At home, Cara hurried from the truck and went inside the house to collect documents she might need to admit the child to the hospital. Driving alone, she wished she had gone with her father to learn the procedures he followed when laborers were injured and hospitalized.

Inside the hospital, she spent nervous minutes filling out forms, hoping the child was not unattended in one of the emergency rooms. As she finished, Clay entered through the front door.

"You must have flown," she said.

He smiled. "There's no traffic on Sunday and no cops around." He checked his watch. "I guess I did fly. What's going on?"

"The child's in the emergency room. Let's go see what the doctors are doing." She picked up copies of the papers she'd signed, and they walked to the waiting room where Luisa sat, María's head resting in her lap. Luisa pointed to the room where nurses had taken the child. The door was open, but curtains hid whatever action the nurses and doctors were taking. Cara walked in, peeked behind the curtain, but retreated when a doctor growled and told a nurse to get rid of her.

"I should call my brother. I need to check on Dad, and maybe Howard can talk to the doctors down here to suggest a surgeon for the child. He must know someone at Children's Hospital in Albuquerque. I suppose the rescue people can fly her there?"

Clay nodded, handed her his mobile phone, and followed her down the hall to a quiet place where she dialed her brother's number. Cara was not prepared for Howard's shouted question. "Where have you been? I've tried reaching you for hours."

"I went fishing. Why were you calling?"

Howard's voice lowered and he choked. "Dad died this morning. He kept asking for you."

Cara could not speak. She must have misunderstood. Her father could not have died. He was not that sick when he left yesterday. Her breath came in gasps. "What happened?"

"It was his heart."

"No. No!" Cara thrust the telephone into Clay's hands. "Tell him *no*," she cried and ran down the hallway to the outside door.

Clay followed her, the telephone to his ear, his breath bouncing back from the receiver. He heard a man speaking.

"Is someone there?"

"Yes. This is Clay Thompson. I live on the ranch. Cara's too upset to talk. What's going on?" He listened in shock as Howard explained his frustration at not reaching Cara before their father died. Howard asked him to explain to Cara that her father's body would be brought to the ranch late Tuesday, for burial Wednesday in the nearby church cemetery. Her sister Emily would arrive at the ranch tonight, driving from Taos.

"Tell Cara to call me when she calms down," Howard said, and Clay heard the telephone click.

He found Cara leaning on the side of her car, hiccupping sobs. Pulling her jerking body into his arms, he kissed her brow, the way he comforted his six-year-old daughter when she cried. Cara began to relax.

"I'll take you home," Clay said. "Howard said your sister would drive up from Taos tonight."

Cara pulled away, confused. "Shouldn't I go to Denver?"

"You couldn't see him tonight, Cara, even if you went." Clay voice dropped. "He won't be at the hospital. Your brother said they'd bring his body here late Tuesday."

Cara began crying again, her thoughts tumbling. Why hadn't she called Howard before she left to go fishing? If she'd stayed home, she could have flown to Denver and perhaps seen her father alive for the last time. Why had the stupid bears come out of the mountains today? And what parent would allow her child to play alone in the meadow behind the cabins?

She wiped her tears and tried to control her anger at the migrants, at the bears, at the doctors who had failed her father, and yes, even at Clay, who failed to understand her need to be with her father immediately. Her jaw tightened. Her whole body ached. She had to get home.

"I can drive myself," she said and left Clay standing in the parking lot, alone.

3

The Burials

By the time Cara reached home, her emotions had calmed, and she regretted her inexcusable theatrics. She'd left the hospital without knowing what happened to the child. She'd left her brother hanging. She'd left Clay without thanking him. What had come over her?

"Lupe!" There was no answer to her call, and she wondered if Lupe already knew of the death and had gone to find Tony.

Lupe had come to America as lady-in-waiting to Consuelo, Cara's mother; following Consuelo's death, Lupe stayed as the housekeeper and second mother to the children. She too would be devastated at hearing of Dave's death.

Cara picked up the telephone to call the hospital and waited for the slow transfer to Rosita's room, hoping to catch Luisa. While she waited, the scene at the migrant camp flashed before her eyes like a video: this latest load of migrant workers—strangers—carelessly allowing the little girl to play alone in the meadow, then slaughtering the mother bear and cubs. What legal consequences would the ranch suffer? She should call her attorney for advice. Luisa's voice interrupted her thoughts.

"Habla Luisa."

"Bueno, Luisa. Cara Morgan here. Sorry I had to leave the hospital. What does the doctor say about Rosita?"

In broken English, Luisa explained that it could have been worse. The child would have scars on her face, but the doctor said they would be small and could be improved cosmetically. The wound on her arm was deeper. She would have to stay in the hospital. They didn't have money to pay the hospital bill.

"Don't worry about the bill. I will pay it . . . and when she gets out of the hospital, she and her mother can stay here at the ranch house until she gets well."

There was a long pause and Cara wondered if she had said something wrong.

"That's the bad part, ma'am. The sheriff came by and . . . well, he told us the county will put Rosita in a foster home when she gets out of the hospital. María's got no green card, and the sheriff yelled at her and said she should be deported—that she can be charged with child abuse for letting Rosita play with the bears." Luisa's voice cracked and Cara could hear the mother sobbing in the background.

"Luisa, tell the mother I'll call my lawyer and he'll talk to the judge. We'll do everything we can to keep them from taking Rosita or from sending María away."

Cara left a message on Frank Wallace's answering machine, asking him to call. He had to be notified of her father's death. She'd let him worry about María's status, also. Her brother's weary voice sounded forced when he answered her call. He listened as she apologized and said he understood. As he described the events preceding their father's death, Cara realized Clay had been correct. She could not have gotten to Denver before her father died. She should stop feeling guilty.

As she finished her calls, Lupe appeared at the door, her eyes swollen from crying. Not speaking, Cara ran to her and they embraced, weeping. Dave had served as both father and mother to his children after Consuelo's death. Cara could not imagine life without him. Even today, his strong, quiet demeanor would have calmed the workers in the camp and solved problems with the sheriff and Immigration Service. Time would tell whether she had handled them appropriately and whether he would have approved.

In her room, Cara hurried to shower and change before Emily arrived. The pulsing hot water rolled over deep chest scars and she cried out, reaching for the cold water spigot. Her skin continued to burn, bringing back memories of the day she and Howard ran into the kitchen, where

Lupe was frying chicken. Ignoring the cook's warning, Howard had rushed in front of Cara and reached for a piece of chicken from a plate she was not tall enough to see. Refusing to let him push her aside, she pulled on the handle of the skillet, spilling a wash of hot grease down her chest. Cringing at the memory, Cara wondered again why her mother, who was so feminine, had not demanded that she undergo restorative surgery. And why had she succumbed to a child's angry refusal, knowing how important breasts would be to her developing womanhood?

In the kitchen, Lupe sat at the table, still sobbing. Cara put her arms around the woman who had treated her like a daughter.

"Please don't cry, Lupe."

"¿Qué va pasar con nosotros?"

Cara paused, aware Lupe often reverted to her native language when under stress. Who knew what would happen to Lupe and Tony following David's death? Cara hadn't stopped to think of such consequences, even to herself, but it was true. The Los Lobos might go the way of the old Mexican landholdings that, when divided into small farms among the children, failed to produce enough income or food to support the growing families. The same thing could happen to the Los Lobos. Where would Lupe and Tony live? Would she lose them, also?

Cara stood and sucked the warm kitchen air into her lungs. "We'll have to work it out later. After we read the will. Let's not worry about it now."

Lupe nodded, dried her eyes. "We have to prepare the bedrooms for the children. Emily can sleep in Howard's room. He and his wife can take your father's room. ¿Sí?"

It wasn't a problem Cara had considered. Howard hadn't spent a night at the ranch since remarrying. "That ought to work," she said as Lupe followed her down the hall. Inside Dave's bedroom, Cara leaned against the chaise lounge where her mother had sat to read romance novels or to write letters to family in Mexico City. Cara closed her eyes, remembering the reclining figure in her frilly gown and robe. "Let's clean this room and change the sheets. They'll have to sleep here or go to a motel."

Lupe began dusting the bookcases and night stands as Cara moved pictures aside. Forgetting the cleaning, she picked up her parents' wedding picture and searched the face of her mother as a young woman.

Those eyes suggested hidden, mysterious thoughts, filled with a young rebel's excitement. If the picture accurately revealed her feelings, the newlywed was excited about her conquest. She was the perfect bride, Cara thought—rich, beautiful, unflawed. No wonder she didn't understand the daughter who argued against breast replacement surgery after the accident. Cara sighed. No wonder she herself became a tomboy, safe from competing with female perfection.

Cara kissed her mother's picture and placed it back on the bedside table. She reached for another, taken after her father brought his bride to the Los Lobos Ranch, away from society as her mother had known it, away from art and music. In the picture, she was elegant, seated sidesaddle on a beautiful white horse, wearing a leather skirt with a white ruffled blouse and holding a stylish roll-brimmed hat. Her husband sat beside her, mounted on a black gelding, dressed in heavy corduroy pants and leather jacket. He sat tall in the saddle, as if he had become owner of the greatest prize in the land. Cara knew his adoration of her mother never wavered. The one comforting thought about his death was that the two lovers were now reunited.

Down the driveway to the right of the ranch house, Ramón knocked at the back door of a small home facing County Road 84. Tony opened the door, threw his arms around his nephew, and motioned for him to sit at the kitchen table. The two men were similarly built, Tony now bent with age. Lupe smiled at Ramón. He was a picture of how Tony had looked when she married him, forty years ago.

"I need the lowdown on what you're doing here," Tony said. "Cara's gonna find out about you sooner or later, and it's sure to get me into trouble."

"If I tell you what I'm doing, you'll have to keep it a secret. You can't tell Cara." Ramón paused, as if not sure how much he should reveal. "I'm working for the INS."

Tony's face paled and he slumped in his chair. Lupe gasped and covered her mouth to smother her shock.

"How could you do that?" Tony shouted and stood up, pacing the floor. "Isn't it enough to have one member of the family in prison? Do we have to have a traitor too?"

"My father was not a criminal. He went to prison because he wouldn't testify against innocent men in his office." Ramón's face turned an angry red. "I'm not a traitor to Mexico. I'm not turning our innocent brothers over to the INS. My job is to find the dirty sons-of-bitches who lure them across the border for enormous fees, then let them die in the desert or later suffocate in the vans that break down on the side of the road. We know that half the time those *coyotes* are bringing in drugs. They're criminals. I expected you to fight on my side."

Tony walked to the stove and refilled his coffee cup. Lupe followed him and pulled cream from the refrigerator.

"I'll get fired if Cara finds out what you're doing."

"She doesn't have to find out. I'll be living with the migrants. They don't know, and I don't plan to tell them."

"What are you looking for, if it's not unregistered workers?"

"You read the papers and talk to the Mexicans who arrive here. You know how much money it takes to get across the river and to get a van ride up here. It's a rip-off. Once they get here, the American Mafia takes over and smuggles them across the country to other states. I'm trying to stop that."

"How do you know all this? The guys coming over don't talk about it."

"They don't know or they're afraid to talk. But it gets in the papers. You should have read about it. It's true, the U.S. is more interested in stopping the gangs than in protecting the workers."

Tony relaxed and surveyed the young man in front of him. So like his father, who went to law school and became somebody instead of running away from home as Tony had when he was a teenager. However, Renaldo's smartness hadn't kept him out of trouble, and here was his son, threatening to follow in his father's footsteps. Tony felt helpless to stop him.

"So what do you want from me?"

"I'm becoming friends with the companeros. I will learn from them who the Mafia leaders are, where the stash houses are, and who's shipping the extras out to other states. They're the ones we want to catch."

Lupe had remained quiet, looking from husband to nephew. "It sounds bad. What can we do to help?" Her eyes sparked the way they did when she thought she was in the right.

Tony looked at her with eyes straining against their limits. His woman had lost her wits. She should know to stay out of man talk and wait until they were in the privacy of their bed before she expressed an opinion. What was she thinking?

Ramón smiled. "Let me know if Cara Morgan makes a move to cooperate with the sheriff in arresting migrants. Word is the ranch welcomes anyone willing to work and tries to protect them, but that she's no longer willing to go out on a limb. So if they get caught, they're on their own."

"You're being pretty hard on her."

"I'm repeating what the workers say."

Tony screwed his mouth into a side grin. "And what do they say about me?"

Ramón's smile reflected his admiration. "That you're much like Cara's father. They trust you." He rose from his chair, kissed the top of Lupe's head, and held out his hand to Tony. "I have to go. Please assign me to work with the three new employees who came in on the van. They are the ones with the information I need." He disappeared out the door, leaving Lupe and Tony to worry about his safety.

Cara sat on the portal watching for Emily. Seeing her sister would make the world seem real again. She hurried out to the car when Emily arrived, and they stood embracing, without words, until Emily released her hold. "I'm sleeping with you," Emily said, and they headed for the stairs.

Cara grinned for the first time during that tragic day. The sisters had always been close, although they had such different personalities. She envied Emily's ability to see the positive side of every situation. She never worried whether day-to-day bills were paid, and in her early twenties she left college for an artists' commune in Taos, where she honed her inherent skills. She now painted portraits of the rich and famous and made more money in a year than Howard did as a doctor.

In the privacy of Cara's suite, they hugged again and wept at the shock of losing the one person who had held the family together. They also recalled the times they had confounded him with teenage antics. In the midst of their happy memories, Howard called and confirmed that the hearse would arrive at the ranch on Tuesday around five o'clock.

Waking early the next morning, Cara left Emily asleep and crept to the kitchen, where Lupe brewed coffee. She found the daily paper on the table beside her plate and opened it cautiously. She expected to find the announcement of her father's death but was surprised to see on the upper half of the front page a picture of three animal carcasses hanging from tree limbs. The headline shouted the news of the bear attack. Cara scanned the story, which described in detail the living conditions at the migrant camp. It ended by stating that Rosita's hospital bills would be charged to the county in accordance with state law. More upsetting was the revelation that María faced possible child abuse charges for failing to keep the child safe.

Cara groaned. She had told the hospital she would take care of the bills. Why must this issue make front-page news? And how could they charge María with child abuse when her child was innocently playing with a puppy? True, yesterday she had been willing to blame María, but she realized now that the young mother was no more than a child herself. She also recognized she would not make it to the hospital today, as she had promised. She made a mental note to ask Clay to go instead.

She searched for the editorial page. As expected, the lead editorial mentioned the front-page story, haranguing the laxity of enforcement of immigration laws by the sheriff's office, the police, and the INS. Cara threw the paper aside, shuddering to think of the letters this editorial would spawn in the days to come. Every rancher in the valley depended upon the pipeline to the Mexican workforce. Even though they had been warned that the government would be cracking down on the employers who hired undocumented workers, she would be blamed for bringing the issue to the public's attention.

In the meantime, work on the ranch had to continue—and fast. If a crackdown was coming, she needed to get those fifty acres of hay baled while she still had workers available. She walked to the barn and into Tony's arms, as she had when she was a child. He patted her shoulders and they both wiped away tears.

"Don't worry about a thing," he said. "The calving is going well, and we still have plenty of vaqueros riding the fences. I sent out two more vehicles so they can cover more territory."

The day's obligations provided no emotional relief, as Cara and Emily took phone calls, received casserole dishes from neighbors, and arranged flowers for the mass.

Tuesday was like a bad re-run of Monday, and Cara felt drained by the time the hearse pulled into the driveway, followed by Howard's

Lexus. Cara walked into the living room as the casket was placed in front of the fireplace. Howard bent to kiss her cheek. Emily joined them, and they stood quietly as the funeral representative opened the casket for the family's private viewing of the man who had held this empire together for over forty years. Howard, who dealt with death on a daily basis, was glad that his father had not suffered a long and painful death. For Emily, his death closed a door she had hoped to enter someday, where the two of them would share their deepest thoughts, where she would receive his blessing and approval of her way of life. Now it was too late.

Cara's thoughts were chaotic. Memory of the bear attack flitted in and out of her consciousness at inappropriate times. The knowledge that Clay was overseeing Rosita's hospital care consoled her. With Frank's legal advice, he had convinced a judge to allow María to be placed in the Hispanic home of church members instead of being jailed. No wonder her father had liked and trusted him.

Howard interrupted her thoughts. "We should tell Frank to bring Dad's will when he comes."

Cara blinked tears from her eyes. She dreaded learning the contents of the will, which she knew would define the bleakness of her future. One thing was sure—she had run the numbers—her third share of the ranch no doubt would cover the ranch headquarters and mountainous areas, with little irrigated acreage left on which to plant crops. The Los Lobos would fall to the same tragic destiny other ranches had suffered when the land grants were divided among family members. "You tell Frank to bring the will," she said to Howard. "I have to go find Tony to see how many of the crew will come for the wake. I'll be back in an hour or so." She ran upstairs to change into her riding clothes.

On the way to the stable, she realized for the first time she was now the boss of Los Lobos. That meant her relationship with Tony would have to change. He would have to accept her as the boss and pass that attitude on to the crew. She could think of no better way to assume the role than to commandeer her father's horse, a tall Andalusian gelding that he had trained and allowed no one else to ride. As of today, like Tony and the other employees, the horse should learn that she was the person in charge. Cara searched for Pepito, and he came running when she called.

"Pepito, has anyone ridden Dad's horse this week?"

"¿Gus? No, señorita."

"Catch him for me, will you? I'll get the saddle."

"Sí." Pepito hesitated before turning to get Gus from his private corral. He led the horse into the stable and stopped where Cara directed him, near a bale of hay. She threw on the saddle blanket and stepped up on the hay, lifting the heavy saddle to the horse's back. She shortened the stirrups and swung into the saddle. The gelding snorted and his muscles trembled as he anticipated a run.

A grin spread over Pepito's face, his eyes wide, as he led Gus out of the barn and handed Cara the reins. When he opened the corral gate, the horse whirled in a circle and neighed as he tried to interpret the signals from an unfamiliar rider. Pepito jumped behind the gate to avoid the horse's hooves. Cara leaned low over the horse's neck and pressed her knees against the saddle. Gus leapt forward and headed for the back pastures.

Cara's heart pounded as the horse sped past the barns. There was no comparison between the strength and stride of this horse and her beloved Buck. Now she understood why her father had refused to let others ride him. There was little room for mistakes on the rider's part. She caught her breath, sat up, and pulled on the reins. Riding Gus was like sailing, her father had said. She now understood what he meant. She pulled the horse to a smooth trot, heading toward the irrigated pastures. When they reached the meadow leading to the hay fields, she allowed him to stretch into a gallop. Cara relaxed and leaned forward, feeling a connection similar to her relationship with Buck. She slowed down and searched the landscape for Tony. He and another rider came toward her from the hay fields, the dogs chasing ahead of them to greet her. Gus snorted and pawed at the yelping dogs.

"Cougar! Sadie!" Tony yelled, and the well-trained Kelpies retreated behind his horse. As Gus pranced to a stop, Cara recognized the other rider as the man who had saved Rosita's life after the bear attack. He wore Levis and boots instead of ragged cotton pants and worn hiking boots. A Stetson now replaced the baseball cap he'd arrived in. He had shaved and looked less professorial without his reading glasses but not exactly like an everyday vaquero either. Cara was not surprised at the confident, almost arrogant ease with which he sat in the saddle. That was the way he had approached caring for Rosita, and she guessed taking charge was an inborn part of his personality. He removed his sunglasses as they approached.

Cara felt her face warm, annoyed at being caught returning the stare of Tony's companion. She recalled a similar scene with Clay on the trail Sunday. What was happening to her?

"Why you riding that horse?" Tony asked.

She turned to Tony and spoke as if there were no question about her riding any horse she wanted to. "He needs exercise."

"You know your dad wouldn't approve. Leave him in the corral. I'll find someone to exercise him." He tipped his head to the right. "This is Ramón. He can do that."

Cara shook her head, gritting her teeth. This was what she had anticipated from Tony. He had given her orders all her life, knowing her dad would back him. She was a kid in his eyes, but things were different now. The decisions were hers to make. "That won't be necessary," she said, smoothing the horse's mane. "He'll get used to me. I came out to see whether plans were set for tonight. Are you bringing the workers by the house for the wake?"

"Yes, ma'am," Tony said, the firmness gone from his voice, surprised at her rebuke.

"There will be food for everyone, and a glass of whiskey."

Tony permitted himself a smile. "Ten men, with esposas."

"I'll see you tonight."

Tony nodded. "Yes, ma'am." Cara's glance slid over to Ramón, who was replacing his dark glasses. She expected to see him among the celebrants.

Cara tapped Gus's rein against his neck and he jumped to the right, where she let him have his head. Let these men see she could ride Gus as well as any man.

A brilliant sunrise seemed out of place, shining on the sadness at the ranch as the family prepared for the funeral. Tony insisted that Dave would want his casket conveyed to the graveyard on a wagon pulled by his favorite draft horses. No one objected. Behind the wagon, Tony led Gus, who pranced under the weight of a silver-laden saddle.

Cara felt a pressure on her heart, and she breathed with difficulty. The truth was coming home. She no longer had a father to consult with or to support and encourage her. The most important man in her life, the one person in the family who shared her love for the ranch, was gone. The three siblings climbed to the buckboard seat, Cara in a calf-length split skirt with a full-sleeved blouse, clothes from her mother's closet.

A long two hours later, the mourners moved from the cemetery behind the church toward their cars parked along the road, visiting in small groups. The family followed but paused as Tony walked over to take Gus's reins from Ramón, who had adjusted the stirrups on the saddle to accommodate Cara's height. Tony led the gelding to Cara and handed her the reins.

"Gus is yours. Ride him home."

There was a restrained murmur from the crowd. Tony's face showed no emotion, but it was obvious he was challenging her to prove in public that she had the cojones to take her father's place. Cara saw it as a "put-up-or-shut-up" moment. The mourners quieted, expecting her to lead the horse back to the ranch, but when Tony held out his cupped hands, she stepped into them and swung into the saddle. Howard coughed and backed away. Emily raised an eyebrow and controlled her smile. Gus reared, fighting the bit he chomped between his teeth. Cara leaned forward, patted his neck, and spoke to him until he quieted. Glancing toward the graveyard where the past was buried, Cara recognized she had a long way to go, all on her own. Her eyes brushed past Clay, who had come to stand beside Ramón, and both leaned against the wooden fence surrounding the cemetery. She pressed her knees against the horse's ribs and together they led the procession away from the church.

As the crowd dispersed from the burial ceremony, Clay reached out to shake hands with Ramón, whom he remembered from the bear incident. He nodded toward Gus and his rider. "I'm not sure I'd want to ride that bastard."

"You are wise. Tony pled with her, but it seems she has a mind of her own. He says no one but her father has ridden the horse, and for a new rider, it is like breaking him to the saddle again. It's dangerous for a woman, because the horse can barely feel her weight." He shrugged, gazing after the procession. "She made it plain to Tony yesterday that she is now in charge of the ranch. Not many women would dare take over such a role."

"Yep. Looks like she won't take a back seat to anyone, man or woman," Clay said. "See you around," and he walked over to join Tony.

From the churchyard, Ramón waited while the crowd left. Finding private places to talk without being overheard had proven difficult. He dialed a safe number to report to Roger Scott, his supervisor at the INS.

"Roger?"

"Ramón, how are things going?"

"Fine. As I told you, I had no trouble crossing the border, and I've maintained a good relationship with the migrants who were dropped off on this ranch. I've already determined Los Lobos is not the site of a stash house. However, I lost contact with Pablo Mendoza, the man who signed me up for the trip, and with the *coyote*, Raphael Cruz. They left this ranch along with four other men who had banded together in a pack on the trip up. My impression is that Mendoza is clean. He made this one trip to get his sister and her baby out of Juárez. However, since he left them here and disappeared, he raises suspicions. I'll keep watching for him. Anything else needed while I'm here?"

"No. This is the information we need. Find out where Cruz and Mendoza are, if possible. We know the Mafia has contacts in Chama, working to set up a stash house, so be watchful."

His report finished, Ramón pocketed his phone and glanced around at the small number of gravesites. Flowers covered Dave Morgan's grave and mourners had laid single stems on many of the other sites. The trill of nesting birds made him smile. This country was unlike any place he'd worked in the past few years. He had joined the INS following the publication of a book he authored about immigration problems on the border between Mexico and the U.S. He signed up, anticipating the experience would foster another research project suitable for publication. Academic life had been pleasant, and he often admitted only a fool would have given up the camaraderie of professors and inquiring students to live in the barrios of Juárez as an undercover agent, in constant danger of exposure and "elimination."

The same danger existed in New Mexico, but the living conditions were better. He liked the migrants, who were happy to have jobs and to be able to send money home to their families. He felt welcomed and loved by his uncle, Tony, and by Lupe, who was stuffing him with good home-cooked meals on the sly.

He looked toward the ranch house. The one person he had encountered who left him befuddled and unsure of himself was the woman riding the Andalusian. She was his boss, and to preserve his migrant-worker status, he should avoid eye contact, a test he had failed at least twice in her presence. He vowed to correct that error the next time they met, but he felt a sudden need to complete this INS job, change his worker status at the ranch, and get better acquainted with Cara Morgan. There was something challenging about the way she looked at him, and he, like many men, would not back away from the possibility of tangling with a wildcat.

Larry and Lucille Martin eased out of their truck and walked toward their neighbors who gathered for the traditional meal following a funeral mass. Larry carried a casserole of green beans topped with onion rings, and Lucille cradled the blackberry pie he had urged her to leave at home. "They'll have enough food there for an army," he'd said. "No one will miss a blackberry pie."

Lucille paid no attention. She liked being told her pie was the best dessert on the table, but laudatory comments from the living were secondary to Lucille's secret wishes for the day. She had gone to the mass and burial, watching part of her history being laid to rest in the grave next to Consuelo Marquez Morgan. She felt victorious; time had conquered all.

Life had been good to her, thanks to her ability to maneuver around unfortunate happenings when they challenged her goals. She had expected to marry Dave Morgan after they graduated from high school and was infuriated when he left her "high and dry," as the saying goes, following their coupling after the senior prom. She had planned that event as the coup d'état, certain that he was an honorable man and would marry her to save her reputation should she become pregnant. Before she could spring the trap, however, he ran away to Mexico, leaving a note saying he was sorry for what happened, that she should not blame herself, but he could not settle down before seeing the world.

Her grieving was short-lived. She simply called her second choice, Larry Martin, whose family ranch lay on the western border of the

Morgan ranch. She assured him she'd thought about his offer of marriage and had decided they should elope. He was shocked but delighted, having believed Dave Morgan owned her heart. Wouldn't his pal be surprised when he returned from Mexico and found them married?

Throughout the years, the Martins' marriage remained solid. They had one child, Larry Jr., born eight months after their elopement. Fortunately, Larry Jr. resembled his mother's side of the family, and there was never a question in the minds of friends or family about his paternity. With her secret safe, Lucille's revenge became a two-pronged campaign to have the neighbors shun David's Mexican wife and to make sure her son inherited an estate larger than the one David was creating for his three half-breed offspring. The biggest barrier to her goal was the fact that Larry's ranch sat bordered on all sides by longtime owners who wouldn't sell. Today there was fresh hope. With Dave dead, she anticipated the Morgan empire would crumble. If she were successful in obtaining the better portion of the Los Lobos, her son would become rightful heir to a fortune larger than the Morgan grant. When that happened, she would return to the graveyard to place flowers from her garden between the graves of Dave and Consuelo Morgan. Let Father Angus and the rest of the community think they were intended for the couple. Only Lucille would know they commemorated the night of the senior prom.

4

The Will

The ranch house seemed ominously quiet as the last neighbor said goodbye to the mourning family late in the afternoon. Frank Wallace reached for his briefcase and nodded for Cara, Emily, Howard, and his wife Wendy to follow him into the office. Heavy lines shadowed his face, revealing the depth of pain he suffered. His relationship to Dave Morgan had been as much friend as lawyer. Their Saturday afternoon domino games and political discussions, warmed by Wild Turkey, lay buried in the cemetery. Today, Frank seemed out of sorts, uncomfortable, with his neck bulging over a tight shirt collar, his stomach stretching against the buttons of his shirt. Sunburn from standing outside at the graveyard flushed his face like the ripe skin of a tomato. He wiped perspiration from his brow as he shuffled through the documents.

Cara surveyed the room. Emily and Howard had packed their luggage before the funeral, anxious to return home. Her eyes rested on Howard, the handsomest member of the family. He got his dark good looks from their mother's Spanish ancestors and his height from Dad's Texan relatives. He reminded Cara of a television star instead of a family doctor. She had worshiped him as a child, but he quit coming to the ranch after his sudden divorce from her good friend and his subsequent marriage to Wendy, a petite nurse from his office. His wife sat beside him now, her blond hair pulled into a French knot, her hands twisting in her lap. Cara regretted the near-estrangement with her brother. Just two years apart, they had grown up like twins, until her accident. The tragedy left Howard feeling guilty and angry, but Cara suspected the real problem with their present relationship lay in their competitive spirits. As children, they fought with flying fists or small, flat rocks from the creek bed, only to make up as best friends by bedtime. Following the kitchen accident, Howard refused to make physical contact with her, but they continued to battle with words that left injuries more serious and longer lasting than black eyes. Cara refused to let him win their battles without reprisals, and as he grew taller and heavier, she rarely won the physical competitions. She resorted to besting him with higher grades in school. It was a tenuous peace they held.

Emily abstained from their rivalry, going her own happy way. She now wore her hair long, pulled from her face and clasped with a large shell conch. Her appearance came from Dad's side of the family. She resembled Grandma Morgan, standing as a bride with her hand on Grandpa's shoulder, handsome in his World War I uniform.

Cara's attention shifted back to Frank as he loosened a dark tie and unbuttoned his shirt collar. He shed his jacket, throwing it across the back of their dad's chair, then handed each of them a copy of the will.

"As you will recall," Frank began, "your mother left all her assets to your father with the understanding—though not an order—that the family estate not be divided but should remain with the three children." Frank peered over his glasses. "Such a wish is not binding. Your father remained free to do what he wanted with his property after his death. This is it." He lifted the will and dropped it on the desk with a solid clunk. His voice took on a professorial tenor as he read the legalese that took care of debts, burial expenses, taxes, etc. Cara's mind wandered as she recalled the same boilerplate paragraphs he'd inserted into her own will.

"Whaaat?" Howard's voice pulled her attention back to the reading. Why hadn't she been listening? She glanced at the will, wondering which paragraph he questioned. "Can he do that?"

Frank nodded in Howard's direction. "It's not unusual to add a clause stating any beneficiary who challenges the will receives only one dollar. It takes away the incentive to contest the wishes of the devisor. Of course, there are a few loopholes to overturn this paragraph, but we don't need to go into those." He turned the page, concluding the matter.

Cara let her copy of the will fall to her lap. She closed her eyes and could see her father dictating words to his lawyer, but they soon opened wide, unbelieving, as Frank continued reading:

"Howard's medical degree was financed from the profits of the ranch. Those, in turn, were a product of the labor and expertise his sister, Cara, contributed to the ranch. To my knowledge, Howard is independently wealthy and does not need a share of the family ranch. The same is true of Emily. At the insistence of Cara and against my better judgment, Emily was supported for years by income from the ranch. I was wrong. She is now a successful artist, supporting herself. I am proud of her.

"In consideration of the above facts, I make the following devise, knowing it goes against the advice of many estate planners, who claim it will create divisions among those who expect to share in the family estate. My hope is you children will accept the long-held dream of your parents that the Los Lobos Ranch continue on for many years as a living symbol of our love."

Frank paused and peered over his glasses to make sure everyone was listening. His voice took on the powerful boom of a lecturer intent on proving his thesis. "These next paragraphs are a lesson for any of you who may not understand why your father was so attached to the idea of preserving this estate. He trusted this reminder of its history would help you to see why it was so important to him. He wrote:

"The territory on which the Los Lobos Ranch is situated has a long, rich history. Your ancestors were a part of the metamorphosis the territory underwent from the days of the roaming Native American Indian tribes and the Pueblo Indians to the day I inherited it. You should remember from history classes that in the sixteen hundreds, New Spain attempted to settle and missionize this new world they'd captured from Mexico, until that country eventually rebelled against them. Thanks to the United States' claim of Manifest Destiny—however wrong it might have been—this land became available for settlement by your great-great-grandfather, Colonel John Lester Morgan, when he retired from S. W. Kearney's Army of the West after it invaded the Mexican territory in 1846. Because of his outstanding service, he was awarded one of the territorial grants the government offered to honorable military staff to encourage settlement. Col. Morgan passed ownership to his son, Judge Darius Lee Morgan, in 1890, who deeded it to my father in 1930. I inherited it at his death in 1984.

When he lived here, there were no fences. Today, our borders are well marked. Your mother and I want to keep them that way."

Frank looked up from the document he read to a speechless audience. He continued reading.

"With those considerations in mind and based on our state's history of declining family estates following their division by grants to each child, I have come to the conclusion that to save the Los Lobos Ranch as a family estate, which Consuelo and I intended it should be, I must and hereby do bequeath all my real property, consisting of approximately ninety-five thousand acres, now known as the Los Lobos Ranch, to my daughter, Cara Rose Morgan, such devise limited by the legal description of the property as recorded in Book 105, page 92 in the Recorder's Office of Rio Arriba County, State of New Mexico. This devise includes all houses, barns, sheds, livestock, and personal property owned by me at the time of my death."

Frank stopped reading and Cara tried to stop the uncontrollable shaking of her head. Howard's lips clamped into a straight, grim line. Emily nodded and laid her hand over Cara's tight fist.

Could it be true? Cara wondered. The whole ranch was hers? "What did he say?" she whispered to Emily.

"Dad left the ranch to you. He says he and Mother agreed it shouldn't be divided."

Howard stood and walked back and forth behind the chairs. He rubbed a fist into the palm of his other hand, then whirled toward Frank.

"Is that all?"

"Just about," Frank said. "He's giving the ranch to Cara to keep as long as she lives, provided she stays on the ranch. If she moves off the ranch, she has to sell it and divide the proceeds between the three of you. If she stays on the ranch and marries, the ranch goes to her immediate family when she dies. If she remains single, it will go to you and Emily when she dies."

"And you say if we contest this will and lose, we'll get only one dollar? I can't believe this was Dad's idea."

Cara sat, as shocked as Howard. In all the conversations she'd had with her father, not once had he hinted that if she came back to the ranch after she graduated from college the ranch would be hers when he died. In fact, he had urged her to find another career, pointing out the isolation and loneliness of living on a ranch, where the closest neighbors were ten miles away and where it was typical that all the other young people her age would leave home for city jobs. He wanted assurance that she was not returning to the ranch from a sense of duty to care for him in his old age. Another time, he wondered aloud if she were depressed.

Cara had laughed at his worries. "Do I act depressed?" she'd asked. "I'm here because this is where I want to live. If I've ever been depressed, it was when I was living in the city while I was in college. But if I'm imposing on you, please tell me and I'll leave."

It was the only time she'd seen her father cry since her mother's death. "Don't go," he'd said, and from that day on, although they acted as partners, they'd never discussed what would happen to her when he died. She had not worried about it at the time, assuming she could survive on a third of the estate. Over the years, with inflation and the changes in rural economy, that was no longer possible. She kept the books. She knew how many acres of pasture and how much bottomland under cultivation it took to meet their budget. As he said in the will, the neighborhood rancher or farmer could no longer survive on a small acreage.

"It's too bad you're disappointed, Howard," Emily said, "but I can understand why Dad wouldn't partition the ranch. He wanted to preserve the dream he and Momma had when they married. You know as well as I do, he was able to expand our acreage because our neighbors couldn't make it on smaller farms. He bought them out. He didn't want that to happen to this place."

"I'm sure he didn't make that decision alone." Howard glowered at Cara, then spewed his anger toward the lawyer. "It seems to me this should have been discussed with the rest of the family before Dad died."

Frank closed the file and leaned back in the leather chair, relaxed, as if a heavy burden had fallen from his shoulders. "Your father knew what he was doing, Howard. He didn't tell you because he guessed you'd be unhappy with his decision. He didn't want to leave this world with harsh words between the two of you." Frank closed the will. "Your dad expected you to respect his feelings after he died."

"By making sure I couldn't do anything about it." Howard dropped his copy of the will into his wife's lap.

Cara had heard all she could tolerate. She hurried out the door and crossed the dining room into the kitchen, where Lupe stood at the sink.

She ran into Lupe's arms and kissed her on each cheek. "Lupe, we can stay," she whispered.

"What do you mean?"

"We can stay here. Dad left the ranch to me. You and Tony won't have to move."

Lupe backed away, her hands flying to cover her cheeks. "The whole ranch to you? I can't believe it." Her eyes widened, her mouth opened.

The screen door from the back porch squeaked. Tony and Clay, who had been helping with construction of a new corral, hung their straw hats on deer prong racks and greeted Lupe in the kitchen. Both men were tall—Tony dark complexioned with heavy, broad shoulders and narrow hips, stooping with signs of age; Clay, young and healthy, with less wear and tear on his body, both full of life.

"Dinner ready?" Tony asked. "We're hungry as a pack of wolves."

Cara ran to Tony and threw her arms around his neck. His eyes shifted to Lupe for an explanation.

"We can stay on the ranch," the women said in unison.

"Frank read the will. Daddy left the ranch to me." Cara was blinking tears from her eyes.

Tony hugged her to his chest, kissed her cheeks, then pushed her into Clay's arms while he grabbed Lupe and whirled her in a circle around the kitchen, his boots clicking a Mexican dance rhythm on the tile floor. "That old son of a gun," he shouted. "He fooled us all."

In the excitement, Cara looked up, joining in Clay's laughter. His thumbs brushed tears from her cheeks and he kissed her lips. "Congratulations," he said.

Cara pulled away, surprised at herself. For a second time, she had invited an intimate connection with a man she hardly knew.

Lupe struggled out of Tony's arms. "Let me go," she said. "Go wash up. Both of you." She flapped her apron at the men, who retreated to the back porch. From the range she pulled a long pan of hot rolls from the oven. "The bread is done. If Frank keeps going on, everything will get cold."

Cara touched the tingle remaining on her lips and suggested that Lupe not worry. "He was about through when I left." Peering across the bar separating the kitchen and dining room, toward the office where the voices diminished, she told Lupe she'd round them up. She strode past the dining room table, laid with the family's best china and silver, but before she could reach the double doors, they opened, and Emily led the family toward the table.

"Lupe says the food is getting cold," Cara said. "Come and eat."

"I'm not hungry." Howard reached for Wendy's arm. "Let's go on into town." His face turned dark and ugly.

"You can't do that," Cara said. "There's so much food. Lupe cooked all morning to please you. Come sit down." She held a hand out to Wendy.

Emily slipped her arm around Howard's waist. "Come on. We may not see each other again for months. We should talk."

"You take Dad's place," Cara directed and pointed Howard to the head of the table, his back to the open bar. She moved to the other end of the table and sat in her mother's chair. "Frank, you sit here." Cara sat, quite comfortable with her new sense of status.

"Wish I had a nickel for every time we've gathered around this table," Emily said, as she found her place. She rubbed a finger over the scratches that cut into the thick block of oak resting on legs made from carved tree trunks. She spoke to Cara. "Now that Dad's gone, you can get rid of this old stuff."

"I can't imagine doing that. This table is part of what Dad wanted preserved." Cara looked toward the kitchen, where Lupe was handing plates to Tony and Clay. She watched as they carried their food toward the screened porch. She flushed with anticipation. She would remember these days as a special time for the family—the three siblings and Wendy, visiting and eating casual meals together. Surely the will reading could not have suffocated those bonds. Or had their father's wishes ruined all hope of a close relationship in the future? Perhaps his death had wiped away their adulthood, and she and Howard were reverting to childhood struggles over the top-dog position. She saw Emily withdrawing further from the ranch, because she was no longer required, as a dutiful daughter, to make an appearance when Daddy called. Cara shuddered. How would her new position as owner of the ranch change her relationship to the family? Already she felt empowered, no longer just the youngest of Dave's kids. She was an individual—somebody her father trusted to take over his role as head honcho. But was it possible for her to hold the family together? She looked across the bar into the kitchen and nodded to Lupe. It was time to serve her guests.

The conversation in the dining room stopped while a platter of fried chicken, a bowl of mashed potatoes, fresh garden vegetables, and rolls were passed around the table. Howard looked at Frank, "Maybe we should talk about the future of the ranch. I doubt if Cara understands the financial problems she'll have because of what Dad did. Why don't you tell us how much money she'll have to come up with in a short time for estate taxes?"

Goosebumps rose on Cara's arms. She rubbed them, wondering how she could be chilled in July. Raising her eyebrows, she waited for Frank's reply.

Frank laid down a chicken thigh bone he had cleaned with two bites. He wiped his fingers and mouth with a large napkin and looked at Cara. "You and I talked about estate taxes when we wrote your will, and I discussed it with your dad when he decided to leave you the ranch." He surveyed the table, reveling in sharing his expertise. "It used to be families around here were having to sell their ranches when the old folks died, because they couldn't raise enough cash for the inheritance tax. Congress recognized that problem and has passed legislation to ease the burden on the kids who inherit the family farm. I discussed it with Dave, but he brushed my worries aside. He said Cara was smart. She'd figure out what to do. I agreed with him." He reached over and patted Cara's hand.

"Well, the new estate tax laws may have eased the problem, but she'll still have to come up with the cash to pay them. This ranch's value is in the land and the cattle, not stashed in a bank account. In fact, this place stays afloat on bank loans that Cara will now have to negotiate."

"How much in taxes are we talking about?" Cara asked Frank.

"I figure over a hundred thousand after we take off the tax credits."

Cara felt her stomach plunge downward and lie there, dead weight. She'd never dreamed her father would leave the ranch to her, so the idea of being responsible for the taxes had never entered her mind. They used bank loans each year to cover feed and payroll expenses, then paid the loans off when they sold cattle and crops each fall. She knew there weren't thousands of dollars lying around to use for unexpected expenses. She laid her fork on the side of her plate. "This sounds like a problem for another time. Dad was right. I'll take care of it."

"Easier said than done." Howard pointed his fork at Frank. "Maybe we can work something out."

"What do you mean?" Cara interrupted.

"You could sell the ranch to me. You'd get enough money to live comfortably the rest of your life. I'll pay the taxes. I can use the write-off."

Cara envisioned the fist of a small girl slamming into her older brother's face because he was taking advantage of his greater height and strength. She had won many of those battles, before her accident. She blinked the image away. "I don't think that's what Dad had in mind."

"It's your call. Dad didn't make this decision with the expectation you'd go into bankruptcy."

"That won't happen." Her voice was sharp, but Howard refused to back off.

He pushed his advantage. "Paying the taxes is only one problem. Making this place pay its way is a job for a businessman." He beckoned to Frank for support. "Besides needing a business sense, a rancher has to manage a work force. It's not a job for a woman."

Cara felt a calmness settle over her body. Howard had pushed a familiar button. She wouldn't let him release a time bomb. "What you're saying is that you, or another man, could run this ranch better than I can." She laughed. "That's bullshit." She continued eating as if the matter were settled.

No one moved, and Cara realized everyone was staring at her. She had to admit she was a little surprised herself. She usually reserved her foul language for moments when she was alone.

All heads rotated toward Howard, who paused before he answered. "Dad was successful because he knew the ropes. He hired cheap labor, and he kept a tight rein on them. He wouldn't admit it, but half those wetbacks he hired are criminals. Because they're good workers doesn't mean they can be trusted out of your sight."

Lupe stood behind Howard, ready to remove his empty plate. She marched to the kitchen empty handed.

"Howard, you owe Lupe an apology," Emily whispered. "I can't believe you're so thoughtless."

"I wasn't talking about her and Tony," he muttered out of the corner of his mouth. "She knows that. It's the seasonal workers you can't trust."

"The seasonal workers," said Cara, "who are expected to live on minimum wage, and if you kept up with politics, Howard, you'd know this particular cheap labor force will disappear within the next year or two anyway. But you're right. We've survived by hiring undocumented workers from Mexico. That will stop. Dad knew it as well as I do." She stared at Howard. "I'll find a way to replace them."

"Exactly what worries me. Times are changing fast, and it will take real savvy to find a way to survive in the next few years. Dad started with what was left of his family's land grant and developed it back into his great-grandfather's original size. What a shame to see all his efforts go down the drain."

"I beg your pardon, but a lot of that effort came from me. Many of those purchases were made at my insistence. We pursued that dream together, and I have no intention of letting it die. Howard, you have no idea what my business sense is. I've worked side-by-side with Dad and Frank on the financing of this place. I know how it operates better than you do."

Frank coughed and pushed his plate away. He smiled at Lupe, who came to replace it with a plate of strawberry shortcake. "Best meal I've eaten since I was out here last time, Lupe."

Everyone nodded in agreement. The conversation ceased as they ate their dessert. Emily broke the silence. "What will happen to the ranch when you die, Cara?"

Cara chuckled. "That's a pleasant change of subject. I'd as soon talk about taxes and undocumented migrant workers."

"I'm sorry," Emily said, "but Dad said in his will he expected you to leave the ranch to me and Howard if you died first. Unless you got married, of course."

Cara glanced at Emily, her eyes widening. She hadn't absorbed much of what Frank said following the words giving her the ranch.

Emily questioned Frank. "I wondered if that would happen automatically?"

Frank grinned. "Are you asking what it will take to get her married . . . or what she has to do to make the ranch revert to you and Howard?"

Everyone laughed except Howard, who snorted. "That's the only fair thing Dad put in his will. He knew she would never get married." He looked at Frank. "Tell us the process for passing the ranch on to the family."

Frank swallowed and cleared his throat, "Well . . ."

Cara's eyes flashed, unaware Clay and Tony were across the counter in the kitchen, reaching for strawberry shortcake and whipped cream. Waiting his turn, Clay lounged against the cabinet, his legs crossed casually while he glanced past the bar into the dining room, not caring that he was eavesdropping on a private conversation. His eyes rested on Howard, then switched to Cara, as if he were reading her thoughts.

Cara was relieved the subject matter had switched from taxes and employment problems to a lighter subject. This was a game she could win, because she held the trump cards. Her getting married was not something her father or Howard could dictate. "What makes you think I'll never get married?" She smiled and lifted her eyebrows.

All movement stopped at the table. Lupe stood behind Wendy, her lips parted, as she stared at Cara. Emily kicked Howard, but he ignored the warning. "You know why you haven't gotten married. I'm surprised you'd bring up that subject," he said.

His words slammed into Cara like a body blow. In her exuberance over inheriting the ranch, she had become different, someone without the weight of scars. This reminder shocked her. "I'm not the one who brought it up," she said.

Ignoring the impact of what he had intimated, Howard rested his elbow on the table and pointed his finger at Cara. "What I find intriguing is Dad's intention that you leave the ranch to me and Emily *when you die.*" He paused and surveyed the table. "If I had such a clause in my inheritance, I'd look both ways, twice, every time I walked across the road." He chuckled, shaking his head.

A pall fell over the table.

"Really, Howard," Emily said. "That's not funny. It's beneath you." She spoke to Cara. "Forgive him. He'll grow up someday."

Howard's face flushed. "Hell. You jump on everything I say, Em. Doesn't anybody have a sense of humor around here? I was joking."

Cara's ears were ringing. She pushed on them with her fingers, closing her eyes. The words hit her like a slap across the face, a threat, no matter how he intended it. Her personal choice to live a celibate life because of her scars was none of Howard's business. She would listen to no more of his insinuations. She stood, flushed with anger, her eyes escaping across the bar where Clay and Tony stood listening to the conversation.

Raising his hand to stop her, Clay set his dessert aside and walked into the dining room as if he'd come to join the party. Tony followed him to the door. Clay laid his hand on Cara's shoulder and nodded a recognition to everyone at the table. When he had their full attention, he spoke. "Your problem, Dr. Morgan, is the subject matter. Threatening someone's life isn't funny, no matter how you look at it. I suggest you explain yourself."

Howard laid down a forkful of shortcake and looked around the table. He swallowed and, glaring at Clay, said, "This is none of your business."

"You're wrong. Your dad and I were fishing buddies and very good friends. I can't imagine he'd expect me to stand by and watch while you verbally threaten his daughter's life."

"I said it was joke. Cara can take care of herself."

"It didn't sound very funny from where I stood." Clay looked at Tony, who nodded, then continued. "Cara doesn't have to take care of herself. If your father were here he'd take you out to the woodshed. He is not here, but he left friends who can do it for him." Clay spoke to Cara. "Are you satisfied that what he says clears up the threat?"

She nodded, too numb and shocked to respond to what was said.

Clay continued to stare at Howard. "One more thing, not that it's any of your business, but you don't have to worry about Cara's ability to run this ranch. Your dad told me she's a better rancher than he was. He trusted her judgment on the crops, the cattle, and the employees."

Cara remained immobilized by the tension between the men. How strange it was to have someone fighting for her. Clay's words released her from the pressure of Howard's attack. More, her father had believed in her, and his friendship with Clay had been well placed. She agreed that he would have thrown Howard out of the house for his insults. If Clay hadn't intervened, she might have done the same. She sat down, flabbergasted.

Howard's face flushed and he started to stand, but his wife placed her hand on his arm. Lamely, he said, "Lupe, I could use more coffee."

Tony spoke to Cara. "We'll be outside if you need us." He and Clay returned to the kitchen and picked up their desserts. Tony threw his arm over Clay's shoulder and guided him toward the table on the back porch.

Howard handed his cup to Lupe as he spoke to Cara. "Who the hell is that guy, and what's he doing in this house?"

Finding it difficult to control her emotions, Cara sat twirling her spoon in the whipped cream on top of her dessert. She looked up. "His name is Clay Thompson. You spoke to him on the telephone after Dad died. He's leasing the servants' quarters over the garage."

"I remember Dad saying a guy was boarding his horses here on a temporary basis. How long is he planning to stay?"

"As long as he wants to." Her strength was returning. She wanted to run after Clay and ask him what else her father had said, but at least she now knew she hadn't been given the ranch out of pity. Her father knew she could handle the employees. Deep down, he must have believed she could also handle Howard. "We're boarding his horses too. It's extra income for the ranch."

Cara looked around the table. "Dad enjoyed Clay's company very much. But the biggest advantage for us is he can send temporary workers when we run short. When he has slow periods in the building industry, his local employees can fill in for the migrant workers we may lose."

"He seems like a nice man," Emily said.

Howard was not so easily pacified. "It must be expensive, bringing help all the way from town," he said. "Where does he get them, anyway?"

"He owns a construction company and a lumberyard. It's been in business a long time, and he has contact with lots of temporary workers who live here."

Frank raised his eyebrows in surprise, peering over his glasses. "Thompson Construction and Lumberyard? That's an enormous business. Don't the Thompsons live in one of those monstrosities up on the hill, west of town?"

"They did. He moved into the apartment over the garage after his wife filed for divorce. She and the children live in the home, I believe."

Wendy touched Howard's sleeve and stood. "We'd better go. It's getting late." Cara watched as he and Wendy left without speaking to her.

Frank rose to follow them. He put his arms around Cara and kissed her forehead. "I'll talk with you next week, honey," he said and followed Howard and Wendy out the door.

Alone, the sisters moved to the living room. "Why is Howard such a horse's ass?" Emily asked.

"You know him. He likes to run things. He expected to assume leadership of the family estate when Dad died."

"Well, Dad didn't see it that way. He picked you for the job."

"And what he wrote in his will is true. I've run this place for years. Howard knows that."

"Of course he does. But he's always resented your position here, even though he wasn't willing to stay and keep the place going himself. I hope he doesn't cause problems."

"I'm surprised at Dad's decision, but when you think about it, he left things pretty much the way they were when he was alive." Cara lifted her arms toward the heavens. "I suspect he's up there right now, telling me it's time to get out to the barn and do my chores." They laughed. "Why don't you come with me and see the new calves?"

"Me? No way. I didn't go to the barns when I lived here." She hugged a pillow, resting her chin on it. "I never dreamed of being a cowgirl when we were little. It's all you've ever wanted. You're stuck here. Why don't you move off this ranch and find out how exciting the rest of the world is? This is your chance to do anything you want. Come to Taos with me. We'd have so much fun."

"I wish I could. You seem so happy. But you know I'm not like you. Ranching is what I love. It's why I came back after college. It's in my blood."

"But you've never known anything else. Nothing holds you here. You'd love Taos."

"Nothing makes me want to move, either. Living in town would kill me. What would I do? I don't have your talent. I don't have your beauty. I don't have your body. I'm who I am."

"You're sure you're not hiding out here in the boondocks?"

Cara raised an eyebrow. "What would I be hiding from?"

Emily frowned. "Yourself?"

"Are you suggesting I'm anti-social? Is that what you think?"

Emily shook her head. "You know I don't mean that. You just don't let anybody get through your armor." She pointed her finger at Cara's chest. "We come from the same gene pool. If you're anything at all like me, somewhere in there . . ." She paused and examined Cara's eyes.

"Somewhere, hidden under that cowboy disguise, is a lot of woman, and it's a damned shame you haven't found her."

Cara's voice was controlled. "You seem to be saying the same thing Howard intimated. That I'm not really a woman. Not marriage material."

"Oh, Cara. I said the opposite." She looked away. "You're still a virgin, aren't you?"

Cara flushed. "I'm surprised you'd indulge in personal insults as Howard did."

"Cara, don't be angry with me. We could talk about these things when we were young. I'll admit we didn't know what we were talking about most of the time, but sex wasn't off limits. Why now?"

"You're not talking about sex. You're talking about me and my inhibitions, as if there's something wrong with me if I haven't had sex."

"I don't think there's anything wrong with you. I'm suggesting you've cut yourself off from a very wonderful part of being human for the wrong reason. Scars are no excuse." She paused. "I'd better shut up before I do make you angry."

"No. Say what you have to say."

"Well, this is the perfect time for you to make changes in your life. Mom and Dad are gone. You've got plenty of money. You'd be a great catch if you'd get out there and meet people. You could even have plastic surgery if it's important to you."

"I don't want plastic surgery and I'm not looking for a man. I guess that does make me weird."

"No. But different from me."

Cara shook her head, smiling for the first time. "You know? You haven't changed since high school. You drove Dad crazy with all your boyfriends."

"He had nothing to worry about, believe me. If I'd known then what I know now . . ." Emily lifted her eyebrows. "We were so naive when we were kids." She checked her watch. "I have to go." As she gathered her purse and headed for the door, she called over her shoulder, "How about that construction guy? You said he was getting a divorce. He certainly seemed interested in you today."

"Emily, he's at least ten years younger than I am, and I suspect part of the reason he comes to the ranch is to get away from women."

"Oh. Too bad. Of course, you could change his mind." She waved her arm. "I need to say goodbye to Lupe. Let's go out the back way." Cara followed Emily toward the kitchen, envying the swing of her hips, the daintiness of her figure. Of course she was alluring to every man she met. In comparison, Cara was tall, brown from the sun, with muscled arms and strong hands made for work, not for flirting. But she agreed with Emily. The real difference in their lifestyles was not in their looks. It was in her mind. She hadn't moved past the trauma of her childhood disfigurement. They hugged and parted.

Cara went to her suite on the second floor of the ranch house, a space she had enjoyed since her college graduation, after she returned, determined to live and work on the ranch. Her father had insisted on building a new suite, a space to call her own. Emily's accusation she was hiding might be right. The upstairs rooms allowed her to get away from the world.

Dressed in jeans and old boots, she heard Buck whinny from the corral as she walked down the path to the barns. Distant thunder rumbled, and she knew bad weather made him nervous. She often wondered if he relived the stormy night he was born, when a wildcat found him wobbling on new legs near his mother. Cara remembered sitting up in bed that night, wide awake for no reason, then grabbing the rifle and running barefoot through the rain to the corral, knowing something was wrong. She saw the predator slinking away; inside, the jittery mother licked her foal's shiny dark coat. Cara fell in love with the colt's three white socks and the crooked blaze that ran from his forehead to the tip of his nose.

From that day, Buck whinnied when she came within his orbit or when lightening sent explosions of thunder rumbling through the valley. Today he pushed his wet nose against her neck as soon as she arrived at the corral.

"Buck! Stop it. I don't need your sloppy kisses." She pushed him toward the water tank and brushed his slobbers from her shirt. She patted each of the other horses as they gathered around her. They acted as if they'd suffered neglect during the past week while she and Tony were too busy to supervise Pepito's work.

Inside, she heard Mouser meowing from the loft. "What are you doing up there?" she called. The large grey cat disappeared without responding. "Well, you climbed up by yourself, you can get down by yourself, I guess."

She was ankle deep in the muck she was shoveling from Buck's stall when Clay and Tony drove up and parked outside the barn at the far end of the stable. They talked, shook hands, and Tony drove off toward home. Clay came striding to the stable to care for his own four horses. As he passed where she was working, he stopped and leaned on the gate.

"Where's Pepito? Vacationing?"

"No, this job is getting too big for one little guy. I'll have to get him some help."

"Looks like you're doing a good job." Clay said. "When you get through here, why don't you go clean up after my horses?" He headed in the direction of the farthest stall, grinning to himself.

"Clay," Cara called. "Thanks for what you said to Howard. You didn't have to do that. I appreciate it."

Clay returned and leaned over the half-door that kept the horses out of the stall where Cara worked. "Somebody had to. Howard's a bully. Too bad he didn't grow up with an older brother who could have knocked those rough edges off."

"That's what Dad always said, but I figured it was his way of expressing disappointment that I wasn't a boy."

"You know that's not true. Your father wouldn't have traded you for half a dozen sons like Howard."

Cara looked up, surprised "No. I didn't know that. What makes you think so?"

"Your dad and I did a lot of talking on our fishing trips—about the ranch, his family. He worried whether it was in your best interest to take over the ranch."

"He talked to you about his will?"

Clay nodded, a little embarrassed. "He needed a sounding board. I just listened. He wanted me to say he was doing the right thing—leaving the ranch to you. I told him I couldn't tell him that, because I didn't know you well enough to judge whether it would be good for you."

"Seems pretty obvious to most people that the ranch is my whole life."

"Yes, but it isn't clear whether you stay here because you love the ranch or because you felt obligated to take care of your dad. It wasn't my place to raise that question with him."

Cara shook her head.

"My concern was your father wanted to pull strings from the grave. He made sure in his will the odds were weighted in favor of your staying on the ranch."

"You mean the part about my having to live here the rest of my life, or else divide it with Howard and Emily?"

"Yeah."

"I don't see it as a burden, since that's what I'd do anyway. What I don't understand is the bit about getting married. Why did he put that in his will?"

"Another manipulation. He was disappointed you hadn't married Frank. He hoped a little push might encourage you."

"Frank?" Cara pictured herself in a wedding dress, tall and gawky, standing beside Frank, round and jolly, with dominos in one of his hands and a whiskey bottle in the other. She threw back her head and laughed.

Clay seemed puzzled by her laughter. "Your dad thought very highly of him."

Cara swallowed her chuckle. "I'm sorry. Frank is a nice guy. But marriage? It never entered my mind."

"That's the point. You father is giving you a reason to think about it. He put a carrot in front of you."

"So the joke's on me," she said. "I was amused when Frank read the part about not contesting the will. I thought it was written to give Dad the last word with Howard. You're telling me I got manipulated too." Cara threw a shovelful of manure into the pile she was creating.

"Your dad wanted grandchildren, and he thought you'd make somebody a damned good wife. From what I've seen, I'd say he was right."

Cara leaned on the shovel, her hands overlapping on top of the handle, her chin resting on her hands. She studied Clay's demeanor, admitting to herself she was flattered by his interest but confounded that her father had revealed his innermost thoughts about family to a man he'd known such a short time. She pushed her hat to the back of her head.

"It's obvious you don't know me very well."

"You're right," Clay said. "And what I've learned in the last few days suggests I may be wrong. I'm not sure any man could live with a woman who casts a fishing line as well you do. Not to mention your being a damned Democrat."

Cara laughed. "And those are only two of my faults."

Clay's voice became soft, almost as if he were talking to himself. "Well, they're problems most men would be willing to tackle, with a little encouragement." His eyebrows rose over inquiring blue eyes. He smiled as if waiting for an answer.

Cara bent over and pushed the shovel into the corner of the stall to get the last of the soiled straw.

"Keep an open mind," he said. "Your dad wanted you to follow in your mother's footsteps. Take it or leave it."

One of Clay's horses whinnied from the corral. "Somebody's hungry. I'll see you later." He left Cara standing alone, leaning on the shovel.

So Dad had plans for her life! But wanting her to follow in her mother's footsteps? She couldn't believe it. He'd known better than to push her around while he was alive. In death, he didn't worry she'd pack her bags and leave. She lifted the shovel and banged it into the gate to remove the last of the manure. Splatters of muck flew like black paste, speckling her clothing.

Buck trotted across the corral adjoining the barn and came into the passageway to his stall. He shook his head at Cara, snorting for attention, then backed away when she held out her muddied hand. She surveyed the mess she had made and shook her head. She'd smell like horse shit for a week. "Oh, well," she said to Buck. "Your stall is clean. If I fail at everything else, I can be a stable boy."

She headed toward the house, surveying the white board fences that ran to the highway. They needed paint, another job for Pepito. She would read *Tom Sawyer* to him some rainy day, so he could appreciate his work. She was excited about all the changes she could make. She didn't need a man around to make those decisions. Her father's "carrot" to encourage her to marry could lie rotting in the field. She headed for the shower in the garage's mudroom.

5

Moving the Goalposts

Cara pulled on a sweat suit and followed the smell of coffee wafting up the stairs from the kitchen. Someone had spilled sugar on the counter and dribbled cream from the pitcher. Tony must have done it; Lupe cleaned up her messes when they occurred. Cara wiped it up, poured her coffee, and headed for the front porch. The Sunday *Times* would be in the mailbox down by the highway.

"Looking for the paper?" Clay's drawl came from a chair at the domino table, where he sprawled, his bare feet propped on a nearby bench. Cara's arm jerked in surprise, splashing coffee down her shirt.

"Sorry, I didn't mean to frighten you." He rushed over, holding out a paper towel he'd used for a napkin, and dabbed at the coffee stain on her shirt. "Did you get burned?"

She backed away, shaking her head, taking the towel from him. He reached for her cup. "Let me refill it."

Cara followed him to the kitchen, wondering if she should put on a clean shirt.

"Cream?"

"I'll get it," she said, forgetting the shirt. "Thanks for making the coffee. I'm spoiled. Dad used to have it ready on Sunday mornings."

"I know," Clay said. "We always had a cup before we went fishing." He refilled his own cup. "This is not as strong as your dad's, but better than nothing. I figured you'd need a little boost to start the day."

His encouraging smile went well with the coffee, smooth like thick cream.

Cara followed him back to the porch, where he pushed a plate of muffins across the table. "Straight from the grocery shelf," he said. "Gives you an idea of how nutritious my meals are on the weekends."

"Mmm. They look good to someone who's too dumb to cook her own. Lupe usually leaves me something to nibble on for breakfast on the weekends. I guess she's been too busy with all the changes we've had this past week." She reached for the front section of the paper. "What are you doing here? The fish must be biting."

"Yeah, according to your dad. I got the feeling he liked to get up early, so he made up that rule to fit his habits instead of the fish's." Cara smiled and peered over the paper she was reading. True, Clay didn't look like an early-morning person. His comb had missed the cowlick over his brow. A day-old beard covered his chin and jaws. The newspaper was scattered in piles on the table.

"Dad wasn't always easy to live with, but he was nice company over the morning paper," she said.

Clay nodded. Cara continued reading. Her eye diverted to a headline about the death of Mexicans who had escaped detection by the border patrol while crossing the US-Mexican border, then died at the hands of their *coyotes*.

"This is what has to stop," she said, slapping her hand on the article.

"What's that?"

"Another truck loaded with Mexican workers was found broken down on the side of the road in Arizona. Seventeen inside, all dead. The driver didn't bother to unlock the van when he hightailed it to save himself. That makes me so angry. Why can't we do something to solve this immigration problem and stop such stupidity?"

"Because employers like you and me hire 'em."

Cara's eyes squinted and her voice was sharp. "We're not the cause. The policy that doesn't allow them to come over legally is the cause. Our participation is the consequence of a bad law."

"You'd agree if we didn't offer jobs, they'd stay home?" Clay asked.

"No, I'm not so sure of that. Their families are starving and being murdered by the drug cartels. Can you imagine sitting by and letting your family starve to death? You'd migrate too, because all you'd have left would be the hope you'd find a job. And you would find one no matter how difficult it was. In fact, I read this week our government concedes that America relies on millions of illegal Mexican laborers to keep our economy going, and the need will be greater in the coming years. That's really why we don't do anything about the laws. We need the workers. All we'd have to do is give them legal worker permits. And, yes, I do hire them because the INS looks the other way. That doesn't mean I like breaking laws just because the government doesn't enforce them."

"What would you do to fix things?" Clay found it fascinating that Cara was so interested in politics. This was not the personality her father had disclosed, maybe because they disagreed on the subject and he chose not to discuss family arguments.

Cara read the headline again, looked up, and said, "Open the borders. Let Americans compete for the jobs."

"You think everybody has the right to come across our borders? How about terrorists?"

"No. They need an organized way to get legitimate work visas. For example, we allowed workers to come from Mexico during the Second World War, when our boys were overseas. We stopped them when our soldiers came home and filled those jobs. Nowadays, Americans don't want low-paying jobs, so foreigners could still fill our vacancies." Cara frowned at Clay. "Why are you smiling?"

"How did your father feel about this subject? He never discussed it with me."

"I'm not surprised. He knew his position was vulnerable. We argued about it all the time. As long as the migrants are here illegally, we can continue to pay them almost nothing for their labor. The cities complain about the high cost of educating the migrants' children and providing health care, but these workers pay taxes just like we do, even social security, which they'll never get back. As to wages, if they earned more, they'd pay more taxes."

"I agree, but they have to learn the English language if they want better jobs. I have to hire a foreman who speaks both English and Spanish, because the migrants don't understand English. I'm sure you have the same problem."

Cara laughed. "Yes. Dad argued we should not teach them to speak English. He said if we did, they'd go find a better job and we'd lose our labor source."

"I'm surprised at your dad, but I shouldn't be. He always looked at the bottom line. That's how he accomplished so much." Clay threw his paper to the table. "Why don't you run for office? If you want something done about these problems, you have to become part of the process."

"You sound like Dad. My problem is I love what I'm doing. I guess that's everyone's excuse, isn't it? We don't want our own comfort level disturbed."

Clay went to the edge of the porch, where he stretched his arms above his head and rolled his shoulders to loosen muscles. "What are you doing today, after you solve the country's foreign policy problems?"

He grinned at her and she found herself wondering what his wife could possibly find wrong with him. He seemed so open, honest, and caring. Must be playing around behind her back, Cara surmised. Although he'd acted the perfect gentleman in her presence, that didn't prove much. She wasn't the sort of woman a man left his wife for.

Cara frowned. "I haven't decided. I need to balance the books before next week. I'm supposed to meet with the lawyer to figure out how I'll pay the taxes." While she talked, she ran her fingers through silky hair and shook her head to separate the strands lying on her shoulders. Clay watched as she braided them into a rope, which she tossed over her shoulder.

"Go fishing with me. Our last trip was cut short by the bear slaughter." Cara didn't respond, and he added, "I'm not a loner. I need motivation without your dad around."

"You really want to go back to the lake? My nightmares are filled with bears hanging in trees. I'm not sure I'm ready to re-live that experience."

Clay sighed, not sure how to approach the subject, but he had to admit he would like to spend more time with her. "When you get bucked off a horse, you get back on. You know those rules," he said.

Cara weighed his comment and could find no argument against it. "I suppose you're right. It won't get any easier, will it?"

"We could do something else. How about going for a swim in the pool at the waterfall?" He grinned again. She felt her pulse throbbing near her ear. She rubbed the area and tried to cover it with loose strands of hair. Clay's eyes were teasing, and she was as flustered as she had been at sixteen when a boy flirted with her.

She stood and stacked the newspapers into a neat pile. "The water is still cold this early." She regretted using the excuse of icy water. How would she avoid swimming later in the day? "I'll ride to the lake with you, but I can't fish. Last week's catch was left in my saddlebag overnight, and it hasn't aired out yet." The decision banished her jitters, and she stared at him, her voice firm. "I'll go for the ride, though, and fix lunch if you'll saddle the horses." She went upstairs without waiting for his reply.

Her hands trembled as she dressed. She knew her worries had nothing to do with the bear attack. Common sense told her Clay wanted companionship comparable to what her father had furnished. He saw her as she portrayed herself, an independent, take-charge woman. Not exactly what a man wanted in bed. So why was she fantasizing encounters going far beyond a fishing trip? She had to admit, in her dreams about men, she was always dressed. Her scars were hidden. One could do that with fantasies. And she had managed it in reality as well—she wasn't a neophyte at courting. She'd learned in college to limit a date's access to her body by meeting in the library or coffeehouses. Choosing the milieu was half the battle. And after college, she'd learned on the ranch that doing the work of a man earned the respect of the vaqueros. If they thought of her as a woman, they didn't reveal it in her presence.

But with Clay, it was different. He ignored her wish to be treated like her father—the person in charge. When he looked into her eyes, she felt vulnerable. He was married. He was a good ten years younger, and he could have any woman he wanted. In fact, he might be seeing other women now, who were flattered to be invited into his stable. However, she suspected he had been a wild mustang too long, preferring to range on the edge of the herd. Cara frowned at the thought she might be one of the women who responded to his charm. And though this was an innocent horseback ride, she felt her guard rising.

Rain had left the path up the mountainside damp. Small animal tracks made patterns in the mud, but no bear scat was evident. Wild flowers blossomed in splattered colors across the meadow at the top of the trail. The horses pulled at their bridle reins, wanting freedom to nibble at the grass growing at the edge of the trail.

"The weather's nicer than it was last week," Clay said. "This sun feels good."

At the lake, they dismounted and unsaddled the horses, leading them out to graze.

"I have an extra fishing rod," Clay said, frowning as he watched her arranging a comfortable reading space beneath the tree.

"No. I brought a book. It's hard to find time to read."

She didn't mention that this ruse would also keep them separated for the major part of the morning.

"I get the rocky overhang this time then," Clay said and ambled off by himself.

Cara nodded and settled down on the blanket, her head propped on her saddle.

When Clay returned, Cara was asleep with her book open across her chest. She woke when his horse nickered a greeting. "Well, it's nice to see somebody missed me," he said as he laid his fishing gear near his saddle. "I don't see any lunch. I thought you were in charge and it would be spread out, waiting for me."

Cara sat up. "And who was your servant this time last year, Mr. Thompson?"

"My wife. Maybe that's why she wants a divorce."

Embarrassed, Cara reached for the bag where she'd stored their lunch. She regretted having brought up the subject. Clay's divorce was none of her business and not a subject she wished to discuss. "How many fish did you catch?"

"Four, but I threw them back in. It avoids any comparisons with what you caught last week."

"So, we're competing? You didn't tell me."

Clay washed his hands in the lake, then stretched out, resting his head on his saddle.

"You don't know much about men, do you?"

Cara paused. "What do you mean?"

"Men have very sensitive egos. From the day we're born, we spend our lives aiming for the top-dog position in the man's world. In our relationship with women, we don't want, nor expect, any competition. We assume women know we are number one, born to be served." Not happy with his effort to be funny, Clay pushed off his hat and let it fall behind the saddle. He surveyed the clouds in the sky as if something were hidden there.

Cara pointed her chin upward and howled like a wolf. Clay laughed and clapped his hands, catching the radish she threw it at him. He popped it into his mouth. "Thank you, woman. Now I'll have a beer."

"For your information, women don't buy your definition of how it's our duty to stroke a man's ego." She pulled an iced beer from the plastic container and tossed it to him. Drops of water splashed across his face as the can dropped beside him. He wiped the water from the can and set it aside to settle before opening.

"Really?" he said. "That hasn't been my experience with women. They seem more than obliging."

Cara hardly knew where to take this conversation; it wasn't going in a direction she liked. "I guess that's why you have no ego problems," she finally said, picking up a sandwich. Clay reached to take it, but she leaned away, put the sandwich to her mouth, and sat looking out over the lake. He sat up and helped himself.

"What gave you that idea?" he asked.

Cara shrugged, wishing she could take back what she'd said, since it couldn't be defended without revealing her own insecurity around men who made passes at her. From the time she was in high school, her life had been one long struggle to maintain her privacy. She became a star athlete and a straight-A student, both positions placing her above the crowd, commanding a public respect that cloaked the need for intimate contact in her life. Boys who approached her took one look, backed off, or started discussing last night's ballgame.

An occasional fish splashed in the lake. A woodpecker hammered in a dying aspen tree to their left. The horses munched grass and snorted when it tickled their noses. The silence between Cara and Clay was broken only by the noise of their eating. Both were frustrated, for different reasons, by the conversation.

Clay leaned over to get another sandwich. "Not to change the subject, but how was your nap?"

Cara heard the tightness in his voice. Still, he was offering a new subject, one less volatile than talking about his experience with women.

"Wonderful. It's very peaceful here. And this is a good book." She pointed to *The Da Vinci Code*.

"I've read the reviews. Is it as good as they say?" Clay unwrapped his sandwich and inspected its content.

He wasn't interested in the book, she thought, but she could make it interesting. "It's intriguing. It suggests that Jesus and Mary Magdalene may have married. She is described as a very powerful woman in the community—not a prostitute." Her smile became a grin. "And I doubt that she sat at his feet, either."

Clay gave her a mock frown. "Sounds like heresy to me. Not what we learned in Sunday school." He chewed, waiting for an answer. "I suspect you went to a Catholic school, where the nuns explained that they, too, were married to Jesus?"

"They didn't claim to have sexual relations with him."

"That's true. Sex wasn't discussed at all, which is another way of teaching. However, knowing your father, I doubt you learned your uptight, iceberg approach to relationships from your parents."

A delicate snort escaped Cara's nostrils, a sound intended to hide the shock she felt at being called, for lack of a better description, frigid. Perhaps she was cold, but Catholic schooling had nothing to do with it. "What gives you the right to judge me?" She turned her head to avoid looking at him.

"I'm sorry. You're right. I had no business saying that. However, I've been living on the ranch for three months, enjoying a wonderful relationship with your father. Most of that time you've pretended I don't exist. Normally I wouldn't spend time wondering what's wrong, but there's something about you that bugs the hell out of me. I lie awake wondering if I've done something to offend you."

She didn't answer, and he opened the book she'd laid aside. "Sorry I brought it up."

Cara watched him thumb through the book, shaken by what he'd said. Of course she had kept her distance, for the very same reason he revealed. Something about him disturbed her, and she lay awake nights assuring herself that avoiding him was the only protection she had against falling for a married man. "It's okay. Sorry if I've seemed rude," she said. "There isn't anything about you I don't like." She blushed. "I mean—well, I mean you hadn't done anything to offend me—until you called me frigid. Women are sensitive about those things."

Clay closed the book and laid it aside. "And that's why I apologized. Your father said you were much like your mother, very private but driven, competitive, aggressive behind the scenes. You have those qualities. I shouldn't have described them as frigid."

Cara sat rolling his words around in her mind. She had never heard her mother described in those terms. "Dad told you that about my mother?" She had trouble believing her father talked about his wife with this man he had known only three months. He had refused to discuss her with his own children. She felt she and her father had become best friends, even buddies, after her mother's death. True, he never discussed his personal feelings and did not encourage her to, but she assumed it was because he was a man, and as a rule, men are not demonstrative. She learned to follow his example. Why had he opened his heart and mind to Clay?

"I had no problems with my mother. She died when I was a teenager." Cara paused. "Maybe I was angry she left me to grow up alone."

"When we talked about her last week, you seemed surprised your father gave her credit for any success he'd had. I got the feeling you had trouble believing that."

"No. I was surprised he compared the two of us. We were both tall and dark, but she was never a tomboy. Instead she was a delicate Spanish beauty. She drank from china cups and wouldn't have let her lips touch a beer can." She had no scars, Cara thought, squinting against the sunlight on the lake. "No one would describe me that way."

"Your dad didn't speak of how she looked. He took her beauty for granted. It was her intelligence and inner strength he felt she had passed down to you, more than the other children."

A delicious warmth spread through Cara's body. She was aware she blamed her mother for being so different, so female, and for not understanding it was okay to be a tomboy.

"You think she's sitting on your shoulder today, warning you against associating with a common, ordinary working man?"

"Certainly not. That's exactly what she did as a girl. Dad was a kid out of high school, breaking horses on her father's ranch. I guess what surprised her was that I was soaking up a lot of Dad's qualities. She worried that I'd become an old maid. It's not something I worry about."

Clay bit into his sandwich, not taking his eyes from Cara's face. He finished chewing. "So, mother's judgments aside, becoming friends with me is a possibility."

"I assumed we were friends. Fishing friends?"

"More than friends," he said. "That's a first step. My real question is whether Mrs. Morgan's daughter has the same free spirit her mother had." He stretched out on one elbow, facing Cara.

She laid half her sandwich aside. "Will you eat this, or shall I give it to the chipmunks?"

"Feed the chipmunks. Then answer my question."

The conversation had left Cara with a feeling of empowerment. She didn't have to continue comparing herself to the ideal woman. She could be content with who she was, a rancher, more at home on a horse than balancing tea cups. A woman who didn't need a man to make her complete. Different but approved of by her father, even accepted by her mother. She felt a new assurance talking to this Romeo.

"Let me save you a lot of time and trouble," she said as she threw the remnant of food outside the circle of their picnic. "I've never slept with a man. It isn't likely I'm going to sleep with someone I hardly know."

Clay choked on his beer.

"What's wrong?"

"That's . . . that's hard to believe," he said, clearing his throat.

"That I haven't slept with a man, or that I don't have any plans to?"

"Either," Clay said, nodding his head. "Both!"

Cara picked up the book. Clay finished his sandwich and brushed his hands together. He reached over and took the paperback from her hands.

"Maybe I should read this," he said.

"Don't bore yourself."

"Who knows? I might learn something. If Jesus got suckered into marriage by this smart, powerful woman, who's to say every man's not vulnerable? Is it possible you're baiting the hook?" He ducked his chin, looked up as if he were peering over eyeglasses, and dropped the book between them.

Cara laughed. "Don't you wish."

"Most women don't hold my interest," Clay said. "Their chatter is boring. Boredom is what killed my marriage. Bette isn't dumb, but you'd never know it from the topics she and her friends discuss. She and I stopped talking after Ashley was born. Pretty soon, even the sex got routine." Clay picked up his straw hat, lay back on his saddle, and covered his eyes. "Sorry," he mumbled. "I sometimes bore myself."

"No. Let's get this straight. You're trying to make me believe my brains are what you find attractive about me?"

Clay removed his hat and looked at her as if testing how far he could go. "It may be more complicated than that. Hummingbirds are attracted to flowers because they're red, but they aren't satisfied just to look. They go for the nectar."

"That's what I thought. And as soon as the nectar dries up and the petals fall, the hummingbirds fly south. I'm surprised you recognize a man's attraction to females is similar."

"With one exception. Some guys are lucky enough to find more than honey when they dip into the flower. That extra something is what keeps us around. Your mother had that. Call it brains if you want to, but it seems more personal than that. You haven't allowed me to get close enough to know what attracts me."

Cara blushed and looked away.

"Despite what you said, I'm still interested in pursuing the possibility of having a relationship with you." Clay said. "I promise not to seduce you on the first date, if that's a bargaining chip."

"You're kidding. There are too many negatives. The age difference is one. And you're still a married man."

Clay threw his empty beer can into the air and caught it. "Okay," he said. "You're proving that you aren't like your mother. She wouldn't have found me too young, if I'm to believe your father. She was five years older than he was when they married. He was still in his teens. She was fiery, a risk taker. She wanted to come to America, and he was her ticket. He said she continued to attract the attention of younger men after their marriage, and he was flattered to know that he was her sole lover. Furthermore, my being married is a bogus excuse you're using. It's a matter of time before my divorce is final." He started collecting the picnic scraps. "However, I respect the rules you live by. Consider the subject closed."

Cara squeezed her beer can until it collapsed. She had accomplished her goal. Why didn't she feel victorious? She feared her position was all talk, that it would be impossible to maintain her neutral man-to-man stance in his presence. His kiss in the kitchen had excited her. And the conversation with Emily about beginning a new life still resonated in the back of her mind. Perhaps Clay was right. Her mother did pursue her father, encouraging him to make decisions that fulfilled her dreams.

If she had lived, Cara might have learned from her how to tame the conflicting emotions that buffeted her. She frowned at this conclusion of their conversation. The truth was, she didn't want to put an end to Clay's pursuit.

They rode back to the ranch without speaking, but after the horses were unsaddled, Clay leaned his arm against Buck's stall gate, deterring Cara's exit. "I can't say I understand where you're coming from, but I respect your right to live by your own rules. I'd like to remain friends. And if the rules in your game change, let me know."

At home alone that night, Cara wondered how her mother would have handled this situation. For one thing, she would have controlled "the game" from beginning to end, without floundering around like a fish flopping on dry land. And she definitely would have been open to changing the rules if necessary to reach her goals. Cara's problem seemed to be she was pursuing conflicting goals. And the goalposts kept moving.

6

Legal Maneuvers

In a sense, she did sleep with Clay—he pestered her dreams all night. Rising sluggishly, she stood under the shower until she relaxed. Her head ached from trying to wipe away a nagging concern that yesterday's conversation with Clay required a future conclusion. As she dressed, she closed her eyes until her undershirt was tight against her chest. She stepped into her jeans but left them low, covering her ankles, while her eyes measured her muscled thighs. These were the petals that hid the nectar, no doubt about it. And all this time she had been shielding that part of her body, assuming it was a lost treasure. Clay had made it clear that he was attracted to her and was offering new vistas outside her enclosed world—vistas she had denied wanting all her adult life. Today her body insisted there was no good reason to deny herself the pleasures Emily promised were out there if she'd only stop hiding in the boondocks. Suddenly, she realized this was what his pursuit was all about—Clay was asking for the key to the boondocks.

Downstairs, Lupe reminded her that Frank had left a message yesterday, saying he wanted to see her right away. When could he come out? Cara wondered why he had been working on Sunday. His law business must be picking up. She dialed his office, but there was no answer. She left a message asking him to drop by for supper that evening.

Frank knocked on the back door of the ranch house at 6:00 p.m., and Lupe welcomed him inside.

"Cara home?"

"Sí, señor, she's here."

Cara came into the kitchen with a smile. "Lupe," she said. "We have business to take care of. Please leave our plates in the oven and we'll eat later."

"I can stay, dear, if you need me."

"No, we may be late."

Frank's shirt was wrinkled after a day at the office, but it showed signs of having been washed and starched at a laundry. His striped tie was a garish red and blue, loosened, along with the top button of his shirt. He nodded and smiled in a lawyerly sort of way. To Cara, he was family. He had appeared each Saturday to have lunch with her dad, sitting on the front porch in the summer and in the kitchen during the winter months. They read the paper, cussed the Democrats who were ruining the state's economy, played dominos, and by late afternoon were mellow from drinking whiskey.

"Shall we go to the office?"

He nodded and lifted his briefcase over the kitchen chair. "Your dad always insisted on handling business in the office." Down the hall he added, "I get a power surge when I come in here. Does it affect you that way?"

"Yes," Cara said. She knew what Frank meant. While Dave lived, she had been in awe of the power he wielded behind his desk. Now she sat on the throne. She liked the feeling and was sure her father would approve. For this discussion, she needed his strength.

Frank seemed reluctant to begin the discussion of problems she'd face on the ranch. He wandered around, looking at the wall hangings. He stopped before the mural separating the bookshelves behind the massive desk. Dave, proud of the relationship between his wife's grand-mother and Pancho Villa, commissioned the painting, set against the backdrop of New Mexico's mountain peaks, with saw-toothed red rocks standing like skyscrapers across the valley. He insisted that Pancho Villa be pictured on the mesa, surrounded by his rag-tag army. The general was pictured as a tall, stern man surveying the massive log ranch house that dominated the flatlands spreading eastward to the river. His interest lay not in the rich hay fields and barns. He stared at the cattle and the well-fed, restless horses in the corrals and at the women embroidering under the portal. Cara's grandmother, Carmen Villa, had bragged that Pancho preferred to dance with her instead of the other señorítas who adored him.

Cara was glad Pancho had never actually set eyes on the Los Lobos Ranch. He was known for taking what he wanted. She sat down behind the desk, knowing if she was to be in charge of her life and the ranch, she had to take on the trappings of the man who used to sit here. Frank pulled a book from the shelf and thumbed through it, reminding her of her father's love of history. He slapped the book closed. "I'll take this biography of Pancho home, if I may. Your dad was fascinated with that man." He sat in front of the desk. "Let's get on with our business."

"Have you figured out how much in taxes I'll owe?" she asked Frank.

"That's part of the bad news. This place is valued at millions of dollars. The estate tax laws related to farms and ranches fill books, and I can't come up with the exact amount you'll owe right now, but as Howard predicted, it will make a big hit on your cash account no matter how you look at it. I'm guessing even with all the available credits that will reduce what you'll owe, you'll hold the bag for a good three hundred thousand." Frank stopped to check Cara's reaction.

She leaned back in the tall leather chair and moaned. "You predicted a hundred thousand before." Were taxes the stealthy predator that could take down the Los Lobos, as it had the small farmers who homesteaded on the Morgan Grant?

"There is good news. Your dad was carrying a load of insurance, two hundred thousand dollars' worth. When I checked into it, your dad had changed the beneficiary the week before he died. Left Howard and Emily out in the cold again. The agent said the old man told him it was for paying the estate taxes. I figure your dad must have suspected there was something wrong with his heart and he was preparing for this situation. Did he ever mention having a problem?"

Cara straightened in her chair. "No, and this is hard to believe. Have you talked to Howard about the insurance?"

"Yeah. He was really pissed off again. He's going to see a lawyer, but there isn't much he can do about it. It was your dad's decision to make."

"That still leaves a lot of money I'll have to come up with. Where will I get it?"

"Sell a few cattle. Maybe land. Larry Martin begged your dad to sell him that forty-acre chunk across the river every time they met. I'm sure he still wants it."

"That's the best, irrigated bottomland we own."

"That's why he wants it."

"How much time do we have?"

"Again, the statutes take into account that ranchers live on credit. They allow installment payments, and in some cases you only have to pay the interest for the first few years. We can take advantage of all those laws."

"Well, that sounds doable. I just hate to be in debt. I'll think about selling to Larry, but let's look at all the alternatives. And I'll call Howard. Maybe I can placate him over the insurance."

"I have more bad news."

Cara frowned. "Now what?"

"I just heard through the grapevine that Howard has hired a big law firm in Albuquerque to review your father's will."

"He what?"

"He asked if it could be overturned. I doubt any law firm will say no to a potentially money-making deal like that."

"I can't believe he'd do that."

"You know how upset he was the day I read the will."

"Yes, but we're family."

"Greed has a way of diminishing family ties."

"I don't think it's greed with Howard. He just can't believe Dad would put the ranch in my hands. He is the best-educated member of the family. He's older than I am. And he's a male. His thinking is that Dad should have divided the estate equally or, better still, left him to manage it."

"I'm a little surprised he decided to do this so soon after Dave died."

"Yes, you said he had three years to decide to sue. I thought he'd get over it in that length of time."

"He seemed consoled that your father said you had to leave the ranch to him and Emily when you died, if you haven't married. I suspect he's concerned about how quickly you're changing lifestyles."

"Lifestyles? Such as?"

"He probably worries you'll get married, which could wipe out any hope he has of getting a share of the estate. If he can get the suit heard before that happens, his chances will be better at convincing the judge that the estate should be divided between the three of you now."

"I don't understand."

"It can be complicated. The will says if you get married, the ranch will become marital property. By law, the spouse inherits the community property, and the only way to keep that from happening would have been for Dave to award you only a life interest in the ranch. Once you died, it would go to the other living children. I explained this as a way he could leave it to Howard and Emily if you died after marrying, but he was not interested. He wanted it to stay with your family if you married so that the grandchildren he assumed you would have could carry on the family heritage. I also told him you could sign a prenuptial agreement when you marry, directing that the husband will have no claim to the ranch if you divorce or die. That would allow it to pass on to Emily and Howard if you have no children. He waved that idea aside and said it was yours and you could do with it whatever you wished. By the way, I recommend a prenuptial agreement even if you do want your assets to become marital property."

Cara stared at the picture of Pancho contemplating the risks of stealing some horses.

Frank cleared his throat. "I hear Clay Thompson is spending a lot of time at the ranch these days."

"You know he's boarding his horses here, and Dad invited him to rent the apartment over the garage after his wife kicked him out."

"I also hear he's bought a big house in town. Maybe he's thinking of getting married again once the divorce is final. I understand from Bette that there are several women lined up, hoping to take her place."

"Frank, I fail to understand why we're talking about Clay Thompson."

"Well, I'm not interested in his situation just because he'll soon be prime marriage material. I've been hired by his wife's divorce attorneys to suggest a financial settlement."

"You mean you're advising her on how they should divide their marital property? You must be kidding. Isn't it wrong to work for Bette when you know Clay was one of Dad's best friends? It looks like a conflict of interest."

"What conflict? I know neither of these people, although I am curious about what Clay's interest is, or might be, in Dave Morgan's ranch."

"Dave Morgan doesn't own a ranch."

"That's what I meant."

"And your point is?"

"Have you been to his new place?" Frank's tone hardened with each new question.

"What does that have to do with anything?"

"I'm your attorney, Cara. I have to base my advice on realities. I'd like to know if you're shacking up with the guy. I can't very well make suggestions on how to divide his marital property right away if there's the possibility his property interest will improve in the near future. If he gets his hands on this ranch, it will make a big difference in his property values."

Cara pushed her chair back. "There. You've just proved that there is a connection between your handling of the Thompson divorce and your knowledge and legal handling of this ranch. You know as well as I do Clay has no interest in the Los Lobos Ranch, and your suggestion that any interest he might have in the future should be considered in their present division of assets is ludicrous. You're only probing for information that is none of your business."

"Listen. What you do with Clay is no concern of mine. I've only seen the man once. I've never spoken to him. What I know about him is what his soon-to-be ex-wife tells me. Don't expect her opinion to be unbiased."

"Frank, this boils down to one thing. Clay was a friend of my father's. As our attorney, I expect you to honor that friendship."

Frank laughed. "That's ridiculous. A lawyer can't limit his practice against friends of one of his clients. In this small town, we'd go out of business in a week."

Cara rose abruptly. "Let's go eat." In the kitchen, she opened the oven and placed two hot plates on the table. They sat without speaking, giving all their attention to the food. Cara laid aside her fork. "Let's talk ethics."

Frank kept chewing and spoke over his food. "There is no ethical problem in my representing Bette Thompson and you at the same time."

"How about friendship? I thought you and I were friends." She shook a bottle of salad dressing and unscrewed the lid. The oil spilled on her shaking fingers, and the lid rolled across the floor. Frank picked it up and washed it under the faucet. His stubbornness surprised her as much as her own angry response. He had always acted in the family's best interest. When they needed legal advice, he gave it; when they needed emotional support, he was the first to respond.

Now his voice was heavy with sadness. "I've come to the conclusion you and I were never friends, Cara. Your father and I were friends. Every time I tried to get close to you, I got the brush off."

Cara knew he was right. She had never allowed him to think he was more than her father's buddy. She watched as he refilled his wine glass. He seemed not to understand why she was angry, or worse still, he was treating her concerns like a child's tantrum.

"Clay said if Bette would agree, they could get their divorce now and divide the property later. Is that true?"

"Yes. It's called bifurcation. If both parties agree, the law allows the court to issue the decree three months after the petition is filed. That's so people can remarry before the property division is final, if they're hot to do so." Frank chewed on a mouthful of liver and onions. "I suppose Clay falls into that category."

"There are many reasons to finalize a divorce. Mainly it's difficult for the children."

"Are you telling me Clay wants the bifurcation?"

"I can't speak for Clay. Ask his lawyer."

Frank gulped his wine. "You've no idea how hurt I am by the knowledge you're shacking up with that man. Your father would be outraged."

"I am not 'shacking up' with anyone, Frank. I can't believe you'd use that expression with me." Her voice was raspy. "If Bette told you I was sleeping with Clay, she's lying."

"I apologize for the language, but it doesn't change the facts." He continued talking with his mouth full. "It's good you didn't come right out and tell me about an affair with Clay, because legally that leaves me clear of conflict charges. Don't blame me for knowledge of hanky-panky I learned by looking into your eyes."

"I imagine you could be charged with slander, however, if you start spreading lies around, based on what you think you see in somebody's eyes."

Frank snickered. "Very funny."

"If you're my lawyer and I'm sleeping with Clay, does that keep you from representing Bette in the divorce?"

"Not necessarily, but I'll take your word that you're not. If all his girl-friends keep mum until the divorce is final, there should be no problems."

Cara picked up her plate and dropped it in the sink. The china broke, exploding the tension inside her head. She leaned against the counter. "That's enough. You're not my father. I don't need your advice anymore. I'll find another attorney to handle Howard's lawsuit. That's the only issue left, isn't it?"

Frank slumped as her message sank in, then squared his shoulders. "We need to finish the estate business. You're making a big mistake, Cara. Your dad would be furious."

"My dad doesn't run this ranch anymore. I do, and I won't put up with your insults."

Blood drained from the lawyer's face. He seemed lost for words. He pushed away from the table. "It won't be difficult for another attorney to finish the estate work. I'll get the file ready. Where do I send it?"

"Here, to me."

Frank reached over to pick up his briefcase. He started for the door, then stopped and gazed around the kitchen. "I didn't think my relation-ship with the Morgans would end this way. Your dad wanted me and you to get married. He didn't count on your falling for a guy young enough to be his grandson."

Cara flushed but didn't respond to the illogical accusation. Frank went to his Porsche and backed across the driveway. The tires threw gravel as he headed for town.

Cara threw her napkin across the room. Frank was probably right. As much as her father liked Clay, he would not have considered him a possible son-in-law. But he wasn't the one in love. She shivered. Where had that thought come from?

She checked her watch, worried about how she could resolve the problems with Frank. First, she'd have to find another attorney. She opened the telephone book and flipped through the ads. This time she'd look for a female attorney who understood her problems.

Trace Leader's name stood out among the women listed under "general practice." Cara liked the name. It sounded tough. She called to make an appointment for an interview and was told how lucky she was.

"Ms. Leader is just finishing a trial and could see you first thing next week. What time would you like to come?"

7

The Wolf Pack

Frustration fueled the routine beginning of Cara's day. Opening the door to a possible suitor had been a silly thing to do, plus she had fired her father's best friend and family attorney without thinking through the obvious problems that created. She heard the phone ringing downstairs as she peered into the mirror. Maybe she should cut her hair. She pulled a silver strand from the crown and threw down her comb. What did it matter whether the part of herself she showed to the world was attractive? Beauty was all a facade. She hurried downstairs to begin her day's work.

As she entered the kitchen, Lupe placed coffee beside a plate of ham and eggs, then pulled golden biscuits from the oven.

"Thanks, Lupe, I may live. Supper didn't sit so well last night."

"Is that why you broke your mother's china plate? What was wrong with supper?"

"It wasn't the food, Lupe. Frank made me angry. I fired him."

Lupe shrugged her disapproval. "I talked to Ramón yesterday," she said. "Rosita is going to a foster home. She can't be returned to her mother because María has no job or a safe place to live. I don't know how that can happen without a green card."

"Well, Clay said he and Bette had hired her to babysit the children and that she and Pablo would be living in a little house on his lot. That should take care of those concerns. Where's Tony?"

"He's at home making telephone calls. He went to the camp this morning. It's almost empty." Lupe's voice was low and worried. "All the new workers left in the night, afraid of the sheriff."

Cara set down her cup with a splash. "They're gone? All of them?"

"All of the undocumented men in the camp. Word is out the sheriff is coming. They're afraid they'll be arrested. That's what they told Tony."

"My God! We hired them to bale hay this week." She headed for the door.

Lupe followed her, wringing her hands. "Come back, Cara! Tony will fix it. He's calling other ranchers to send extras."

Cara stopped. "Are you sure? When will he be back?"

"Pronto."

"Who was on the phone this morning?"

"The sheriff. He's coming out to check on the bear."

"Today? That happened a week ago."

"Tony says it's just an excuse to look over the camp."

"For heaven's sake. What did you tell the sheriff?"

"I told him you'd call him back."

Cara slumped, frowning.

"This whole mess scares me," Lupe said.

"I know, but don't worry too much. The sheriff was a friend of Dad. He's always cut us slack." She picked up her coffee cup and headed for the office.

At the same time, Lucille Martin was cleaning turnips at the sink when the phone rang. "No," she said to Tony. "Larry's out at the barns. Can I give him a message?"

"Ma'am, I just wondered if any of my workers showed up at your place looking for jobs?"

"No, I don't think so. Larry didn't mention it if they did."

"Well, we're hard up this week. Already got the hay cut, and it'll be ready to bale tomorrow. I wonder if y'all could spare a few men to help us?"

Lucille's voice lowered. "I'm sure Larry can spare a few. I'll have him call you as soon as he comes in for lunch." She paused. "You must be shorthanded for vaqueros to ride the fences," she said. "We lost calves last week to the wolves while our lazy bums were sleeping on the job."

Tony cringed. He'd never cared for the sharp tongue on this woman, but, as Lupe said, she was Larry's problem. Tony just wished she'd keep her thoughts to herself when it came to criticizing the immigrant workers. They were doing her a favor. Now he needed a favor, so he tried to sound sympathetic. "Sorry, ma'am. That can happen. I'll have to pull my fence riders off for a few days, till we get these men back. Maybe you all can keep an eye out for strange trucks. Tell Larry I need to talk to him, please, ma'am."

Lucille laid down the phone and smiled. What a shame. Cara Morgan was having all sorts of bad luck. Maybe she'd have to sell land. Chuckling, she searched her desk for Rafael's number. This was news he could make use of, and if he did, it might accomplish what she had not been able to do through negotiating with the Morgans.

In her office, Cara tried to remain calm as the sheriff's receptionist switched her call to Matt Placer.

"Cara, how are you? Everything getting back to normal since you buried your dad?"

"We miss him, of course, but things are back to normal. Lupe said you wanted to talk to me."

"Hmm. I'm . . . I'm just checking up on what happened out at your place last week. Sounds a little unusual for a bear to attack like that. I thought you could fill me in on all the details."

"A sow and her cubs walked right into the workers' camp and grabbed this little kid who was playing out in the meadow. I happened to be fishing on the other side of the lake when I heard the racket. We got her to the hospital in time to save her arm."

"That's good. What happened to the bear?"

"You must have seen the pictures in the paper, Sheriff. She was shot."

"That's what I called about. Who shot her?"

"One of the ranch hands."

"What make of guns do them migrants carry?"

"They don't carry guns, Sheriff. The camp supervisor keeps a rifle for emergencies."

"Guess he has sharp knives, too, from the looks of those carcasses pictured in the paper." Cara didn't respond.

"It's my job to investigate, you understand. Huntin' bears is against the law. I gotta report it to the Game and Fish Department."

"Seems to me the facts are clear, Sheriff. The bear was shot in self-defense. That's not a crime. I'm happy to answer your questions. What else do you need?"

"I figure I should come out and look over the scene . . . check out the rifle."

Cara could hear her breath as she contemplated how she could satisfy the sheriff's needs without inviting him onto her property, where he would scare off any remaining workers. "I was just on my way up to the camp, Sheriff. I'll see what I can find out for you. Shall I bring the rifle down?"

"Guess I should see it. And any knives layin' around." He paused. "This whole immigration problem is spiraling out of control. I guess you saw the story in the paper today about the Mexican woman here in town who got her throat slit. The police say it looks like revenge from one of the Mafia groups working this part of the country."

"Revenge? What Mafia groups?"

"Well, this area has always been one of the rest stops on the way from El Paso to the Colorado stash houses. Now the *coyotes* are dropping their loads off here instead of taking 'em on to Colorado. It's big business in the U.S., and as you might expect, the Mafia is moving in to take over their transportation across the country. We have gangs fighting over who gets the next load. The police chief figures this woman's family picked up a group already spoken for, and this is their punishment. Plus a warning not to do it again."

Cara felt nauseated. Hiring undocumented migrants had changed from run-of-the-mill business to mob activity. Had the last van load of workers included Mafia connections? Could Pablo be connected to the Mafia? And what of Ramón? His education belied his lowly status as a vaquero. Was he an informer for the smugglers, working with Pablo?

"You catch any fish in that lake up there?"

Cara nodded, trying to connect with the sheriff's change of subject. "Sure do. I caught four browns last Sunday."

"I done that a time or two with your dad." He waited, hoping for an invitation. Cara glanced away. "I heard Clay Thompson was out there on Sunday. What's he up to nowadays?"

The question surprised Cara. She grimaced at the thought of connecting Clay to the illegal immigrant investigation. He mostly hired locals, but when business got hot in the summer, he hired migrants. He didn't need a raid at the busiest time of the year.

"Oh, he's boarding horses with us. He used to fish with Dad on the weekends."

"I guess he saw what happened with the bear."

"He wasn't at the camp when it happened." Cara switched the telephone to her other ear, trying not show her nervousness. "He was across the lake fishing. I'm on my way up to the camp now, Sheriff. Why don't I call you back when I find out who shot the bear? And I'll get the weapons for you."

There was a long pause. Cara realized the sheriff was not satisfied with her effort to keep him off the ranch. He was coming out. Maybe he thought the shooting was connected to the murder of the Mexican woman. It would be a feather in his cap to solve that murder.

"Don't put yourself out, dearie. I'm on my way." The telephone clicked dead.

She opened the desk drawer to find Clay's business card. He deserved a warning that the sheriff intended to crack down on the hiring of undocumented workers.

Clay's secretary answered his telephone and asked whether she could give him a message. She took Cara's telephone number.

An hour later, Clay walked into his office, past the secretary, and slammed the door. He had missed a half day of work while attending a custody hearing, where Bette had successfully convinced the court to limit his parenting time based on the newspaper story of a child being attacked by a bear on the ranch where he took the children. He punched the intercom button on the telephone. "Where's Bill?" he asked.

"He's out at the Juniper site. He asked you to call as soon as you got back."

"Any other calls?"

"Cara Morgan called. Said she needed to talk to you as soon as possible. She left a number."

"I have it, thanks." Clay hung up and called his project superintendent. He discovered there were only minor decisions left for him to make, and he made them quickly. He dialed Cara's satellite phone, wondering where he'd find her. She responded, and he sat down and leaned back in his chair with his boots propped on the desk. He was coiled as tight as a metal spring ready to pop. He hoped her call was social instead of business—anything to wipe out the memories of the custody session.

"What's up?" he asked.

"Clay, I'm sorry, but the sheriff called this morning. He wants to talk to you about what happened out here on Sunday."

"Why would he want to talk to me?"

"I suspect he's getting pressure from INS on the undocumented workers issue because of the murder reported in today's paper. Have you seen it?"

"Yeah. I figured that might cause repercussions for the migrants, but I'm surprised killing a bear would cause a stir."

"He's acting on the basis that it's a crime to kill bears, but I assured him it was self-defense. I'm sure it's an excuse to inspect my ranch for stash houses. He says he has to report the bear incident to the Fish and Game Department. My new workers have run away, afraid the sheriff will show up. If he finds out they're gone, he'll assume smugglers picked them up to take to another state."

"That sounds bad. You think he plans an investigation at the ranch?"

"I'm sure of it. The sheriff wants to know what you saw at the lake. He asked how you happened to be here."

"That's simple. Is that all?"

"It's enough. I just wanted to let you know he might be calling on you."

"Thanks for the warning. Anything I can do for you?"

"Well, I'll have to replace those workers, but this is not the time to connect your business with mine. Tony is calling nearby ranchers."

"Sorry about all this. Thanks for calling."

Cara joined Tony and Lupe at the table on the back porch. "Did you find our guys?"

"No, and they haven't shown up at neighboring ranches, so they either left the county or they're camping out until it's safe to return. Ramón is with them, so I figure he'll let us know what's going on as soon as he can. How's Rosita doing?"

"I haven't heard anything except what Ramón told Lupe. I did call Frank last week to see if he could talk to the judge about returning the child to her mother. He said when he contacted the D.A., he was asked if there was a father in the picture. Do you know if María is married?"

"She ain't. Ramón says she had the baby when she was around twelve. Her own father left when María was born, and her mother died a year or so ago. Pablo has been taking care of her and the kid since that time. The story is he recruited migrants for a *coyote* in exchange for free passage for them. He wanted them over here, because it's so dangerous to live in Juárez."

Lupe sat down at the table, her hands clasped under her chin. Her accusing voice interrupted them. "Why did you fire Frank? He's been a part of this family for years."

Tony frowned. "You fired Frank?"

"Howard filed a lawsuit to overturn Dad's will. Frank will be a witness to Dad's state of mind, but he's also working for Bette's attorney. I couldn't make him understand why that felt like a betrayal. I'll get another lawyer."

Tony shook his head. "Can't believe he's a turncoat. What did he say?"

"I don't have time to discuss it right now. We have bigger problems. The sheriff called and wants to know about the last load of migrants we hired. I'm wondering about Pablo and Ramón."

Tony pushed his chair away from the table and bounced his hat on his knees. "Ramón was on the same boat that brought Pablo over."

"Did he know Pablo was in cahoots with the *coyotes*?"

"Yeah. He says it was just like I told you—a onetime deal to get María and her kid over here."

"Was Pablo at the campground on Sunday?"

"He came in the van but didn't stay."

"It's hard to believe he'd run away if he knew the child was going to the hospital."

"He left before the bears showed up. If he's working, he'll get paid on Friday, and I wager he'll be back."

"If he bargained with a *coyote*, he may bargain with the smugglers. Rumor says the *coyotes* dump the migrants here for the smugglers to pick up and move to other states."

Tony's eyes narrowed. "I heard them rumors, but they're overblown. This place is the end of nowhere. Why would anyone pick up illegals here, when there's no good way to get them across the country?"

"That's why. There aren't any INS agents around to see what's going on, so they can bring in trucks or vans to move them without being noticed."

Tony stood so suddenly his chair fell backwards. Embarrassed, he picked it up and replaced it under the table, avoiding Cara's eyes.

"The sheriff also talked about today's news report of a rival gang killing a woman in town because her family poached on their smuggling territory. He says he's coming out to look around because of the bear attack, but you can bet he's checking to see if we're a drop-off place for Mexicans." She turned to Lupe. "Did we get today's paper?"

Lupe nodded and left the room.

"What are you doing to get hay balers?"

"I called Larry Martin. He wants to know if the sheriff's poking around. If not, he'll send Junior and another man over tomorrow, and he'll call the other ranchers. If they come, we can get the hay baled and in the barns before it rains."

"Well, the sheriff's coming out for sure." Cara spread the paper on the table where the headline shouted the news. "Woman's Slaying May Have Link to Mob."

"It says right here that Quail Creek, Colorado, is one of the hubs where *coyotes* drop off their loads of illegal migrants. They leave them there at stash houses, where they later get picked up and moved to other states."

Shaking his head, Tony peered over at the story Cara was reading. She continued, "Matt thinks they're getting smart and stopping here instead of going on to Colorado, where they're being watched." She looked at Tony. "Have you heard anyone talk about stash houses on the ranches around here?"

He shook his head, and Cara closed the paper.

"Can we start baling the hay tomorrow if the sheriff gets out here this afternoon and finishes his business? He sounded like he was on his way."

"Yeah. If the neighbors come through with a few workers."

"If they don't, call Larry and put the baling off for a day. And pray it doesn't rain. The clouds look ominous."

"Hell," Tony said, "The sheriff's got no reason to come out here. He knows this place ain't a stash house. Your dad may have hired illegals, but he sure didn't ship them around the country."

"And if he asks whether our workers have green cards?"

"I don't know nothing about green cards. I'm pure color blind."

Cara laughed. "Maybe you shouldn't talk to the sheriff at all. He's not going to believe that."

"If our workers don't return, I'll have to order another load."

"Let's think about it, Tony. It's getting too dangerous to hire undocumented workers. I'd rather get back the guys we've already hired to finish up the haying, then worry about whether to keep them or hire new ones." Tires crunched on the gravel of the driveway. "Speaking of the devil, here's the sheriff now. Let me do the talking." Tony followed her out to meet the sheriff.

"Howdy, ma'am." Matt Placer opened the door of his Hummer and reached out to shake hands. "How are you, Tony?"

Cara was in no mood for niceties. "I'm glad you made it today, Sheriff. I haven't had time to go to the reservoir. We can drive up together."

"Can we all go in my vehicle?"

"You bet. That thing looks like it could climb Mt. Brazos. The road to the camp's a little rocky in places, but we'll make it."

"Get in," he said. "I'll drive. Not sure I remember how to get there so you'll have to guide me. I hope it's not the trail we took on horseback."

"Not hardly," Cara said.

When they arrived, she was amazed at the change in the campground since the accident. It appeared spotless. No clothing hung out to dry and no personal possessions lay stacked around the cabins or the dormitory. No burned meat clung to the grills. There were no bears hanging in the trees, no tubs filled with entrails. No blood streaked across the ground or puddled where the child had lain. A few women and children, who belonged to the full-time employees, peeked from one the cabins.

Standing beside the Hummer, the sheriff swung his arm around the campground. "Nice place you got here. Is this where all your workers live?"

"This is it."

The sheriff stared at her. "This is a busy season, ain't it? I'm surprised it's not full." He propped both hands on his hips while he waited for an explanation.

A chill spread up Cara's back. The camp was eerie. It appeared like the perfect place for *coyotes* to drop off their loads until the smugglers arrived to disperse them. In fact, it looked like smugglers had just picked up a load and left the camp empty. Could anyone blame the sheriff for reaching the conclusion that the ranch was a hotspot for transporting illegal migrants?

"It was full of long-term workers until last week. The bears scared them off."

The sheriff sneered. "The bears scared them off? I thought they killed the bears."

"Not before the child was attacked."

"Where'd it happen?"

"I don't know. When I got here, the child lay on the table over there, and they were trying to stop the bleeding."

The sheriff listened, wandering farther around the campsite, but Cara refused to follow, forcing him to stay within earshot of her voice.

"I guess the bear was gone when you got here then?" The question was intended to catch her in a lie. Cara wished she could say yes, but the sheriff knew the bear had been slaughtered and no doubt eaten.

"It was dead, but I didn't pay a lot of attention to it. The child was bleeding, so I spent all my time working with her."

"How about you, Tony?"

"He wasn't here at the time." Cara's voice was sharp, daring the sheriff to continue along this line of questioning.

"Clay Thompson made the 9-1-1 call," the sheriff said.

Cara tried to hide her dismay. So that's how the sheriff knew Clay was present. She wished she'd allowed him to question Tony instead of moving to Clay.

"Yes, Clay called 9-1-1 and got the Mountain Rescue ambulance out to the ranch."

"That all he did?"

"What do you mean?"

"What was Thompson doing out here in the first place? How's he connected to the ranch? Maybe the two of you share a work force. Maybe he brings in the illegals and spreads them around to the ranchers?"

Cara's face flushed, her voice strident. "That sounds a lot like the smuggling you were describing, Sheriff. I can assure you neither one of us smuggles undocumented workers. Thompson Lumber and Construction Company and the ranch have separate employees. In hard times, when Thompson has no work available for his temporary workers, he sends them out to us, and vice versa."

The sheriff shook his head and snorted. They walked to the Hummer, and he spit tobacco juice away from her and shifted the wad to the other cheek. While he pontificated about the problems the county had with the invasion of more and more Mexican nationals, she worried about the connection he was trying to make between the ranch and Thompson Construction Company.

"How do you get your workers?" he asked.

"We usually go through the employment office in Santa Fe."

"Guess they all have green cards." His lips recovered from the sneer and became a smirk. His stare remained hard, unfriendly. He looked over his shoulder at Tony.

Cara interrupted. "We check for green cards. A few may slip by without coming through the office. I won't swear we're squeaky clean, Sheriff, but we're cleaner than most. You know how the system works."

"Yeah, I know how it works. Your dad was a stickler for the law. I 'spect it's harder, being a woman."

Cara was dumbfounded, her voice icy, recalling her brother's prediction that she couldn't handle the employees. "What's your point, Sheriff?"

Fearing Cara's temper, Tony cleared his throat.

The sheriff flushed. "I'm just saying, ma'am, you've taken on a man's job. We didn't have these problems when your dad was alive. Taking over his job can't be easy."

"Right now, Sheriff, it's a woman's job, and I've had no trouble handling it at all."

The sheriff looked at Tony for backup but couldn't catch his eye.

"Just one more thing then, and I'm finished here. When you find that gun and them knives, have Tony bring 'em in."

They climbed into the Hummer and returned to the ranch house without speaking.

She and Tony stood watching as the sheriff eased down the driveway and gunned the Hummer onto the highway.

"Probably won't ever find that gun and 'them knives,'" Cara mused.

Tony untied the reins of his horse and swung into the saddle. "He'll probably forget he asked for 'em."

Lupe laid down the potato she was peeling as Cara entered the kitchen. "María's brother, Pablo, he came by while you were gone. He was looking for María."

"Is he still here?"

"No. When he heard the sheriff was here, he said he was heading for town. He's been working out here for Larry Martin and in town for Clay."

"Does he know where the other vaqueros went?"

"Down by Junction Creek, he said. Hiding until this blows over."

"Good. The sheriff's gone. I'll ride down and tell Ramón to get them back in the fields."

"You can't go down there by yourself. It's not safe."

Cara headed for the door. "I know. It's a man's job."

"You could be killed," Lupe called. "Them men don't know what the laws are here. In Mexico they get away with kidnapping women and girls all the time!"

"We haven't had any of those problems here, Lupe. That's a different country. Here, they're afraid to break the law. They'll be deported."

"Tony told me he was worried about this last load of workers. They haven't worked over here before. They came right from Juárez, where the law pays no attention to their crimes. They live like wild animals there, preying on women and children. He wouldn't let you go if he was here."

Cara adjusted her hat as she started out the door. She hated to see Lupe so upset, but her worries seemed unjustified. There were no instances of crime in the migrant camp. Even María had not complained of harassment, and she was young and beautiful. She turned to comfort Lupe. "Tony said Ramón was with the migrants. He will protect me if necessary. Don't worry. I'll be back soon. I'll get that hay baled if it kills me."

Buck took off at a fast gallop, but soon Cara slowed him to an easy lope and guided him through the meadow's tall grass, heavy with seeds. A covey of quail burst from the depth of the brush like pellets from a shotgun. Buck jumped sideways, diving away from the noise, pulling Cara forward over the saddle horn.

"Dummy," she said, jerking the reins until he slowed to a walk. "You act like you'd never seen a quail."

They neared a clearing in the woods where Junction Creek rushed south beside the cliffs and emptied a few miles further down into the Brazos River. Cara let Buck have his head. Dammit, Pablo could have told us which direction they took. Buck leaned forward, reaching for the cool, clear water with his muzzle. His nose disappeared and there were no sounds except the bubbles from his breathing and the lapping of waves against the rocks. Birds had stopped singing. An eeriness settled over the shadowed tree line. Cara pulled Buck's head from the water, where he was playing instead of drinking. The logical place for a campground was at the natural pool on the creek, a half mile to the south. The best way to get there was straight south from where she sat.

Heat waves rose from the grass where the dew had evaporated. The hay should be dry by now and the borrowed crew hard at work. She had to get her own men back into the fields so the neighbors' workers could return to their own crops by the end of the day.

Buck pushed through the tall grass, breathing short snorts of air, his head bobbing. Twenty minutes down the trail, foamy sweat formed white borders around the saddle blanket. Cara moved the horse closer to the trees for the occasional shade.

She listened, hoping to hear voices. A splash in the water broke the silence. Frogs, not fish. She directed Buck out of the trees, across the meadow toward the sharp turn in the waterway, where she could hear the noisy falls dumping into a pool below the rocks.

Around the corner, Buck reared to a stop on the bank of the swimming hole. Cara gasped, surprised and embarrassed. Below her, the migrant workers were swimming nude, laughing and splashing in the water like children. Two of them grabbed a third and dragged him into the deeper water, hollering while he struggled to get out.

She yanked Buck's reins away from the pool, kicking him with her spurs. His rear legs danced around, but he didn't respond to her pull on the reins. She looked over his head into the eyes of a man who held Buck's bridle. It was Ramón. He wore no shirt. A dirty pair of jeans hung from his narrow hips. He was barefoot and his hair was untied, hanging in ringlets to his shoulders. Unlike his former appearance, today he could pass for one of the vaqueros who worked in the fields. His dark eyes flashed sparks as he pulled Buck's bridle with both hands, turning the horse's rump to the water hole, steering Cara's view away from the vaqueros. That done, he looked at Cara, his lips drawn into a tight line. His voice was calm. "Buenos días, señorita."

Cara jerked hard on the reins. Buck lifted his front feet and struggled to balance Cara's weight against the pull on his bridle. She reached for her rifle, but Ramón's strong hand covered hers, as he pulled the gun from the scabbard. In the struggle, she dropped one of the reins and he retrieved it. Backing away from the pool, he held onto the horse's rein and cradled the rifle at his elbow.

The scene was surreal. The man holding her captive bore little resemblance to the Ramón who wore glasses and worked to save Rosita's life, or to the vaquero who rode beside Tony and came to her father's funeral mass. He resembled the other feral-like, brutish men coming to join him. He had not shaved for days, and his heavy mustache hung toward his jaw.

Without glasses, Ramón squinted, his thick black lashes almost hiding the dark brown of his eyes. The men scrambled from the pool and pulled on their pants. They began circling around the horse and rider. Ramón stood taller than the other migrants, strong, composed, sure of himself. He ordered the others to back off, and they slunk out of his way.

"What are you doing?" Cara demanded, trying to pull Buck's head from his grasp.

His grip tightened, his lips clamped as he pulled the horse's head to his chest and whispered, "What the hell are you doing? This is very dangerous. Do what I say!"

The other employees gathered around him, yelling their approval of his capture. Cara felt her face burning. This was the man she had expected to protect her. He turned and laughed with the other men. She gritted her teeth and spurred the horse again, urging him to run over his captor. Buck whinnied, trying to spit out the bridle bit cutting into his tongue. He could not move his head. Cara relaxed and changed her tactics. She could deal with Ramón as an equal—a woman speaking to a man in a language they both understood.

"How dare you assault me. I own this ranch. You tell the men it is safe to return. The sheriff inspected the campground this morning and left. Everyone is needed in the hay fields immediately." She spit the words out like bullets.

She bent over to retrieve the bridle rein, grabbing it at the edge of the bit. As she leaned over the horse's neck, Ramón allowed her to straighten to a sitting position, then he pulled the rein tighter, dragging her forward. Bent forward over the saddle horn, Cara's face was within inches of Ramón's. "Don't be an idiot. Follow my lead," he whispered.

She dropped the rein and sat up, trying to hide her trembling. Her nose flared, making way for short, cropped breaths. The swimmers watched attentively, edging in.

She focused on her captor. "Give them my message and let me go."

"¿Por favor, señorita?" he asked loudly enough for the men to hear. He turned and smiled at them as if they shared a joke. Turning back to Cara, his smile disappeared and his eyes glinted. She recognized her tactical error. Ramón would not take orders from a woman in front of the other men.

One of them called to Ramón, words she could not understand. He replied in Spanish and the others guffawed and nodded, making vulgar gestures.

"Please," Cara said through clamped teeth, not looking at him. She reached for the rein. The men closed in, reaching out to touch her, pushing each other aside.

"¡No la toquen!" Ramón shouted to the men. They backed off, muttering.

Ramón took a step backward. "Well, it seems I must defend my manhood or lose face with my friends. The alpha male cannot take orders from la gringa. We will resolve this my way."

Cara understood by the tone of his voice he was implying she was a woman with loose morals for having sought out the migrant camp. The men cheered and blood rushed to her face. Jerking Buck's reins and spurring him viciously, she fought to break Ramón's grasp on the bridle. The men moved in, grabbing for the reins.

Ramón turned, barked orders, and pointed toward the hay fields. Cara understood most of his words and knew he was telling the men to break camp and return to work. A few hung their heads and shuffled, one at a time, toward the campfire. Others stood their ground, urging

Ramón to pull her from the horse. They whistled and howled like wolves. Ramón smiled at them and made a hand gesture Cara didn't understand. They nodded and began collecting their possessions as if they planned to leave.

Cara hoped for a reprieve. It seemed logical that the vaqueros wouldn't harm her if they planned to go back to work.

Ramón threw the rein he held over the horse's neck. He caught it with his other hand and yanked Cara's boot from the stirrup. He stepped into it with his bare foot and swung behind her saddle. She was crushed between his arms as he held both reins in front of her and at the same time pushed to clamp the rifle back into its scabbard.

"Stop it," she cried, pushing against him with her arms. His grip tightened and he kicked Buck with his bare heels, urging him to move. Buck fought to gain his balance under the weight of two riders and headed south.

"You're going the wrong way," Cara said.

He ignored her and spurred Buck to a faster pace.

Cara's hope that they were returning to the ranch house faded. Her only hope was to stay on Buck when Ramón dismounted and race to safety.

"Where are we going?" she asked.

He cursed and dipped his head to the side. "Get your hat out of the way!" he said, and she raised her arms as if to do his bidding. Instead, she swung her shoulders into his body and pushed backward, to jostle him off Buck's rump. His arm tightened around her waist and she was pulled backward to the sharp rim of the saddle. They balanced precariously as Ramón yanked Buck to a stop.

The horse snorted and swung his head toward the riders, his eyes wild. His legs shook, and he stumbled from the unbalanced weight.

Ramón thrust Cara back into the saddle and pulled his own body against hers, holding on with one arm. "Stop your fighting," he said. "We're out of sight. This won't take long."

He sailed her hat into the tall grass and it rested there, waving on the heavy-headed weeds. Pressing his heels into Buck's flanks, he allowed the horse to walk forward, gaining his balance.

Cara felt numb. She was no match for Ramón's strength. She became aware of his cheek rubbing against her face, his whiskers scratching each time Buck took a step.

Ramón glanced back toward the camp, which had disappeared from view, then guided Buck under the trees near the river. He slipped off horse's rump, holding only one of the reins. Cara quickly spurred the horse and jerked his head toward the meadow. Ramón cursed and put all his weight on the other rein, pulling Buck's head to the ground. Cara swung her leg over the saddle and slid to the ground, running on impact. Ramón's bare foot tripped her, and she fell on her face.

"Stop being stupid!" He tied the reins to a tree limb.

She rolled over in the musty leaves and stiff needles underneath the trees. "Please don't hurt me."

"I have no intention of hurting you, if you cooperate. I'm trying to save you from these men who were criminals in Juárez. They ran drugs and committed rapes and killings. You must have read of the wolf packs and drug cartels who run things there."

Cara closed her eyes. She knew of the wolf packs who captured women, took them to the desert, raped and killed them, later leaving them for the wild animals to eat. "This is not Mexico," she said. "I need the workers to return to the fields."

"Tony could have brought that news." Ramón's voice was harsh with anger.

"Tony is busy with the baling crew."

"Ma'am, you are either brave or stupid. I know Tony. He would not have allowed you to come alone."

He held out his hand and she took it, too weak to boost herself. As she swayed in front of him, he lifted her chin and stared into her eyes.

"You will not like this, but I have one way to save face. I told the men you were my woman. They will not challenge that ownership, but we have to convince them I have taken you as my mate to guarantee your safety."

Cara slapped him across the face. He grabbed her hand and she cried in pain.

"Listen to me. There is more at stake here than your reputation. It is imperative that I maintain my cover. I'm an agent for the INS, sent here undercover. The men don't know that, and it has to be kept a secret. I need them to trust me until I find out who's running the smuggling and Mafia gangs. This plan is the only thing that will protect you and keep my secret."

"You must be crazy to think I'll cooperate."

"Would you prefer I hand you over to them? Your death would seal my secret."

Cara slumped against the tree and grabbed his hand as he pulled at the top button on her shirt. "No," she said.

He stopped at her command and dropped one hand to the ground where he picked up a handful of dirt and brushed it across her cheeks. Cara choked on sobs. "I'm sorry," he said. "But they have to believe I took you for my own. It's what the gangs do in Juárez." She clawed at his face with her free hand. He cursed and captured her wrists again.

Her screams echoed through the trees. Ramón dropped his hands, backed away, and wiped his lips. Cara lunged toward him, screaming louder and leaving nail marks across his forehead.

"That's enough," he said, "They will believe I slept with a tiger." Cara collapsed, squatting against the tree. Ramón stood unmoving until she stopped crying, then he reached out, pulling her up. She swayed as he smoothed hair off her forehead.

She spat in his face and he smiled, wiping his fingers where it landed, touching them to his lips.

"I hate you. You'll die for this. Mark my word."

He shook his head. "You don't know what hate is. And it is not in your best interest to kill me. I will order the wolves never to speak of this incident. They live by a gang code and they will treat you with great respect and protect you if you cooperate. On the other hand, if you deny you are my mate, you become their target." He paused. "I will not worry when we meet again."

"We won't meet again. You get off my ranch."

"We'll see, after you've thought about it and considered what's in the best interest of the Los Lobos. If you kick me out, the INS will assume you're hiding information." He pulled Buck's reins from the tree limb. "Let's go."

Cara stumbled to Buck's side, but she was too exhausted to pull herself into the saddle. Ramón lifted her, one hand beneath her armpit and the other beneath her crotch. She settled in place, and he mounted behind her.

"Don't tell anyone what happened here today. Not even Tony. And give thanks that you're alive."

Cara shuddered, hugging her arms to her body for comfort. She didn't resist the sweaty heat from Ramón's body, but rested in the circle of his arms, his hands holding the reins. When they passed the patch of grass where her hat perched, Ramón guided Buck near it, leaned over, and plucked it up without pausing.

At the camp, a roar of approval from the men lingering by the river greeted Ramón's return. Maneuvering the horse so that the men could view his trophy, he pointed to the scratches on his face. They cheered wildly. He pushed Cara's hat onto her head and wrapped her fingers around the reins. Dismounting by pushing away and landing on the ground behind Buck, he punched his fist high above his head in a victory salute, then spoke to Cara. "We will arrive at the fields in an hour."

He slapped Buck's rump. "¡Arre! ¡Veéte!" he yelled.

Buck jumped forward. The wind whipped Cara's hat into the air and it sailed to Ramón's feet. He reached down, picked it up, and slapped it against his thigh. The horse ran as if his life depended upon it.

At the ranch, Buck galloped across the road, past the house and the garage to the stables. Cara unsaddled him and left him loose in the corral without his usual rubdown.

She slipped into the garage shower, hoping to hide the dirt from Lupe. She pulled off her shirt and hid it below the trash in the container near the door of the garage, then dropped her filthy jeans into the dirty clothes hamper.

In the shower, tears flowed as the hot water seared her body. She felt the grit under her feet after it washed from her hair and face. She kicked the side of the shower and then beat on it with her fists. The water became tepid, then icy. Cara gasped and the tears stopped. She dried her aching body and reached for Clay's robe without apology. Wrapping it tightly, she hurried to her bathroom upstairs, where she found painkillers for her head, salves for her scratches, and eye drops to mingle with her tears.

Going to look for the vaqueros by herself had been stupid. Her actions probably proved Howard's point that she could not handle the migrant work force. She had been suspicious of Ramón, but if he indeed was an agent for the INS, she should have been informed. She kicked a wastebasket out of her way. This wasn't a crime she could report. But she could learn from it. She had to start over and act smarter next time. She had told Howard she would find a solution to the undocumented workers problem if the government began clamping down on ranchers who hired them. Today she suffered the consequences of not following through on her claim. Tomorrow she would find a way to replace the wolf pack.

In front of the mirror, she used makeup to cover the rash where Ramón had brushed his beard against her face. With her little finger, she touched Vaseline to her lips, still red and tender. There was little she could do to improve her eyes. They were bloodshot, and the lids were swollen and reddened to the point of looking bloody. She reached again for eye drops.

A fingernail was broken on the hand she'd used to scratch his forehead. She smoothed the remaining nail with an emery board and dug dirt the shower had not found from beneath the other nails. The scratches on the backs of her hands surprised her. She didn't remember how she got them. She applied makeup there also.

Her body was a mess. Inside, she was still shaking. Rummaging in a drawer, she found lightly shaded reading glasses she could get away with wearing in the house.

8

The Bargain

Cara carried Clay's robe to the kitchen and threw it on a chair near Lupe's ironing board.

"What happened to you?" Lupe asked.

"What do you mean?"

"You found the vaqueros."

"Yes. They are back in the fields by now."

"What happened to your face?"

"Buck ran under some low-hanging tree limbs." Cara poured a glass of milk and found cookies in the jar on the counter. She sat at the table, resigned to dodging as many of Lupe's questions as she could.

"What do you want for lunch, dear?"

"A sandwich sounds good." Lupe went to the refrigerator and gathered the fixings.

"Why were you riding under the trees?"

"It's a long story, Lupe. I don't have time to talk about it."

"I warned you."

Cara felt blood rising up her cheeks and flooding her face. She'd had enough problems today. She didn't need to quarrel with Lupe. "It's over, Lupe. Let it go." She snatched the sandwich and tore into the first bite, hoping the questioning would stop.

"Clay is a good man," Lupe said as she returned the food to the refrigerator.

Cara swallowed the tender roast beef, glad Lupe had given up on the vaquero question but not happy discussing Clay. "So?"

"I talked to him this morning. He is very concerned about you."

"Why were you talking to him?"

"I called to find Pablo."

"And?"

"He said Pablo and María had moved into the carriage house, and Pablo is working up in the mountains."

Cara was astonished. Lupe and Clay were taking charge of her problems behind her back, and all she could do was create more. "Anything else I should know?"

"Tony called and said the migrants are back in the fields. You can stop worrying about them."

Cara controlled her pleasure at hearing the news. It worked! she thought and left a puzzled Lupe watching her as she stalked out the door toward the barns.

At the stables, she found Buck standing alone in the corral, his head drooping, while the other horses stood in the shade of a tree, flicking flies.

"I'm sorry, fellow. You had a rough morning." She led him toward his stall, but at the gate he stopped and snorted, pulling against the halter.

"What's the matter?" she asked, and then she saw the hat she had lost at the river, hanging from a nail on the gate to his stall. She froze.

"He smells a wolf, señorita," Ramón said from the hay loft, where he sat on the top step of the ladder, Mouser in his lap. The cat blinked at Cara, then lifted her head, aloof. "Don't mind her. She has a nest full of babies, and she doesn't want you to find them." He ran his hand down the cat's back and she purred her appreciation.

"Don't give me your 'señorita' garbage. You speak English as well as I do. You're not from Mexico."

"I was born in Mexico, but you're right about my education. I was sent to an American academy at the age of eight. I became an American citizen when I was eighteen."

Cara ignored the cat, but Ramón's presence enraged her. "You have your nerve, coming back here. How do you know the sheriff isn't on his way?"

"A smart woman would have sense enough not to call him. I'm guessing you're very smart."

"I should shoot you. That's what you deserve. It would be self-defense." She showed him her hand. "I have the scratches to prove it."

"I told you not to fight."

"I don't take orders from you. I want you off this ranch today, or I will call the sheriff."

Ramón suppressed a smile. "Now you're acting like a helpless woman, not a smart leader who makes rational decisions for the good of her people."

"I am a woman, but I'm not helpless. You treated me with disrespect in front of my employees, and I will not put up with that."

"I apologized for what I had to do, but you have to admit it worked. The migrants will give you the respect you deserve now."

"If what you say is true, they will show respect to their leader's mate. I don't fill that position."

"True. But they don't know that. I will respect you as my boss as long as I work on the ranch."

"You no longer work on the ranch."

Ramón sighed, pushed Mouser from his lap and moved down the ladder, his eyes focused on Cara's. He had bathed in the creek. A faded denim shirt hung open to his waist. The mustache was heavy above his lip, hanging past the corners of his mouth. His self-assurance angered and frightened Cara. He had assaulted her, and now he was invading her space again, as if he belonged here. As if he were her equal.

He stopped at the foot of the ladder, and Cara noted with satisfaction she had left jagged scratches across his forehead and serum seeped from a cut on his lip. They didn't speak as she pulled Buck's halter, urging him into the stall.

Ramón sat down on a lower step of the ladder, his elbows on his knees, relaxed, as if they were business friends closing a deal. "I'm sorry to hear that, because it means I can no longer protect you from the migrants, nor negotiate for you with the INS."

"I don't need anyone to stand between me and the INS. I'm sure they know I'm not running a stash house and I'm not smuggling migrants."

"You do have migrants without green cards."

"You'd stoop to blackmail?"

"Call it what you wish. I can have your workers picked up tonight, and your hay will lie in the field, if that's the game you want to play."

"Why did you come to my ranch?"

"I came because Tony is my uncle. I thought, with that connection, there would be fewer questions about my presence."

"Does Tony know what you're doing here?"

"He knows I work for Immigration. I asked him not to tell you."

"Let me get this straight. You want me to act as if you hadn't assaulted me this morning, and you want me to enter into a conspiracy against the people who work for me."

"No. The people who work for you aren't guilty, but they can lead me to the people who are. I can't imagine you would object to our catching international gang members who deal in drugs and trafficking humans. I would like to continue my work here because what happened today—despite the trauma it caused you—put me in solid with the migrants. They trust me. My work can be completed in a very short time if you'll allow me to continue."

Cara stared at Ramón as if he were a stranger. Which he was. At the site of the bear attack, she had admired his competent treatment of Rosita's wounds. On a horse, he struck an imposing posture. At her father's mass, he had made friends with Clay and mingled with the leaders of the community. Today, he'd turned into the leader of a wolf pack.

Her head whirled. "How do I know you're telling the truth?"

"You'll have to trust me."

"Today's paper said a woman was murdered in town because her family moved into another gang's territory. The sheriff thinks I'm running a stash house and presumably cooperating with gangs who may also operate in the territory. What's to keep the gangs from coming after me if they find out you're here?"

"There are no guarantees in this world, but I wouldn't stay if I thought I was endangering your life, or Tony's and Lupe's. As I said, the *coyotes* and smugglers know where the stash houses are. They know they aren't on your ranch, even if the sheriff doesn't."

Relieved at some of this news, Cara picked up a brush and began grooming Buck. "What about Pablo? I know he's recruiting migrants. He brought María and her child . . . and you, I presume."

"Pablo is small-time. He's not a smuggler."

"How do you know?"

"I don't have proof, but he's just a kid. The INS is not after small fry. We want the Mafia. We can find them through the *coyotes*."

"Do my workers know what you're doing?"

"I hope not. They don't ask questions."

"Show me your credentials."

"It would be dangerous for me to carry credentials. I can ask my supervisor to get in touch with you. It will take a day or two."

Unable to concentrate on the grooming, Cara set the brush aside. "I will cooperate with you only if you get rid of the troublemakers. I won't allow criminals to hide out on my ranch."

"I'm getting my best information from the bad guys. The *coyote* keeps in touch with them. He's the one who will lead me to the Mafia."

"It seems we're at an impasse. I won't have them on my ranch."

Ramón walked away, rubbing his forehead. He turned. "What if we had Tony move them up to the pastures you lease from the government? They'd like that, and I could go with them. I'd be aware of any contacts they made off the ranch."

"That might work for a few weeks. We'll be selling those cattle within a month. How long will it take you to get the information you need?"

"Not long. The INS is closing in."

"I want them fired as quickly as possible. Then we'll need to hire workers who can stay through the harvest and move the cattle to winter pastures."

"That won't be easy. Most of the people who come over are undocumented."

"You know as well as I do that the government has always turned its head when ranchers hired undocumented workers during our busy seasons. This present crackdown puts us in an untenable position. We have to find other people who need jobs." She paused. "You say you taught at the university. What do those students do for summer jobs?"

"They work at McDonald's."

"I can pay more than McDonald's does. Also, I'll give them more than thirty-hour work weeks, so they can be put on our health insurance plan. They'd get to live in the country, ride horses, fish in the lake, bring their wives or girlfriends—whom we can also hire. If we fire those four, I'll need to replace them quickly."

Ramón frowned "I doubt that you'd be happy with college kids. Not many male students still need a job at this time of the year, and women aren't qualified to do the labor required on a ranch."

"That's a strange thing to say. I assume you've noticed I'm female, and I've worked here since I was a teenager. You also underestimate the young people who may never have lived on a farm or ranch but are now having trouble finding summer work in town. They can learn and they're industrious."

Ramón flushed. "All right. What you say is probably true. I don't want to argue about who gets hired—what concerns me is that you are firing the very men who will help me find the gang leaders and Mafia bosses. That will destroy all the progress the INS has made in the past few months."

"If I can't control the men who are working on my ranch, they will destroy all I and my family have worked for, for many years. My brother, like you, thinks I can't control the migrant workers. I told him I would or else I'd find replacements. I suggest you allow me to do one or the other, or else get off my ranch."

She watched as wheels seemed to turn in Ramón's brain. He finally conceded.

"I understand your problem. I'll remind the men that you are the boss and they have to give up their lawless ways or leave. If we move them up north, they won't be able to cause trouble, and if they quit, you can offer their jobs to the wives of the documented workers who stay."

"And I'll hire the older women to form a daycare for the children." Cara struggled to hide the smile at the resolution to her problem. "Get it done immediately, and have Tony report back to me."

"Am I to assume I've been re-hired?"

Cara walked toward the barn door. She turned and spit out, "Against my better judgment."

"Thank you. You will not be disappointed. There is one other thing. These people need to learn enough English to fill out forms. I have time in the evenings to teach, but I need pencils, paper, books. Can you get them for me?"

Pride aside, reading and writing classes for the migrants was a good idea. She had suggested it to her father, but he had vetoed the idea, afraid migrants who could read and write English would not remain on the ranch or would expect higher wages. She wondered what he would say about the decisions she'd made today. She studied the man with whom she had compromised. Her father would have killed him—or had a heart attack trying. Perhaps this was the best solution under the circumstances. Satisfied with the peaceful resolution, she would deal with her own injuries in private.

"I can find pencils and paper at the house. I have no schoolbooks." She paused. "That will require a trip to town."

Ramón carried Mouser to the ladder and sat stroking her back. He touched the cut on his lip. "I'll wait here for you to get the supplies you have."

Cara hesitated, torn between doing his bidding and telling him to go to hell. She tried to think of a reason to discourage starting a school for the Mexican nationals. She could think of none.

As she started toward the house, Ramón called after her. "Ma'am, maybe you could bring me a book to read for pleasure."

She continued as if she hadn't heard him. And it was true, lending him a book to read was low on her list of priorities. Right now she was grinning inside. Wait until Howard found out how she had solved the employee problem!

At the office, she opened the doors to the supply closet, kicked aside empty boxes she'd piled there, looking for one small enough to hold what she needed. Loading the box with pencils and paper, she remembered with nostalgia her first day of school, when the bus, filled with noisy children, came by the ranch house. She loved the smell of new tablets, long, sharpened pencils, unbroken crayons. She pulled a package of yellow legal pads off the shelf. Without counting, she opened a box of yellow pencils and pushed them one by one into the electric sharpener. They'd need a small hand-held sharpener, which she found buried in a junk drawer, along with colored pencils she hadn't used in years. This is kindergarten for adults, she thought. She added a large plastic container of worn and broken crayons.

She reached to the library shelves, looking for books Ramón might read for pleasure. She pulled out her copy of Hemingway's *For Whom the Bell Tolls.* Ramón would have read this book many times, but his students would like hearing about the Spanish Civil War. That should keep him busy. She headed back to the barn with the supplies.

Ramón was asleep, his head on his arms propped across his knees, Mouser at his feet. Cara cleared her throat twice before the man woke with a start. She took pleasure in the panic in his eyes.

He jumped up and took the box from her. He glanced at what she had collected and said, "You're an angel."

"That sounds like a step up from 'mate to the alpha male.'"

The pleasure on Ramón's face disappeared. He closed the box. "I know you can never forgive me for what happened this morning, but I forgive myself, because I did it to save your life."

Cara couldn't argue the point. "I'll pick up workbooks when I go to town, and I'll leave them with Lupe. Please don't bother me again."

"I understand."

Cara watched as he slipped out the door, heading up the trail to the camp. She relaxed, satisfied with their agreement. The hay would be saved, and the criminals in her work force would be removed to the furthest edge of the ranch, then fired. Now all she had to do was convince herself that she, not Ramón, had handled the situation appropriately.

9

If the Earth Moves

Cara spent the next morning in the office, assisting Tony in preparing work schedules for the ranch. "It's a good thing you found the vaqueros," he said. "We'll finish baling hay this week." He handed the completed schedule to her. "It took guts to hunt down those Mexicans. It could have turned out bad for you, but you've proved you can handle this place. Your papa would be proud." As if embarrassed at speaking his mind, Tony turned to leave.

Cara's stomach burned with a heat that spread to her face. Tony's opinion was important to her, and she wondered how he would react if he heard the full story of her fiasco with Ramón at the river. If he had heard, he was keeping it a secret. He had grumbled when Cara insisted that Ramón's schedule should take him to the far north side where the corrientes were pastured.

"That's not the best place to use him," Tony had said. "Anyone can watch for coyotes and wolves. I need Ramón to manage the crews."

Cara pretended not to hear him, unwilling to tell Tony the real reason for sending Ramón away.

She busied herself in the office after Tony left. She expected her plan to be carried out promptly. She wanted Ramón's leadership diminished so that he could not take charge of the workforce.

What angered her more than his assumption of leadership over the workers was her inability to ignore or deny his power to ignite emotional sparks between the two of them. She feared her efforts to remain aloof proved there was a connection. As she completed the work schedule, the telephone rang and she found herself listening to Roger Scott of the INS thank her for allowing Ramón Chavez, nephew of Tony Chavez, to complete his important work on her ranch. He hung up without further explanation.

She threw up her hands. Some confirmation! Roger Scott could be any drinking buddy Ramón might know, fulfilling the promise to verify his legitimate place in the INS. He must think she was stupid, and perhaps she was, but she preferred to think she was just tired of fighting this battle. At least his time here was limited.

Hoping to put an end to her obligations to Ramón, Cara drove to K-Mart. She filled two sacks with beginners' language workbooks and children's readers, which she lugged to the car.

At home, she stacked the supplies on the back porch, explaining to Lupe that Ramón would pick them up. Disgruntled by the realization she had delayed his teaching of English to the workers by sending him to work at the far edge of the ranch, she saw no way to remedy that situation. He wouldn't return to the camp until the weekend.

By late afternoon on Thursday, she had tired of seeing the books she'd piled by the door, constantly reminding her of Ramón. Knowing he wasn't at the camp, she decided to deliver the books so that he would have no reason to come down the mountain. She asked Pepito to pick them up and fill as many saddlebags as necessary to get them to the camp. While he was doing that, she finished working on the office ledgers to find assets that could be liquefied to pay the taxes. As she prepared to quit for the day, Clay's truck pulled into the driveway outside her window. She chided herself for the feeling of excitement flooding over her as she pulled eye drops from her desk drawer, hoping the medicine cleared the red streaks on the whites of her eyes that still lingered; Clay watched her too keenly. To cover them further, she put the shaded glasses back on and went to the kitchen, where Lupe stood looking out the window.

"He brought the children back," she said. "They're headed out to the barn. Going riding, I guess."

"Good," Cara said. "They need to get away from town occasionally."

"I see Tony at the stables. He'll be hungry soon. Will you eat with us?"

"No. Go ahead without me. I had Pepito pack the schoolbooks in saddlebags, and he'll load them onto Buck. I want to ride to the camp while it's cool. Ramón will need the supplies this weekend for his classes. If I start now, I can get back before dark."

Lupe frowned. "You got no business riding to that camp alone. Ramón can get his own books."

"I know, but he's working on the far side of the ranch and won't come back to the camp before tomorrow. This will give him more time to teach. It is safe, Lupe. There are women and children in the camp."

"You don't know what it's like in their homes. Besides, many of the men left their wives in Mexico. They have no women to control them."

"Lupe, this is my home. I'll go where I want to go."

"Ramón could send one of the men to get the books."

Cara smiled at Lupe's persistence. "You're just full of good ideas. I'll tell him to do that next time."

"Huh." Lupe didn't sound appeased.

Two days of rest had left Buck with more energy than Cara could muster. She felt tension in his muscles. Did he know where they were going? A half hour later, she rode into the camp where the vaqueros, with women and children, sat on rocks arranged around a campfire. Stanchions held pots over the coals. Spoons clinked against tin plates as they ate. Ramón sat on the tallest rock, reading aloud from the book she'd loaned him. She pulled Buck to a quick stop. What was he doing here? She considered leaving, but heads were turning. Ramón laid his book aside and strode out to greet her. Buck reared as Ramón reached for his bridle, forcing him to back away.

"He has a good memory, and he doesn't like wolves."

Ramón waited until Buck's agitation calmed. "I will win him over, given time. I'm not so sure about his mistress."

Cara had no intention of getting into a dialogue with Ramón. "I brought the school supplies. Get them out of the saddlebags, please."

Ramón moved to Buck's flank and struggled to untie the straps Pepito had knotted. Impatient, Cara swung to the ground and began working on the other strap.

"Why don't we just take out the books and leave the saddlebags in place?" Ramón asked.

Cara gritted her teeth. "Fine. Just get them out. I'm in a hurry."

Ramón lifted the covering flap and pulled supplies from one of the bags. His arms full, he turned toward the campfire and signaled for the men to come. They stood, not sure of his request.

"Don't bother them. I'll carry a few." Her orders came too late. Before she could move she was surrounded by the migrants, their outstretched hands frightening her. Ramón filled every hand that reached out with books, pencils, crayons, and paper. Cara was lost in their midst. A few of these men were potential rapists and murderers. Why hadn't she listened to Lupe? To her surprise, the noise turned to quiet expressions of wonder as the migrants examined the gifts. Loud laughter and shouting dissolved into ohs and ahs.

"Gracias," they said, over and over as they left, wandering back toward the fire, fingering the treasures, showing them to each other. Cara found herself standing alone, wondering at the change in their demeanor. Ramón's voice awakened her from her reverie.

"We were reading from Hemingway when you came," he said "They love to hear about the Spanish Civil War. Perhaps you could read a page to them in English—to show the music of Hemingway's words." He pointed to the vaqueros. "They won't understand the meaning, of course."

"No, I can't do that. It's getting late." The sun's globe was sinking near the horizon, and she judged that she had just enough time to get to the barns before dusk.

"Don't worry. I'll go back with you if it gets dark. Please. Read a page or two." Ramón's fingers encircled her elbow, as if she had agreed, and he guided her toward the campfire.

"Lea, lea," the vaqueros called, and Cara found herself in a dream, walking to the rock where Ramón had sat. He opened the novel to the page where he had turned down the corner, handed it to her, and walked to the shadows behind the circle of migrants.

Cara began reading with hesitation. But the smell of the heather on the mountain, as Hemingway described it, was intoxicating. Her voice became stronger, rising and falling with the words describing the flowers that brushed against Jordan's leg, warming with the sun on his head, sailing with the breeze from the snow of the mountain peak, cool on his back. Cara's voice lowered. *And in his hand, he felt the girl's hand firm and strong, the fingers locked in his.* She swallowed, unable to go on. The story was approaching the love scene, which she refused to read aloud even though the migrants wouldn't understand. Ramón would. She closed the book and handed it to him. "That's enough." She nodded to her audience. "Buenas noches," she said, and hurried toward her horse.

Ramón followed her. "Thank you," he said. "You captivated them." He touched her elbow as she started to mount.

She jerked her arm away and glared at Ramón. "I suspect you were the one who was captivated."

"That's true. But please don't be angry. You must have noticed that the people were moving to the rhythm of the words—the music of this love song from a woman's voice. They heard it, and responded, even though they didn't understand the words."

"And what did it do for you?" She wished she hadn't asked.

Ramón smiled and his eyes became dark pools, dancing with lights that beckoned her to plunge inside. She hurried to mount Buck.

"The same as for Jordan." Ramón touched his chest, then pointed toward Cara. "For both of us," he said. "The earth could move for both of us, no?"

"No," she said, "and why aren't you riding the fences where Tony sent you? You were not supposed to be here."

"Tony had us herd the cattle to another pasture this week. There were enough vaqueros working there."

Angry that she wasn't consulted about this move, she put to rest one last issue between them. "Roger Scott called today and confirmed that your work with the department is legitimate. For your information, I still have my doubts. This school is my last effort on your behalf. Don't ask me for any more favors."

She slashed the ends of the reins in an arc between them, hitting Buck with a loud snap. He jumped forward, galloping out of the campground. Cara's heart pounded to the beat of his hooves. She had successfully shown the migrants she was not afraid of them, but she had failed with Ramón. Trembling, she pulled Buck to a walk, afraid he might stumble on the rocky path. The trees beside the trail were almost hidden in the shady dusk. Buck snorted as if he sensed the presence of danger, and she spurred him on, weighing the fear of the unknown against the chance the horse might fall on the rocky path.

10

Wolves and Pheromones

In the stable, Cara's fingers trembled as she fumbled with the saddle cinch. Her victory at making peace with the migrants was overshadowed by her inability to handle Ramón. She pulled harder on the leather strap. Buck took a deep breath and pushed out on his chest and belly, tightening the cinch.

"You bum," she said. "You're doing that just to irritate me." She slapped him on the rump and waited until he exhaled so she could pull the strap loose.

"Were you talking to me?" Clay asked, walking in from the corral.

Cara jumped. Her answer to Clay carried anger she felt toward Ramón. "No," she said. "But if the shoe fits . . ."

Clay scratched behind Buck's ears. "Fellow, you and I need to talk. Getting this woman angry is a bad idea. Especially when I planned to invite myself over for a nightcap." Clay took the saddle from Cara and stored it near the stall. He leaned against the boards and smiled at her. "You know, if you keep beating up on me like this, I may come to the conclusion you don't like me."

"Sorry," she said. "It's been a tough week." She took warm water and sponged the sweaty salt off Buck's body.

"Sounds like you could use a nightcap too. I've had more than my share of crises this week, so we can cry on each other's shoulders."

Cara had to smile. He knew his strengths well. Did anyone ever say no to him? She began to relax. She'd often allowed herself to believe the worst of Clay, of men in general, because they held all the cards, deciding at their pleasure when to play them. She dried Buck's coat and threw a light blanket over his back for the night. "I'll meet you on the portal. What can I fix you to drink? Bourbon?"

"On the rocks," he said.

"You got it." She went to the kitchen for ice and glasses. Taking bourbon from her father's stash in the office, she brought water to weaken her drink and settled down on the porch, determined to put Ramón out of her mind.

"The kids are dead to the world. They enjoyed their ride," Clay said, as he climbed the stone steps to the porch and dropped into a chair beside her. She looked to the left to avoid his seeing her face. It was getting dark, and she'd had to remove her dark glasses.

"You must have turned on the charm for that psychologist," she said.

"You may be right, but I'd like to think my obvious parenting skills made it a no-brainer. She spent an hour testing me and watching me with the kids and saw no problems. She thought bringing them out to ride horses was a plus."

He took a long drink and looked at Cara. "That's my story. Now it's your turn to tell me why you're hiding behind dark glasses." His voice was gentle, as if he were almost afraid to ask.

"I was riding down by the creek and ran under low tree branches."

"Both eyes and hands?"

Cara hid her broken nails. "The same," she said.

He looked away. "Lupe called on Tuesday to find Pablo. She said you were riding to the river alone. Were you on Gus?"

"No."

"Well, the whole thing seems very strange to me."

"Are you questioning my story?" Her voice rose as she realized it did sound farfetched.

He smiled and pulled her hand to the arm of the wicker chair where he examined the scratches. "I didn't say that."

She retrieved her hand and tightened it into a fist. She had made up her mind to keep Tuesday's happenings a secret from Tony and Lupe. Her failure would color every decision she made in the future. But perhaps Clay would understand, and she did want to unburden herself. "You want the whole story?" she asked.

"I'm curious."

"Howard's right about my inability to handle the migrants. I rode to their river camp to order them back to their jobs, and I failed miserably." She relaxed and waited for the confession to make her feel better.

Clay leaned forward, elbows on his knees, listening to each word. "Why didn't you wait? I could have gone with you. Pablo came into the office soon after Lupe called. He could have come too."

"I didn't think it was a big deal." She sipped her drink and placed the glass on the table, lacing her fingers together in a fist. "Besides, I wanted to prove I could handle them alone."

"What happened?"

Cara described her misguided trip to the river, and Ramón's humiliating rescue. Even now she had difficulty talking about it.

"You say he pretended to rape you to get across a message to the other men?"

She nodded.

"It sounds like a sexual assault to me. Did you report it to the sheriff?"

"Of course not! And neither should you." Cara was suddenly dismayed at her openness with Clay about her private life. She had no idea what he would do with the information, and it was important it not become public.

He turned to stare at her. "Cara, I'm your friend. You know I wouldn't say or do anything without your approval. I do find it difficult to understand your relationship with Ramón. I'm not surprised he's attracted to you. I'll admit I'm a little jealous. The problem is I don't understand what it is that keeps you and me at arm's length. Is it Ramón?" He waited, watching her widened eyes. "I'm sorry. Forget I asked that." His voice turned angry. "Despite how you may feel about me, what Ramón did makes me mad as hell. Why didn't you fire him? Or have Tony kick him the hell off the ranch?"

Cara was stunned by his outburst. "Please don't read too much into what happened with Ramón. I needed help and he gave it to me in a way that the migrants would understand. It's over and done with, and it won't go any further. I told you about it because I wanted to share it with a friend who would understand. I didn't know it would upset you."

"Why did you allow the migrants back into the camp? They sound like a band of criminals."

"You sound like Howard."

"Maybe your brother is smarter than I give him credit for."

"Thanks a lot. The truth is, I've moved the troublemakers up to ride herd on the corrientes. They are no longer a threat. You and Howard might do it differently, but it works for me."

"I'm surprised at Ramón. Maybe he isn't a gang member, but he can't be controlled, either. Are you sure you're safe around him?"

"He saved my life by quick thinking. He managed to get me away from those men under rules they understand. Believe it or not, criminals live by rules. Ramón said once the wolf pack is convinced I belong to him, I'm safe from predators."

"That whole theory sounds hokey to me. What if they find out he's tricked them? That you aren't his property?"

"How could they?"

"I don't know. Secrets have a way of leaking."

"Well, I don't have time to worry about it. My job is to save my ranch. This is my best hay crop, and I need to get it baled before it rains."

"On the other hand, you can't afford to keep them, if your life is in danger."

"Ramón agreed to identify the bad guys and get them fired. We'll do that immediately."

Clay refilled his glass and sat down at the table. "I'm sorry. I feel damned angry that these guys got away with what they did."

"Clay, I had to do it my way. Howard is pressuring me to give up the ranch. One of his arguments is that I can't handle the employees. If I make this incident public, he'll use it against me."

"It sounds to me like blackmail."

"Maybe, but I can live with that, if I save my money crops."

"Not if it's eating you up inside."

"Are you suggesting a man could have done it better? The sheriff intimated that as well."

Clay laughed, dipped his fingers in his drink, and flipped the bourbon in her direction. "No, that's not what I'm saying. You aren't a failure. I don't know of any man who could have pulled off what you did. There would probably have been a war with gunshots if a man had been in charge. You got your workers back. You're safe. We should drink to the positive things that came out of this."

Cara nodded. "I was lucky and I'm thankful for that, but I want to be right instead of lucky. My confidence in decision-making has taken a big hit. I used to feel I was right all the time."

"No one's right all the time. And good could come out of this. You could take a second look at the rules you laid down up at the lake about your personal life."

"What do you mean?"

"Well, let's forget the employee problem. We know you can handle that. I'm more interested in the very strict rules that govern your relationship with men, particularly me. You turned me down when I suggested our friendship should go beyond merely fishing together. I'm saying if you can modify the rules regarding employees, why not for your personal life? I haven't heard from you that you're working on changing those rules."

Cara gasped and then laughed. "That's a very sneaky way to open that discussion again."

"It doesn't compare to what Ramón came up with. I concede he's smarter than I am."

"Hmm. Maybe smarter, but not as charming. I'll work on it."

He rose to go. "It's a good thing you're worth waiting for. Let me know of any progress."

"Clay, what did my father tell you about me?" She needed to know if hiding her scars was an act of futility. Maybe he already knew about the accident, and it wasn't important to him, although she found that hard to believe.

Clay stopped and leaned again the porch railing. "That you're very smart, and he didn't understand why you hadn't married." Clay paused. "I guess I don't understand that about you either. You send out all the right vibes. I'm sure I'm not the only man who's responded. Ramón for instance?"

Many faces flashed before her. From high school through college, she'd turned away from men when they insisted on intimacy. Was Clay suggesting she was sending signals that she was an easy lay?

"What sort of vibes?" she asked.

Clay came back to her, leaned over, and brushed his lips against hers. His tongue slipped briefly between her lips. She pulled away.

"Don't act so surprised. You've been asking for this to happen since the first day we met."

"You read minds on the side?"

"I didn't read your mind. I got bombarded by pheromones. They tell me I'm a man and you're a woman. That's more scientific than reading minds."

"You're making this up," she said.

"Nope. It's scientific, and it convinces me that, as two healthy human beings, we have feelings that ought to be encouraged. But it takes two to tango, as the saying goes."

Cara didn't reply. She wanted to dance, she wanted to say yes, but it wasn't in her vocabulary. The man in front of her was gentle, patient, and open. He was promising her nothing except an animal coupling. Perhaps she had been sending out vibes, if that's what you called the urge to be touched and to be held in his arms.

Clay walked to the edge of the porch and stepped down. "Truth is, I respect your position. You make decisions about your personal life the same way you handle business: cautiously but intelligently. That's another reason I admire you."

Cara's heart ached as she watched him disappear around the corner of the house. She was confused by all that had happened this week. She felt her eyes begin to burn, a warning that tears were on the way. She snatched her dark glasses from the table and went inside. To hell with wolves and pheromones.

11

Women in Charge

Cara sat in the reception room of the lawyer's office, holding the file she had received from Frank's office. This office space differed from Frank's downtown suite in the bank building. It was an old house, set back from the road, with tall pine trees shading it, suggesting family law, not a corporate practice.

Was she making a mistake coming to a lawyer who had no partners to support her? Was a woman able to hold her own against multiple lawyers from a large Albuquerque firm, if Howard chose to sue? Cara felt ashamed for questioning a woman's abilities. If she could run a ranch as well as her father, a woman should be able to stand strong against male attorneys.

Trace Leader appeared in the doorway, holding Cara's information log. She spoke her name with a smile genuine and personable, and asked Cara to follow her to the office. Hanging on the wall behind her desk were certificates showing she had graduated from the University of Oklahoma Law school and that she had been editor of the American Indian Law Review. Way to go! Cara thought.

"What can I do for you?" the lawyer asked as she opened the file folder Cara produced and surveyed a copy of the will.

"My father died this summer. He left most of his estate to me, including a ranch. I have a brother Howard, who is a doctor in Denver, and a sister Emily, who is an artist, doing well in Taos. Howard has threatened to sue to overturn the will. He may not go through with his threats, but I'd feel more comfortable having an attorney on board in case he does. Also, I'll need someone to finish the probate issues for Dad's will. I owe estate taxes due in March."

"What's his basis for overturning the will?"

The story had become old for Cara, but she relayed it as truthfully as she could. Trace's eyebrows lifted in surprise as the story unfolded. "Did he leave nothing to the other children?"

"Not much." Cara explained her father's reasoning concerning his investment in the siblings' careers. "I'm sure he gave the ranch to me because I've lived and worked here for years, and he thought I'd keep the ranch the way he left it."

"And he reasoned that leaving the ranch to you was equivalent to the investment he made in the other children's careers?"

"Well, not equivalent in actual value. He paid for my education too. But what he gave them made it possible for them to earn an equivalent estate, yes. I came home to work on the ranch after I graduated from college. He thought those were equivalent investments."

"I'll search for precedent law, but off the top of my head, I'd say your brother doesn't have a legal leg to stand on, unless he can prove you used your influence in the writing of the will. Parents aren't required by law to leave anything to their children. It's standard practice to leave them a little something, even a dollar will do, just to recognize that they exist and explain why they get nothing. Your dad seems to have done that." Trace continued to read the will. "Who is your brother's attorney?"

Cara leaned forward and pulled Frank's letter from the pile of documents. "Parker, Lampton, and Wiley. They're in Albuquerque."

"Yes. I know. And Frank Wallace, here in town, wrote your father's will?"

"Yes."

"Well, I know him. That's his area of expertise. Why are you seeking different counsel?"

Cara had practiced what she would say to answer this question. She found it embarrassing to reveal what she thought was Frank's conflict of interest as she described Clay's divorce proceedings.

"You aren't a witness in the divorce case, are you?"

"No. The husband boards his horses on the ranch. Dad offered to let him rent our guesthouse as long as he needs it . . . until the divorce is over. He has two children and shares custody with his wife, so I expect him to move back to town as soon as the custody is settled."

"I don't see any conflicts," Trace said. "What divorce are you talking about, just to make sure? I often get appointed as a guardian ad litem for the children in a divorce."

Cara's voice lowered. "Clay and Bette Thompson."

Trace searched Cara's face, then shook her head. "No. Not my case." She laid the papers aside. "We'll need to sign a contract and get releases if you wish to hire me." She shuffled the papers. "No petitions have been filed, so we'll just wait to see what your brother does. I'll need to talk to Frank, since he wrote the will. Is it all right if I inquire of him about your father's state of mind at the time?"

"Of course. I'll call Frank's office and let them know I've hired you, and they're to expect your call." After signing contracts and releases, Cara handed Trace a check for the retainer fee and left the office, heading north to the ranch. This was one problem she could forget about for the time being.

It was easy to move from legal problems in the lawyer's office to her own desk at home. Bills had to be paid and checkbooks balanced. The lawyer's questionnaire took hours to complete. She had barely finished when she saw Tony on his way to oversee the herding of cattle back home from the pastures south of the mesa. She saddled Buck and spurred him to the top of a rise, where Tony sat looking down on the opened gates of the holding pasture. Vaqueros popped their whips above a slow-moving herd of cattle, driving them through the double gates that led to a new grassland. Dirt, flying into the air, muddled with dribbles of sweat rolling through the dusty hair, leaving dark, wet lines down each cow's back. Vaqueros pulled neckerchiefs over their nostrils, straining the dust from each breath, muffling their shouts. A stray calf butted its way through the crowded herd, bawling desperately for its wide-eyed mother, who was horning her way toward her offspring. The chaos made progress haphazard and frustrating.

These were the prize Highland cattle Cara had chosen despite her father's skepticism. He was a Hereford man and questioned whether this new breed would live up to its hype. Cara insisted on keeping the Highlanders separate from the mixed breeds brought from Mexico that roamed the leased Bureau of Land Management land adjoining the ranch, and from Dave's Herefords that for many years reigned as the most popular breed for beef production. She had argued that the Herefords he took such pride in required richer pastures to keep their bodies in top shape for breeding and sale value and that instead, the Highland folds could thrive on the drought-damaged pastures that had been developing over the last few years. She'd convinced him the long-haired Highlands, cross-bred with Charolais bulls, were the breed of the future, producing the finest quality beef available on today's market.

"They're beautiful, aren't they?" Cara asked.

Tony nodded. "This is the best herd we've had in years. The Charolais bulls made the difference."

"I was sure they would. Dad said I was making a mistake when I bought them. He wanted to wait another year."

"Your dad and I come from the old school. If it works, we stick with it. You're young. Willing to try new things. Look at that one." He pointed to a calf, heavy with a fuzzy coat that made him look like a fat teddy bear. "He'll bring a lot more than the calves we get from the Herefords."

"I'm hoping we have a few head left after the taxes are paid." The thought of taxes reminded her that she had delayed too long in calling her brother to discuss their father's purchase of an insurance policy to pay for the taxes. She had not heard from him since her father's death.

Leather squeaked on Tony's saddle as he jerked his horse to the right, rushing out to recover another stray calf. Cara followed him, and together they brought the stray back to the herd. Their horses pranced in place, eager to enter the fray again, but the riders pulled them to a halt and sat watching as the last cows crowded through the gates.

"We need to inventory this herd to get an estimate of how many yearlings we have. A number of the cows and heifers must go, too. Can you do that?"

"You bet. And Ramón is available." Tony pointed to the far side of the herd, where Ramón shouted directions as he snapped a whip in the air above his head. "He's good with numbers."

"Ramón?"

"Yeah. We make good partners. He's book smart. I have the ranching know-how."

"I thought he had taken some of the men up to herd the corrientes. What is he doing here?"

"He finished up there."

"Where are the men he was working with?"

"He told me to fire them. They were troublemakers."

"Are we short-handed then?"

"Not right now. The hay is baled, so we're good for another month until the next crop comes in. I've ordered three more."

Cara stared at Tony's weathered face.

"Ramón tells me he's your nephew."

Surprised, Tony spit into the grass, killing time. He inspected the movement of the cattle as Ramón maneuvered them through the gates. "Yep. He's my brother's son."

Cara looked at the vaquero, tall in the saddle, like Tony. Why hadn't she guessed the first time she'd seen them together? Their dark, deep-set eyes, even their smiles, heavy chests, and shoulders showed a familial connection. She surveyed the older man leaning against the saddle horn, chewing tobacco, pretending this revelation between them was routine, like discussing the purchase of new bulls. He came to the United States with her father, both as teenagers, and he became the right-hand man—the manager of the ranch—from day one. She loved him like a father, and he treated her with the same devotion. Like her father, he never spoke of personal matters. What she knew of his family came from Lupe.

"He also told me he was working for the government—trying to find out who's making money transporting undocumented workers and drugs across the country, after they cross the border. What happens if the people who oppose what he's doing find him on my property?"

Tony's eyes darkened. "He won't be found. He's too smart."

"Even smart people get caught."

She stared across the herd at the man who had puzzled her from the day they met. She had learned a lot about him, most of it troubling. Was he passing on information to the sheriff and the INS that would reveal incriminating labor practices on her ranch? It wasn't possible to verify every green card she approved, and she had no wish to do so. These people needed jobs. They were hard workers, and she needed them.

However, no matter how admirable Ramón's employment appeared, she had no desire to go to jail or lose her ranch to protect a mole.

"Tell Ramón to get me the number of cattle available to market this month." Her voice was brusque, and she didn't wait for an answer but spurred Buck toward the barns. She moved to the easy rhythm of Buck's stride, disturbed by the irony of allowing the wolf to be in charge of counting her cattle.

At the ranch house, she headed to the office where she found a note from Lupe that Clay had called with a request that she drop by his office after work. She frowned, wondering what he wanted.

First, she really must call Howard. His greeting was cool, and she wasn't prepared for the belligerent accusations he made about her influence in the writing of the will. It was her fault, he said, not their father's, that he and Emily had been left out of the will. Their father was incompetent at the time he died and not capable of making independent decisions. Howard repeated his demand that Cara correct his mistake by selling the ranch and dividing the assets equally. His final threat was to sue to overturn the will if she refused to cooperate. He said he had talked to lawyers, which was no surprise to Cara.

"Do what you have to do, Howard. I will be following Dad's wishes."

She laid down the telephone and stood looking at it as if she expected it to come alive and continue the outrageous spewing of accusations. She sat down at her father's desk and closed her eyes, searching for the source of Howard's venom. Why had their father left her the ranch? She knew he loved all his children. Had he considered the possibility that his actions would split the siblings apart? Was preserving his heritage more important than keeping the family together? And should she give it the same priority?

She looked at the painting of Pancho Villa evaluating the wealth he saw in the corrals below. Her father had taken pleasure in imagining Villa coveting his wealth. She knew he would expect her to protect his estate with the same vigor he had.

As she rose to leave the office, she noticed a neat pile of paper stacked on the corner of her desk. Beside the sheets were the books she had loaned to Ramón. She sat down smiling. She was better at interpreting what people wrote than what they shouted over the telephone.

Dear Ms. Morgan, she read on the first sheet, and the same greeting topped each page thereafter, all in letter form. She laid them down, looking around the office to see if she was alone. She fingered the pages again and carried them to a window seat. Trees shaded that side of the house, but light from the noontime sun glanced off the driveway and fell onto the pages. Several of the migrant students had written letters using a mixture of bright crayons. Her heart began a soft rat-a-tat. Could these letters serve as evidence that she was part of an underground network supporting the movement of illegal Mexican migrants into American society? Teaching them to use the English language was a definite step in that direction, which was why a number of politicians objected to adding such classes to the American school system. Were the letters written to connect her to mob activities? Had she fallen for Ramón's plan because of her innocent belief that education was good—that everyone would benefit from the sharing of a common language?

Thank you for paper and pencils. Ramón is good teacher. José.

Thank you for music. Soon we learn words. Johnny.

Please forgive bad acts on river. Your friend. We talk when learn English. Pedro.

Cara laid the papers aside, unable to finish reading. She had become a part of something volatile. What if José, Johnny, and Pedro became teachers? Great writers? Or what if they used those talents in terrorist acts? She heard her father grumbling over her shoulder. Teaching migrants to read and write doesn't make sense. Just runs up their going price. As soon as they get a diploma, they'll refuse to work on farms and ranches. Isn't that what happened to the US work force?

She threw the papers down on the desk. Teaching the migrants English was one thing. The question remained, was Ramón teaching more than just reading and writing? What if his interest in teaching was a cover for the gangsters who were transporting drugs? What if agreeing to fire them was just a cover for his real motive? Perhaps he'd just moved them to another ranch.

She reached again for the letters. When she lifted the last one, written in beautiful script, her frown deepened. It bore Ramón's signature.

Dear Cara: I trust you appreciate the sincerity of my students' messages. They worked late into the night, rewriting them many times. You will forgive my presumptions, but I assured them you would respond.

Under Lupe's watchful and disapproving eyes, I borrowed two more of your books. I will return them pronto. With warmest regards, Ramón.

P. S. The colored pencils are now worn down to stubs.

Cara shuffled the papers into a neat stack and hurried to the kitchen, where Lupe bent over the open oven door.

"When did Ramón come by?"

Lupe put her hands on her hips and faced Cara. "This morning, early. He met Tony, and they went to count the cows. I told him to leave the papers with me, but he went right past me into your office, as if he owned this place. He took your books too."

Cara patted her shoulder. "It's all right, Lupe. I told him he could borrow the books."

She hadn't told him any such thing. She knew he was pushing the boundaries of their agreement, as if it were his right to intrude on her space. She'd set stricter limits the next time they met.

12

El Paso Street

At five minutes to six, Cara parked in front of Clay's office, responding to his invitation to come see his new house the following Tuesday. She had spent half an hour at the hospital, talking with the physical rehab staff about Rosita's progress. She learned they were pleased with the mobility of the arm but anticipated continuing to work with Rosita for several weeks, perhaps months. They were aware María had moved into the carriage house behind Clay's home, that she had a job babysitting, and they hoped that Rosita would be returned to her soon.

Cara had spent another half hour at the bookstore, collecting supplies and the next set of workbooks in phonics and writing for Ramón's students. She remembered his postscript about the stubby colored pencils, and despite her reluctance to submit to his undisguised bidding, she selected five boxes of colored pencils. She was too deep into his project to back out now.

Clay tapped on her car window before sliding in beside her.

"Where are we going?"

"909 El Paso Street."

"That's in the historic part of town, right?" Cara pulled out into traffic, following his pointing finger.

"You're right. It was built in the 1940s by one of the early mining tycoons. Needs updating in the kitchen and bathrooms, but the structure is perfect. It's around the corner from where Bette's living, so the kids can move back and forth whenever they want."

"I thought she kept your home."

"We sold it. It was too expensive and too far out of town."

"Is she pleased that you're buying a house just around the corner from her?"

"She's beginning to understand there are two sides in every divorce—ours and the kids'. Since I get to keep the kids almost half the time, it's better to live where it's easy to move them back and forth."

"Is joint parenting time the same as joint custody?"

"Yep." Clay pushed his fist above his head in a victory salute. "I won!" His grin was infectious.

On a corner lot off a broad street, the house sat surrounded by a half acre of lawn, shadowed by huge cottonwoods and pine trees. It stood two stories tall. Cara parked near the curb.

"First impression?" Clay asked as they got out of the car.

"I love it."

Clay opened one of the two massive doors, and they stepped inside an entranceway of custom-made tile. The ceiling was high, and a curved stairway leading to the second floor dominated the north wall. On the first floor, an arched opening revealed a sitting room, beyond which spread out a dining area large enough to seat twenty people. French doors opened onto a patio of red slate mined from surrounding mountains.

"The size is unbelievable. What will you do with all this room?"

"It's not all that much bigger than yours. It looks bigger because it's empty and because of the high ceilings. The kitchen is a disaster, very small, because they had few appliances in those days. But there's room to extend it into this dining room." Clay pointed to the right. "Let me show you upstairs."

They took a back stairway to the second floor and entered a room that spread across most of the west side of the house. An expanse of windows granted views of the mountains showing above the tall trees in the sloping backyard, where a gazebo overlooked a swath of wild grass that sloped to a small house built for servants.

"What do you think?"

"I can't believe it. The view is fantastic. I can just imagine a huge, full moon sitting on the top of that peak. Is this your bedroom?"

Clay nodded. "My get-away. A place to hide."

"I know what you mean. I love my upstairs suite. I'm having trouble convincing myself I should move into the downstairs bedroom now that Mother and Dad are gone. I'm doing better adjusting to Dad's office. It's peaceful working in there." She opened the door to a smaller room adjoining the bedroom, expecting a closet.

"That's a nursery. Handy, isn't it?"

Cara closed the door and leaned against it. Her own home had never had a nursery. Emily, Howard, and she had slept in her parents' room until they were old enough to share the room of a sibling. The thought of a nursery scared her. It would be filled with baby things one saw in store windows—cribs, diaper tables, mobiles. Not to mention babies. The list went on forever. As the youngest in her family, she'd never been around an infant. Her breasts had never developed after the accident, so she'd avoided the thought of motherhood.

"Clay, why are you getting a divorce?"

He turned and walked to the window, his back to her.

"I'm sorry to be nosey," she said. "I'm just trying to understand why this place appeals to you. It's made for a big family, don't you think?"

"I have a big family. My sister has five children, my brother has three. My parents are still alive, retired down south. So I hope they'll all come at one time or another."

"If you're so committed to family, why did your marriage fail?"

"The divorce wasn't my idea. Bette asked for it. She complained I worked all the time, didn't spend enough time with the kids, didn't pay enough attention to her. She was jealous of every woman I met."

The sun lay on the horizon, slipping behind the mountains, the last rays of the day streaming into the room, outlining his body against the glass.

"*Every* woman?"

Clay put one foot on the wide window seat and gazed at the mountains. "Well, not all of them. And the women are ancient history," he said. "Bette and I got married when we were kids. It wasn't easy for a guy that age to say no to a pretty woman. But I've learned my lesson."

"Are you sure?"

"You doubt me?"

She laughed and walked over to sit on the window seat, facing him. "Remember you said you had read my vibes from the first day we met? I don't recall sending out any vibes when I met you. Maybe you're just programmed to respond to any available female."

Clay removed his foot and sat beside her. "I can see why it might seem that way to you, but I haven't been with another woman for over a year. After Bette asked for a divorce, I cleaned up my act. I tried to save my marriage, but things had gone too far. Now I'm a committed father, but I want to get married again. I'd like to have more children. I won't make the same mistakes again."

"That sounds promising."

"I told my lawyer to file for the divorce right away, and do the property issues later. Maybe if the divorce is final, Bette will be more agreeable to settling everything. In the meantime, I plan to go on with my life."

Cara nodded.

"The decree should be final next week. I was hoping you'd celebrate it with me."

"Really? What did you have in mind?"

"I know how to grill steaks. We could have dinner here." He hesitated. "You won't be too surprised if I ask you to spend the night will you?"

Cara laughed. "You've forgotten our conversation at the lake."

"I assumed you made those rules before you met me. Times change."

Cara looked away, not willing to admit she had dreamed that he might ask her and knowing she still might say no. "Why don't you call me when you get the decree? We can talk about it."

The sun disappeared behind the mountains, leaving the room in a soft, gray cocoon. Cara inspected her watch. "I need to get home. I love your house. When will you move in?"

"Not long. We've re-finished the guesthouse. María has moved into it already, and Pablo will be here this weekend. We'll start renovations on this house tomorrow."

Outside, he pointed down a slate-covered walk to a small house in the corner of the lawn. "That's where María lives."

"So Pablo is in town?"

"He's lying low, working on one of our projects up in the mountains."

"I'm glad he's here for María. She's lucky to have a job with you. The hospital staff said Rosita would be kept in foster care until María's case is decided. They will be happy she has a job."

"She's a good worker. I can't say I've adjusted all that well to being a single father. Do you know what it's like trying to find babysitters and getting meals on time? We've been eating pizza and McDonald's hamburgers."

"I can't imagine what it's like. Lupe has always prepared my meals."

In the car, Clay slumped down and looked up beneath the brim of his ball cap. "So you don't cook?"

"No."

"You don't do laundry either."

"How would you know that?"

"My robe never smells like detergent after you've worn it."

"Umm. Lupe told me. You should have complained. I wear it to avoid streaking across the lawn, scaring the wildlife."

Clay ran his finger along her cheek. "I'm sure we could solve that problem if we thought about it seriously."

Cara's breathing stumbled. "Don't worry. Lupe took care of it by hanging one of my robes in the mudroom shower."

"You should tell Lupe to mind her own business."

Cara laughed. "I have. It does no good."

"This is my weekend without the kids. I'll work on the house in the daytime, but my nights are free. Want to do something?"

"Such as?"

"I don't know. We can play it by ear. I'll bring out a pizza and rent a movie. What do you like on your pizza?"

"Everything. You pick the movie. Just make sure it's not set on a noisy planet."

Clay smiled and shook his head. "How about something romantic?"

Cara felt herself blushing. She pulled the car over in front of his office. "Get out," she said, pretending she was rebuking him for his thoughts.

He leaned over and kissed her cheek. "See you, babe."

Surprised, she watched him sprint up the steps. "Babe" left her speechless, though her thoughts whirred. I'm thirty-six years old, and I don't think I've ever qualified as a "babe." I'm not even sure what I just agreed to, but my guess is that it was more than pizza and a movie. Well, as Emily would say, it's time I grew up and decided whether I'll live the rest of my life by the dictates of my head or my heart. She might also say it's time to add some nice lingerie to my wardrobe.

13

The Lawsuit

Cara was surprised when she received a large brown envelope from her attorney a few days later. She opened it and sat immobilized. Howard had filed the expected lawsuit asking the court to find their father's will invalid. He charged that the will was written at a time when their father's mental capacities were weak and that the devisee, Cara Rose Morgan, used undue influence to persuade David Morgan to leave all his assets to her.

The accompanying letter explained that Trace needed to file an answer and to begin preparing for trial. The lawyer asked Cara to make an appointment through her secretary.

Cara laid the envelope aside. Her day was full. She'd ride with Tony to make the final decision about the cattle for sale. Prices weren't as high as February's would be, but by selling them now she could avoid the long months of feeding during the winter. She glared at the envelope. She refused to allow the lawsuit to change her plans.

It was mid-afternoon when she re-entered her office, the letter demanding attention. She picked up the telephone to call Trace. The secretary informed her that the attorney was in court but could see her tomorrow. She set an appointment, then laid the file aside. Not only had she lost her father, she now knew she'd also lost her brother.

She sighed at the sound of Lupe's footsteps. "I forgot to tell you Emily called this morning," Lupe said.

A weight lifted from Cara's shoulders. She could make it through this crisis if she had Emily's support.

"Thank you, Lupe. I'll call her now."

"What's wrong?"

Cara wiped her eyes and blew her nose.

"It's okay," she said pointing to the papers. "Howard is suing me to take the ranch back. He says I tricked Dad into leaving everything to me."

"How can he say that?" Lupe asked. "I'll have a talk with that boy."

"I don't think you should talk to him, Lupe. You'll be listed as a witness for my side, which means neither he nor his lawyers can talk to you. But don't worry about it. I'll see my attorney tomorrow and know more after that."

Lupe left the office mumbling to herself as Cara dialed Emily's number. Her warm and welcoming voice made Cara feel better. "Sorry I missed your call. Tony and I were running an inventory," she said.

"That's okay. I'm covered with paint, but this is a good time to stop. I wanted to tell you I got a call from Howard's attorney asking me to join in a petition to overturn Dad's will. I told him no, of course."

"Well, he's doing it by himself. I just got a copy of it from my lawyer. I go in to see her tomorrow."

"You know I'm on your side, Cara. Tell Frank to call me if I'm needed. I can't believe Howard's doing this."

"Thanks, Emily. I'm glad you're in my corner. Did I tell you I fired Frank and hired a woman attorney?"

"No. What brought that on?"

Cara hesitated, wishing she hadn't opened up the subject. She should have called Emily long ago to discuss this issue, even ask for her advice. Now it was a little late. Their conversation went on for an hour. Cara hung up the phone, almost forgetting the lawsuit that had precipitated the call.

In the lawyer's office, Cara relaxed and listened while Trace explained that the cruel words in the petition were not facts to be refuted. They were unproven charges and Howard had the burden to convince a jury with a preponderance of evidence that their father was indeed suffering from a diminished mental condition and that Cara used undue influence to cause him to change his will in her favor. Howard's witnesses would testify that David Morgan failed to handle the financial end of the ranching business for several months because Cara deliberately took over those duties without his consent.

"It's true that I took over the books six months ago and ran the business pretty much by myself. But I didn't do it because he couldn't do it. He said he was tired of book work. Frank can testify to that." She paused. "Now I'm wondering if he'd been having trouble with his heart for a while and just didn't tell me about it."

"You may be right," Trace said. "I talked to Frank, and he will testify that your dad was clear-headed right up to the end of his life. He is still angry at you, but he'll testify that your father believed that his dream of holding the ranch together rested in your hands."

"What happens next?"

"I'll file an answer, denying the charges. The attorneys will exchange evidence and a witness list. After we've reviewed that material, we'll meet at one of our offices to see if we can mediate the matter instead of taking it to court."

"What am I supposed to do in the meantime?"

"You're obligated not to waste the assets or do anything to reduce the value of the ranch."

"How am I supposed to pay the taxes if I can't sell assets?"

"Well, the court understands that, and the judge will approve whatever you need to do in the way of buying and selling."

"I can't believe this is happening."

"I'm sorry, Cara. Envy and greed are two of the seven deadly sins. Few families are free of them."

"Do you think I'm being greedy?"

"No. I had Howard in mind. He has more money than he can use, but he's willing to destroy his father's dream to get more. Of course it may be his battle for power over you."

"Yes, that's what drives him. We competed for Dad's attention when we were children. Momma pampered Howard. Dad was afraid she would make his son a sissy, so he was extra hard on him."

Trace turned to her computer. "I need a lot of information." She began probing, pushing to paint a picture of Cara's relationship with her father, to define the structure of the ranching operation, to name the people who worked on the ranch, the names of neighbors who knew and worked with the father and daughter, and a clear picture of the last days of David Morgan's life.

After two hours, Trace shut down her computer. "It will take me a few days to prepare our answer. You'll need to drop by and sign it. Next, we'll schedule depositions and then meet with Howard and his attorneys to see if we can mediate a settlement. If that doesn't work, it will go to an arbitration judge."

"We won't have a trial?"

"No trial, no jury."

"Is that good or bad?"

"Usually it's good. For one thing, we can get a hearing date much sooner than in a regular docket, and a judge knows to weigh the case by law rather than the prejudices that jury members are burdened with. They promise not to let their prejudices interfere with reaching a fair decision, but we all know how hard that is."

Cara understood. For example, she wouldn't want any of the Martin family on a jury whose job it was to determine the ownership of her ranch.

14

The Rustlers

Thunderclouds were rolling in over Brazos Peak when Cara arrived home, and she rode out to check on the progress of the hay harvesting. The balers were gone, having moved over the fields for a week, dropping large blocks of alfalfa and native grasses bound with wire. Many of the bales lay where they fell because the migrant workers, who should have been loading them onto trailers and storing them in sheds, had not returned in time to keep up with the baling. Today they were hurrying to beat the storm clouds.

The alfalfa bales were a rich green, filled with nutrients that ensured healthy calving next spring. The golden timothy grass, harvested from non-irrigated pastures, contained less nourishment but added needed roughage to the diet. With a little bit of luck, those rain clouds would slow down as they moved over the mountain and wait until the harvesting was complete before dumping the moisture necessary to start the next crop. Cara smiled. She was assured of two more cuttings of alfalfa before fall, reducing the amount of feed she'd have to buy over the winter months. In fact, she'd be able to sell hay this year, because much of the herd was being sold before winter. A small whirlwind whipped through the field in front of her. Past the hay fields, she kicked Gus into a gallop, toward pastures where Tony should be directing the roundup of livestock to be sold.

There was no sign of riders along the northwest fence line, so Cara rode to the top of the hill, where she could see for miles down the southern border that crossed the river. She saw two horses staked out near a clump of trees bordering the highway. One belonged to Tony, and if she wasn't mistaken, the other was Ramón's. She watched as Tony hurried out of the woods, mounted his horse and headed at a hard gallop toward where she sat. She trotted out to meet him.

"What's up?"

"Rustlers. We found the fence cut behind that clump of trees and tire tracks coming from the road. They've been stealing cattle, and they've been here more than once. Probably started last week when the vaqueros left."

"Dammit," she said. "I'll call the sheriff, but I suppose they've left the state by now." Her heart sank as she realized these were the cattle she planned to sell to pay the taxes.

Tony nodded. "Or maybe they've been dropped off on a ranch nearby, getting the brands changed. The bastards took a big gamble. They must have known we didn't have riders on the fences."

"A lot of people knew, didn't they? I thought you told all the neighbors."

"You're right. Ones I didn't have time to call, the Martins did for us. You call the sheriff, and Ramón and I will fix the fence." Tony whipped his horse into a lope heading back to where he'd found the intrusion. Cara sat for a moment watching his departure, wondering whether Ramón was surprised or pleased with the cattle theft.

Cara's call to the sheriff was discouraging. Hers were not the only cattle that had been rustled nearby within the past few weeks.

"Dadburn," the sheriff said. "This is the third report I've had this month. They're using high-tech methods. I talked to the sheriff in Taos County and he says they're cutting the fences, turning dogs loose to round up twenty or so head, running them into a temporary corral they put together, and then loading them on the trucks. They're off and running in fifteen minutes."

"This job looks like it was a pushover," Cara said. "Tony thinks they've been here more than once. They'll be tempted to come back if they think we're still working with a small crew. I'd like to put guns along that fence for a while. Can you spare a deputy overnight?"

"For how long?"

"Up to a week."

"I guess so. Looks to me, though, like it's an inside job. Somebody must have known you were shorthanded, don't you think?"

"You mean one of our men might be connected to the rustlers?"

"Yep. I'm guessing all these jobs are connected by something or somebody. There may be a mole letting the rustlers know when and where it's safe to hit."

"I hate to think so, but it's worth checking into."

"I'll send Joe and Clifford out there to collect tire prints. They can stay overnight. Don't let anybody on the ranch know the plans, in case there is a mole."

"Sure thing. Thanks for your assistance, Sheriff. Tell the deputies to come by the house, and we'll take them to where the fence was cut."

Near sundown, the deputies arrived, and they loaded extra guns and food into the county's Hummer.

Cara stood watching. "Why don't I take the deputies to the site while it's daylight, so they can look for evidence," she said as she turned to Tony. "You bring the horses up." She handed him the ice chest to load into the vehicle.

Tony avoided looking at her, but his words were pointed in her direction. "Me and Ramón will spend the night with them. You better sit by the telephone. You may need to call for extra men."

Cara stared at Tony, glanced at the two deputies, who nodded agreement to what he said. She decided to follow his advice. The men didn't want a woman around. She took one of the rifles out of the Jeep. There were ways to get around their wishes.

"See you in the morning," she said and smiled at the deputies. "Good luck."

In the kitchen, she wolfed down a serving of the picnic supper Lupe had made for the posse, her mind clicking off plans to ride up to the site around midnight. If the thieves showed, she'd call the sheriff from there on her satellite phone.

Stars lay close to the ground, like fireflies, lighting her way as Cara headed for the south pasture before midnight. A half moon headed to the western horizon, impartial to the action below. Venus sparkled to the right, below the moon's forward tip. As she approached the top of the hill, Buck's metal shoes touched rock, so she guided him over to the soft padding of grass. The squeak of saddle leathers rubbing together each time the horse stepped forward broke the silence of the night.

At the top of the hill, she peered down the road a quarter mile away from the damaged fence. There was no sign of the sheriff's Hummer. It must be parked behind the brush. Buck pointed his ears in the direction of the fence, and Cara turned him to the right to avoid getting close enough to elicit a greeting from one of the other horses. Near the upper fence, she dismounted and tied the reins to a tree limb. Preparing for a long wait, she unrolled a blanket from behind the saddle and spread it at the foot of a large tree. From there, she could see any action that took place along the cut fence. Comfortable, she poured a cup of coffee, leaned her head against the tree, and wondered how long she could stay awake if the night remained so tranquil. Moments later, Buck released a warning snort and a hand covered her mouth.

"Shush," someone whispered. Cara tasted blood as she bit the fingers pressed against her mouth. The contents of her coffee cup sailed over her shoulder toward where a face should be. She rolled to her side, and Ramón's body came with her. He cursed in Spanish and straddled her stomach.

"Get off me, you jerk" she whispered.

He let go of her arms and pulled a handkerchief from his pocket to wipe the coffee off his neck and shirt and to dab at the blood on his hand.

"I said *get off.*"

"I heard you. I'll get off when I have your word that you won't scream or make more noise."

"Stupid! If I'd intended to scream, I'd have already done it." She was a little embarrassed to find herself resorting to childish insults. However, it seemed to work.

Ramón lifted one leg from her body and rolled back against the tree. "What are you doing here? Tony told you not to come," he said.

"What are you doing here? You're supposed to be down there catching thieves. I'm not one of them."

Ramón chuckled. "No doubt they'll be easier to capture than you are. Tony sent me to tell you to go home."

Cara picked up the thermos and refilled her cup. "I'm not going home. You can go back and tell him so. How did he know I was here?"

"Did you bring enough coffee for two?"

She glared at the stain on his shirt. "I started out with enough for two."

"Thank you. We can share." He took the cup from her hand and drank the dregs of coffee in one gulp. He reached for the thermos.

"Help yourself," she said.

"Sorry, sorry. It would taste better with sugar, don't you think?"

Cara felt like slapping him. Despite her concessions about the school for the migrants, she was sure she hadn't given this man permission to speak so familiarly. Not that he had asked. And that's what irritated her. Never before had one of the migrant laborers presumed to face her unless he was spoken to, and even then he kept his eyes on the ground. Her father had made sure the Los Lobos Ranch was one of the best places in the county to work. He provided good housing, good food, and decent work hours. No worker wanted to risk displeasing the boss, and they took for granted that showing disrespect for his daughter would be buying a fast ticket off the ranch. Cara admitted that she objected to her father's elitism, what she called his Republican stance. Her empathy was for the worker, unions, and universal health care. It offended her to have the workers treat her as if she might call for their heads if they looked at her. Except for Ramón. She would like a little more deference from him. Instead, he acted as if he'd never heard that employees must respect the lady boss.

"I didn't know I was having a party or I'd have brought sugar."

Ramón backed off. "It's very generous of you to share."

Cara sipped from the cup, and he reached to retrieve it.

"This is a very dangerous situation, you know. You have no business being here. Please go home—as soon as we've finished the coffee." He leaned over and set the cup in front of her.

She picked up her rifle. "I started target practice when I was six years old. I'm pretty good."

"I'm sure you are, but you're not so good at sneaking around. We knew you were here from the moment you came over the hill."

Cara was dismayed. "I came through the trees. How could you have seen me?"

"We heard your horse."

Darn! She should have walked over the hill. "You have only four men with guns," she said. "I'm staying as a backup."

He took her rifle. "You don't get the point, do you?" he asked. "It is a man's duty and privilege to protect his womenfolk. How can we do that if you insist on butting in every time there's a crisis? Besides," he said, "I should have some say-so in what you do. Remember, you belong to me."

Cara grabbed her gun from his hands. "Don't push your luck. No one has ever owned me. Besides, you have your facts wrong. I've been reading about real wolf packs, and it seems the alpha male and alpha female are equal in stature in the hierarchy of the pack. One does not own the other."

Ramón sighed. "Mi corazón. You're always messing with my fantasies."

Cara grimaced. "Your fantasies aren't my responsibility, nor are the new school supplies. They're taking up space on the back porch. Please pick them up."

"No more deliveries?" Disappointment showed in his speech, and he pulled his lips down at the corners, like a sad clown.

"You know the answer to that."

"Why don't I stop by tonight, after we . . . after I finish here?" As he spoke, a truck came from the west on County Road 84 and slowed down near where the cattle had been loaded the previous night. The truck had a two-level trailer, the top used for sheep and goats and enclosed with metal sides limited to small vents. The lower half had metal rails spaced so that air circulated to keep the animals cool.

"That's them!" Ramón said. "Stay out of the way. There may be gunshots." He ran toward the truck with his gun drawn.

Two men jumped from the cab of the truck and released a half dozen Australian cattle dogs. With a short whistle and pointed arm, one of the men sent the dogs scrambling under the fence and across the pasture toward the bedded cattle. A pickup arrived, and two men unloaded sections of metal tubing, which they assembled into a corral large enough to contain twenty to twenty-five head of cattle.

Cara hurried to Buck and pulled the telephone from the saddlebag.

The sheriff, half asleep, assured her he had deputies on alert. "We'll set up roadblocks to stop them if they run. I'll send more men out to the site to make the arrests. Hold 'em for twenty minutes."

Cara checked her watch. At the rate the rustlers were operating, the truck would be loaded and gone before the re-enforcements arrived. She picked up her rifle and headed toward the action. Several yards from the loading site, Cara fell to her stomach behind bushes along the fence, with a clear view of the truck. The corral appeared as if by magic. The truck driver maneuvered the trailer to the back opening of the corral. No more than five minutes had passed when bawling cattle appeared over the rise. Two of the thieves whistled and pointed toward the corral, and the dogs circled the herd straight for the gate, quicker than a horse and rider could have.

Cara frowned as she watched the last of the cows being crowded into the truck without interference from Tony and the deputies. What were they waiting for? She dropped to her stomach, hidden in underbrush, and waited for the first shot. She was the lone person in front of the truck, so she took aim at one of the tires. She'd be damned if thieves were driving off with a load of her cattle while she did nothing to stop them.

The driver of the truck leaned against the fender, waiting for the others to complete their jobs. His cigarette bounced up and down as he talked to the men rushing to close the doors. As she watched, the driver threw his cigarette aside and climbed into the cab. The engine roared, and the driver changed gears as the last cow crowded into the trailer and the door closed. Behind the truck, the remaining rustlers ran to disassemble the corral and load the dogs.

Suddenly all hell broke loose. Tony and the deputies slipped from the woods near the truck with guns drawn. Ramón remained between her and the action. Cara heard a gunshot, and the thieves raised their hands above their shoulders. Black smoke shot from the exhaust of the truck as it began to move. Cara's hand rested steady as she aimed at a front tire of the truck. She fired and smiled as the tire flattened. She reloaded and punctured the other front tire, but the truck continued to move, and she aimed for the windshield. The truck stopped and rolled back into the bar ditch, jack-knifing, causing the doors to twist and pop open. The driver jumped from the truck and aimed a gun toward Cara's gunfire. Cattle spilled out of the truck, pushed through the corral gate and headed away from the raiders into the woods where she lay hidden. She ducked and scrambled backward to the safety of a tree that shielded her from bullets whizzing past her head. She gasped for breath as the noise and smell of frightened cattle breezed past her. She heard Ramón yell from near the truck, "Don't shoot," as other bullets popped like firecrackers around her.

As quickly as the firing started, it stopped. She peeked around the tree and watched as the deputies pushed the truck driver and his companion to the ground and handcuffed them. The other men stood with their hands above their heads. The dogs milled around, running from one side of the road to the other, confused by the array of signals they didn't understand,

Tony's voice reached the late-arriving deputies, and they moved through the fence, their guns drawn.

"Open up that top bed," Tony yelled. "There's banging on the walls."

Cara watched, astounded, as bodies piled out of the top truck bed. They appeared to be migrants, pleading for mercy, begging for water. Cara leaned against the tree for support. That's how the smugglers had been hiding their human cargo—in cattle transport trucks. Her finger tightened on the trigger of the rifle. The thieving bastards should be lined up and shot.

Tony's voice echoed through the darkness, but she had lost sight of Ramón. She moved around the tree and ran toward the truck, flailing through branches and underbrush, then piled forward as she stumbled over a soft, yielding body. She hit the ground on her elbows, rolled over, and reached out to touch—Ramón! Her hand slid over his chest and stopped on a wet, sticky mess below his shoulder. She raised to her knees and screamed, "Tony!"

The noise of the scattered cattle bawling to find their calves faded into the distance.

15

Questionable Moves

While Ramón lay unconscious in a hospital room, Cara sat beside the bed, listening to Tony's repeated assurances that Ramón's injury did not result from her intrusion into the capture of the rustlers.

"It wasn't a stray bullet, Tony. It was aimed at me. Ramón stopped it."

"How could it have been meant for you? No one knew you were there."

"I blew out their front tires and the windshield. They were firing back at me."

"It's just as likely they were returning Ramón's fire."

"He wasn't shooting from where I was positioned. He'd gone back to find you."

Tony shuffled back and forth near the windows of the room.

"How many people died?" Cara asked.

"Just one of the rustlers. It's a good thing we found them guys in the top of the truck though. They wouldn't of lasted much longer. The driver brought them all the way from Arizona with a load of cattle he dropped off in Chama. He planned to take them on to Colorado, but the gang leaders decided stealing your cattle was so easy, they'd fill the bottom of the truck with another load of cows that were needed in Arkansas, and take the migrants over there."

"Does the sheriff know who they are?"

"He's got names. He thinks one of them made a call to Arizona, where migrants were on their way east, and told them to take time to pick up cattle in Chama. The decision was made to kill two birds with one stone."

"I hate to think that one of our people told them about the fences. How can we find out who did it?"

"I'll check to see who hightails it from camp. He won't stick around if he knows the sheriff's looking for him."

"Is there any chance we'll get back the cattle they took last time?"

"Not likely," Tony said.

"There goes my tax money."

"Well, we'll keep working on it." Tony took one more look at Ramón and headed for the door "I'd better get back to the ranch. Looks like this guy won't be around for a while."

"I can fill in."

"You need to go home and rest. There's nothing we can do for Ramón but pray to God."

A lot of good my prayers will do, Cara thought. I haven't been to church since Dad's mass.

Oxygen tubes were attached to Ramón's nostrils, and medicine dripped through tubes to a vein on the back of his hand. Another ran from the side of his chest, draining the liquid between the lung and the chest wall. The doctor had said the bullet only nipped the lung, and repair should be successful. At the moment, she could not discern his breathing, so she touched his pulse to make sure he lived. He sighed and she jerked her hand away. Tony was right—there was nothing she could do. So why was the episode affecting her so? Because, she decided, in a strange way, Ramón was right that a part of her did belong to him. Was it the Mexican blood they shared? She had minimized her connection to her heritage all her life. This seemed a strange time for it to become an issue. But why did she spend all their time together denying those feelings? She'd always suspected her concern for the migrants' problems came from her intermixture of bloodlines. Her father's parents were Anglos, and Cara had long recognized her unspoken sense of superiority in the presence of Hispanics, but she tried to excuse it by empathizing with the migrant workers. Since meeting Ramón, she had begun to question her conflicted feelings and now wondered if they were based on her Mexican heritage. She watched the plasma drip attached to Ramón's arm and wondered if he was getting a cross-cultural kick also. She shook her head. Tony was right. She needed rest. She left the hospital and collapsed on her bed at mid-afternoon.

Noise from the kitchen aroused her, but it was the recollection that she had invited Clay for supper and a movie that sent her stumbling to the shower. No time to wash her hair but the quick, warm, sudsy shower left her smelling of lavender. Dressed in shorts and T-shirt, covering the lingerie she'd splurged for, she felt younger than she knew she was. Emily would have approved.

And so did Clay. Standing by the refrigerator, beer in hand, he whistled when she descended the stairs. "You should lock the door when you're here alone. No telling what low-life might come in and make himself at home." He set down his drink, and she walked into his arms for a quick hug.

"Yeah, who knows?" she said. "I might get lucky."

He nodded. "I was right about that book you were reading. You Magdalenes pretend to be so sweet and innocent, while all the time you're laying plans to catch the unsuspecting. And we guys walk right in, thinking it was our idea."

"You think too much. Are you hungry?"

"Starving. I brought pizza."

Cara peeked in the oven. "Lupe left enough meatloaf for two. Would you prefer that?"

"Are you kidding? We can eat the pizza tomorrow, or late tonight if we work up an appetite." She pretended not to know what he was suggesting.

"I don't know," Cara said. "I've had a rough week. It will take more than pizza to keep me awake. You heard about the rustlers."

"Yeah. It's all people are talking about in town. That and the woman's murder."

"Are they connected?"

"The sheriff thinks so. He came by looking for Pablo."

"Lupe said Pablo was hiding. Makes me wonder what he knows and how he learned it."

"Probably from Ramón. I heard he was shot. How's he doing?"

"He's in no condition to talk to Pablo or anyone else. The sheriff thinks one of the migrants let the rustlers know there were no fence riders on the south side of the ranch. It could have been Pablo or Ramón."

Clay frowned. "Pablo doesn't seem like a bad guy to me."

"Nice guys can turn bad if they're offered money. I'll be angry if we discover he did it."

"Well, he knows his way around construction better than the other workers. I've wondered why he's still doing temporary work. He could supervise if he'd stay in one place long enough."

"He went to Juárez to get María, and he's moved from one place to another since he got back. I wonder why he doesn't keep a steady job."

After dinner, they settled on the leather couch in the living room to watch *Out of Africa*.

"I got this movie because I understand women are suckers for Robert Redford," Clay said as he pushed the DVD into the player and stretched out on the couch, with his head on Cara's lap. He was asleep within ten minutes. Cara smiled as he snored softly. It was obvious why he had picked a movie star with blond hair and blue eyes. He had no doubt been compared to him. She had never watched a man sleep, nor had she felt the warmth of a man's body against hers. It was clear why women were suckers for Clay Thompson.

After the movie, she slipped a pillow under Clay's head, covered him with a light blanket, flipped off the lights, and watched his face in the moonlight filtering through the lace curtains. Hesitating, she bent down and kissed him. His breath spread against her nostrils as he sighed. She wanted to wake him, give him a reason to break down those barriers she had placed around herself many years ago. She wanted him to do what she was unable to do—free her body and soul. Remembering his confession to being a workaholic and heavy sleeper, she rose and left the room, relieved that it wasn't her fault the night hadn't ended as planned.

Cara woke to the sounds of Tony and Clay talking in the kitchen. The back door slammed, and the voices were muffled from outside. She went downstairs to find Lupe folding the blanket on the sofa. In the kitchen, she found pancakes, bacon, eggs, and coffee. The men had already cleaned their plates. She grinned; it looked like the arrangement with Clay had changed from renting an apartment to room-and-board.

Lupe entered the kitchen. "I guess you're extra hungry too."

"Umm."

"Why didn't Clay bring the children?"

"It's his wife's weekend to have the kids."

"So he has plenty of time to waste doing nothing?"

"I wouldn't say 'nothing.' He has his horses, and it looks like he's also out at the barn helping Tony." Cara pointed out the kitchen window toward the barns. The men were loading posts onto the flatbed trailer. "He said he was going into town to work on his new house."

Lupe leaned back on the cabinet, watching with questioning eyes.

Cara picked up bacon with her fingers and laid it on her plate. "If there's anything you want to know, Lupe, just ask. My life is an open book."

"Humph," Lupe snorted and pushed another pancake onto her plate.

Still feeling guilty that her actions may have put Ramón in the line of fire, Cara drove to the hospital and watched his restless sleep. A string of pretty Hispanic nurses dropped by to replenish the medicine and check his oxygen supply. Cara asked how he was doing, but the nurses shrugged and one said she'd have to ask the doctor. Ramón did not wake, and his ragged breathing was frightening. The darkness of his skin had paled. Cara approached the head of the bed, remembering the warmth of Clay's head on her lap. She laid her hand on Ramón's brow and he opened his eyes. Embarrassed, she pulled her hand away and sat down.

"Señorita," he whispered.

Cara paused, surprised. He rarely spoke Spanish to her. "How are you feeling?"

"Better each day. The doctor says I can leave as soon as I find a place in town to stay. Tony is looking."

"Will the ranch house do? You're welcome to stay there."

"No. I can't impose on you."

"We do that for anyone who's hurt on the ranch. The trail to the camp is too rough to maneuver if you've had surgery. I'll talk to the doctor." She rose and left the room over Ramón's protests.

From the hospital, she had one task left, and she headed for Clay's house to check on María and Pablo. She picked up hamburgers and Cokes. Maybe Clay could take time out for lunch. He was standing on the roof, repairing flashing around the fireplace when she arrived. She dropped the food and a blanket on the grass under a huge tree.

"Hey," Clay called.

"Hey." She waved.

"Be there in a minute."

Cara nodded and glanced toward the guesthouse, wondering if María and Pablo were home. She hurried down the walkway and knocked on the front door. There was no answer. She knocked harder. The door opened a slit and María peeked out.

"Buenos días, María. Is Pablo home?"

"No." María backed away from the door.

"¿Dónde está?"

"El ya se fue." María said and disappeared behind the closed door.

He is gone. I wonder where? Cara thought as she stood looking at the door, puzzled. She returned to the yard, where Clay stood washing his hands at an outside faucet at the back of the house. They arrived at the picnic site at the same time, and Clay ducked his head as if apologizing.

"I guess you won't worry about my making unwanted moves after last night, will you?"

"You'll never know how close I came to waking you."

"Why didn't you?"

"I tried, gently, but you seemed exhausted."

"I warned you I'm a workaholic. My body just takes over at times and says it needs to rest. That was one of those times. I feel like a first-class heel, though."

"It's okay. I didn't take it personally." Cara knew she was lying. While she was disappointed that Clay hadn't made a move, at the same time she felt conflicted about how she would have reacted. She had come to the conclusion that she liked this man a lot, and her vacillation about pursuing or being pursued bothered her. She was too old to resemble an unsophisticated teenager when it came to sexual matters. Especially with a man who was much younger than she and the father of two children. He knew all that was necessary to know about women. She knew next to nothing about men.

Clay stretched out on the lawn with his hands behind his head. "I almost came up to your room this morning, but Lupe was in the kitchen. I was afraid she'd take one of those skillets to my head."

"I'm surprised she didn't do that when she found you on the couch. She let me know she knew exactly what was going on between us."

"Maybe she could tell us," he said. "I'm not sure I know." His voice was sad, and Cara felt a twinge of guilt. It was her fault nothing was going on between them. Maybe he was ready to give up trying to reach her.

"I'm sorry. Relationships are not easy for me. Emily said I needed to grow up, get off the ranch, and join the real world. You probably agree."

"That sounds pretty drastic. Most people work things out right where they are. Or they go through life not working it out. Take your pick."

Clay lay back, resting his head on his hands again. "I should talk," he said. "It's taken me months to come to the conclusion that I want a divorce now. I'm tired of the conflict." He sat up smiling. "This may have been the longest week of my life, but it's about over." He pecked her on the cheek. "I gotta get back to work. My crew will be showing up any minute. I have to impress them with how industrious I am. Thanks for the lunch."

"Clay, could you do me a favor?"

"Name it."

"Is there a telephone in María's house?"

"Sure."

"Could you let me see the phone bills she's run up since she moved in? I'm checking up on calls Pablo may have made."

"No problem. Call my secretary. Tell her I said it was okay."

Cara picked up the trash and the blanket as she watched Clay climb the ladder to the roof. If divorces could be put on "rush," maybe growing up could also. And the telephone records should lead her toward a solution to another problem.

Tony was drinking coffee at the kitchen table when she arrived home. "How's our man?" he asked.

"Doing very well. The doctor said he should be out of the hospital in a week."

"I'd better get busy. I told him I'd find him a room with the church people in town. He won't be able to get up to the camp for some time."

"He said you were looking, but I told him he could use Howard's old bedroom. It has an outside entrance."

"Are you sure that's a good idea?"

"Why not? He's too weak to cause any trouble, and Lupe can care for him. We can hire a nurse if necessary."

"I'll talk to him."

Cara smiled. "Thank you, Padre."

"I'm sorry. But you've been like family to me. Now that your father's gone, I feel he'd want me to look after you."

Cara sighed and leaned back in her chair. "When do you suppose I'll be old enough to look after myself?"

"Women shouldn't look after themselves. You should get married."

Cara laughed. "At least Emily agrees with what you're saying. She told me to stop hiding in the boondocks, which I assumed meant I should get out and meet men. I thought I was doing a pretty good job of taking care of myself."

"Marriage is not just having a man to take care of you. You're supposed to take care of him too. Lupe takes care of me." Tony laced his fingers together, resting his arms on the table.

Cara leaned over and wrapped her fingers around his huge fist. "I know she does, and that's what worries me when you talk about marriage. I don't know how to take care of a man the way Lupe cares for you, or the way Momma took care of Dad. Maybe I'm put together wrong."

"No. You just haven't met the right man."

Cara squirmed in her chair, remembering her recent conversation with Clay. He made her feel happy when they were together, but he'd never indicated that he needed someone to take care of him, and she resisted the idea that she needed a caretaker. She sat up and leaned her arms on the table. She smiled at Tony. "If I haven't met the right man, maybe it's because I'm not looking." She was surprised at her comment, coming so soon after almost deciding that she loved Clay. She still wasn't ready to admit that she needed a man in her life.

Tony shook his head. "You're so strong willed, with a mind of your own. I don't know whether there's a man around who's your match."

"Let's assume there isn't and drop the subject." She stood and poured fresh coffee. Lupe came in from the garden and laid fresh green onions on the counter. Cara breathed in the pungent smell before speaking to Tony. "What have we found out about the rustlers?"

"I talked to the sheriff. He's given the government enough evidence to close down a big operation that extends over several states. The guys he arrested are talking. The smuggling combined with rustling could have been a one-time run, but it smells like cartel doings."

"What have they found out about where the rustlers got their inside information on our fence riders?" Tony's face aged in front of her. "What's wrong?" she asked.

"One thing's hard to believe. The driver said Pablo relayed a message to them, which he got from Lucille Martin, telling him our fence was unprotected. The sheriff's after Pablo and figures he's the connection to the mob. No way to tell whether Lucille handed on the information out of ignorance or on purpose. It sure makes me mad that a neighbor would do a stupid thing like that." He turned to leave. "I know there wasn't any love lost between her and your maw. Maybe she still holds a grudge." He walked to the door, shaking his head. "I gotta go to work. If you're sure it's okay, I'll bring Ramón's stuff down from the camp in a day or two."

Cara watched as Tony managed a bowlegged stride toward the barn. She worried about his limping. Old age, he said, but she wasn't willing to admit that Tony was slowing down. It angered her that Lucille's latest actions had distressed him. If she had spread the word that the Los Lobos fences were vulnerable for a devious reason, that reason would have been her hope that the loss of cattle would create a cash problem so serious Cara would have to sell her valuable acreage bordering the river. Lucille and Larry had coveted the property for years.

Cara went to the office mumbling to herself. Larry had always been a friendly, cooperative neighbor. Lucille and her son, whom Cara had rebuffed over the years, were the problem. Maybe it was time to do a little investigating into that woman's intentions.

16

Mediation

Trace Leader had given Cara very little hope that much would be accomplished at the mediation session. Mainly the meeting was intended to serve as a deadline for exchanging evidence and making the parties aware of the weaknesses or strengths of the opponent's case. Cara arrived on time and they drove together to Howard's attorney's office.

"Don't let the posh interior intimidate you," Trace said to Cara as they approached the door. "These guys put their pants on just like the janitors do." Cara smiled at the effort to relax her. Her courage was bolstered watching opposing counsel lose their braggadocio as they greeted Trace Leader. There was nothing false nor vulnerable about her attorney presence. She exuded intelligence, preparedness, and don't-fool-around-with-me in her smile, handshake, and appearance.

Cara stared at Howard, whose lips had disappeared, leaving the thin line that Cara was used to seeing when he was cornered. His next move would be to come out swinging, not believing it was proper to hit a girl but unwilling to stand still while her left jab bloodied his nose. Cara smiled at the childhood memory of their boxing matches.

The negotiations began, and Cara sat fascinated by the array of innuendos and lies wrapped in half-truths that were raised to support the opposition's contention that her father was suffering dementia before he died. Her eyes seldom left Howard's face. He stared at a legal pad, doodling instead of taking notes. Trace's calm voice brought Cara's mind back to the mediation table, and she was pleased to see Howard's attorneys struggling to reinforce weaknesses Trace pointed out in their arguments.

Two hours after they entered the room, Trace stood and shook hands with the opposing attorneys. "We'll see you in court," she said. Cara followed her out the door. "That will give them fodder to chew on a while." Trace smiled as if she were pleased with the way things had gone.

"So we go to court now?"

"There's a weak possibility that Howard will withdraw his petition. He'll do that only if he believes he will lose or wants to quit throwing money down a rat hole. Otherwise, the court will assign an arbitration judge to hear the case, usually within the month."

Cara's head swam. "What's our next step?"

"Just wait. They need time to digest what they heard. They'll get back to us in a few days. I'll be in touch as soon as I hear from them."

At home, Cara sat with her hands on the steering wheel, staring at the dirty windshield. She wasn't sure whether today she had taken a step forward, two steps backward, or whether she was jogging in place.

The week crept by. On Friday Cara saddled Buck and headed for the back pasture, where Tony should know by now how many cattle they had lost to the rustlers. She found him talking to the sheriff, whose Hummer sat on County Road 84, near the repaired fence.

"Howdy, ma'am," the sheriff said. "You're mighty lucky we caught them guys when we did. Tony tells me they may have taken over fifty head."

"I can't afford to lose that many, Sheriff. Are you having any luck finding them?"

"No ma'am. It's like trying to find a needle in a haystack. They took cows that could be mixed in with their own herds in another state. They keep the cows for breeding, so we won't find them at a sale barn. The calves aren't branded, so they'll just put their own brand on 'em and sell 'em this fall." The sheriff spit tobacco juice at a grasshopper sitting on the fence. He missed and grunted his disgust. "That Mexican who got shot—how's he holding up?" the sheriff asked.

"Ramón is an American citizen," Cara said, irritated at the sheriff's intended slur in front of Tony. "He'll be out of the hospital in a few days."

"Too bad he was shot, but he's a sight better off than the guy who got a bullet in his head." The sheriff laughed at his effort to be humorous.

"I understand the men you captured are talking. Have you found out who's behind the smuggling?"

"We're making headway. The Feds have found connections in Colorado and Arizona. They pick 'em up here in the West and take 'em to the Midwest farms."

Removing his hat, the sheriff wiped sweat from his forehead across a thinning hairline. He replaced the hat and nodded to Tony before driving away. Cara leaned on her saddle horn and waited for Tony to mount his horse. "He doesn't seem too interested in looking for my cattle."

"He ain't looking for cows," Tony said. "He's too busy looking for Mexicans."

They rode to the mesa and sat on their horses, admiring the herd of cud-chewing cattle.

"They're looking good," she said. "The steers are ready for market early."

"We can weed out around a hundred anytime you need to. It will leave more pasture for the ones we keep."

"I'll check the market and get predictions for where it's going," she said as they rode to the corral. "Why don't we aim for September? I'd like to get rid of them before we have another disaster. A hundred won't cover the taxes, but I'm trying to avoid selling off the forty acres across the creek."

Tony smiled. "That's good."

Cara spurred Buck toward the barns, where she turned him over to Pepito. The discussion of selling cows and possible land disposal depressed her. Her spirits lifted when she saw Clay's pickup in the driveway and the children's toys scattered on the porch. After supper she sat on the portal, expecting him to join her. Exhausted, she gave up waiting and went to bed, falling asleep immediately.

It took hours for the children to settle down on the first night they had been to the ranch in weeks. By the time they yawned, the lights in Cara's upstairs suite were dark. Clay moved to the top step on his porch stairs and turned his eyes to the big dipper, sitting over the ranch house, tipped as if ready to pour its contents into the parched ground. Shifting his gaze to the moon, half hidden by slivers of clouds, he wondered if there was a predestined design for each life. Was it all laid out like one of the architectural maps scattered around his office, or would he have a say in how his future played out? He had to admit there was a niggling worry in the back of his mind about whether it might be immoral to unleash a passion for his friend's daughter. This woman was different, maybe because she grew up a decade earlier than he did. He wished Dave were here to give him fatherly advice. He knew part of his attraction to Cara was the power she wielded so naturally. He'd never met a woman who excited him in quite this way. He loved watching from a distance as she directed the ranch operations. He could tell that Tony respected her decisions and mimicked her management style. Things got done. He liked watching her ride her father's gelding. Not many women would be at home in Gus's saddle, yet she moved as if she were a part of the animal. Riding beside her, he felt the same excitement she must feel. He stood up as the moon slid behind the clouds and went inside to write her a quick note.

Cara looked up from her breakfast plate as Lupe placed an envelope beside her cup of coffee. She scrutinized the writing, looked up, and shrugged her shoulders.

"Clay left it in the screen door. Why is he writing you letters?"

Cara would rather not guess. She had heard his truck backing out of the driveway at sunup and wondered if he had deliberately avoided greeting her last night. What was going on in his life?

She opened the note. *Cara, sorry I didn't get over last night. The kids were too excited to sleep. Clay.*

She folded the note and slipped it into her pocket. Brushing her disappointment aside, she had to agree that his priorities were in the right place.

"He seems like a fine man," Lupe said.

"You like him, don't you, Lupe?"

"Yes, but there are others."

"There are?"

"Before you fired Frank, he talked to Tony about his chances of marrying you." She paused, looking at Cara over her glasses. "And

Ramón's quite taken with you too, if you'd just pay attention. I can tell from the way he moons around when you're nearby."

Cara's mouth fell open. "Frank spoke to Tony? When did that happen? What did he say to him?"

"Tony told Frank you're a stubborn, independent woman. Ain't likely any man's going to lasso you. 'Course, he's a mite prejudiced in favor of Ramón. If you married him, we'd become part of the family." She looked away as if this were not important.

"You're already a part of the family, Lupe. You know that."

No longer smiling, Cara blew on her coffee. She hadn't bothered thinking of marriage since moving back to the ranch after college. Marrying Frank was a non-starter—and following her father's example of taking a spouse of Mexican descent seemed just as remote. "I've got to get to work. Has Tony already gone to the barns?"

"Yes, he said you told him to brand the calves in case the rustlers return, so he's getting that started today."

"Good. I'd better ride out to see how he's doing."

"They got more than enough workers. The migrants who ran from the rustler's truck the other night showed up at the camp. He's putting them to work." Lupe liked passing on information from her husband. Tony was a talker, which meant she knew as much about what went on at the ranch as he did. Maybe more, since she heard Cara's view of matters too.

"I thought Tony said they captured all the migrants. They should be in jail or the hospital."

"He told me the sheriff didn't have enough men to corral them. A few slipped away while everyone was gettin' Ramón to the ambulance."

"What's going to happen when the sheriff comes out and finds we've hired them?"

"He told Tony he wouldn't bother looking for them. There's no room in the jail to keep them."

Cara shook her head. "So we're now in cahoots with the sheriff's office. And all this time I was worried about an investigation into *my* practices."

Cara reached for her coffee cup and carried it to the office, closing the door behind her. She locked Clay's letter in her desk.

17

The Cow Bell

Tony brought Ramón to the ranch from the hospital, and Lupe tucked him into Howard's old bed, assuring him she would be available to take care of his needs. He ate the lunch she had kept warm for him and fell asleep.

Cara and Tony spent the afternoon inspecting the acreage she might have to sell. The house was dark when they arrived back at the stable, and Lupe was leaving for home as Cara opened the door to the back porch. "Ramón is doing fine, dear," she said. "He slept all afternoon, but he ate a good supper and is reading now."

Cara put her arms around Lupe. "Thank you, Lupe. I'm sorry for the extra work."

"It is nothing. Praise God, Tony wasn't shot. He's a terrible patient." She pointed to the stove. "Your supper is warm. I'm taking a plate for Tony. Oh," she said, "I gave Ramón a bell to ring if he needs assistance in the night. I told him not to bother you unless it was life threatening."

Lifting her eyebrows, Cara watched Lupe leave, wondering how a bell could avoid bothering her, if it rang in the night. She moved through the house and knocked on Ramón's open door. He closed a book over his finger and looked up.

"Welcome home," she said. "I hope you'll be comfortable here."

"Anything's better than a hospital."

Cara laughed. "Well, there are no pretty nurses here, although we can bring one down from the camp if we need to. Lupe said you had everything you needed. Let her know if there is anything else we can do."

"Many thanks."

"She said she gave you a bell. Call if you need me during the night." She went upstairs, tired and anxious to sleep.

At two o'clock in the morning, Cara pushed aside the covers and walked over to the west window, where the full moon shone through the curtains. Her head ached and her chest was tight with tension. She had awaken an hour earlier and could not go back to sleep. Memories of the rustling continued to spiral through her thoughts like a Western movie. Good guys in white hats and bad guys in black hats appeared and disappeared. Were images of Pablo and Lucille hidden under the black hats? She had to know whether Pablo could be trusted, and if not, whether Lucille had tipped him off to the ease with which the ranch could be attacked. His language skills and work history had allowed him to find work at the Martin ranch rather than to stick with Ramón and the other migrants at the river. The connection seemed too convenient to ignore.

She moved from the west windows to the north side of the house, where she noted the guest apartment was dark and empty. She missed having Clay and his children nearby and wondered if he would be out this week to check on his horses.

The clang of a cowbell stopped her meandering. Her hands flew to her heart as she grabbed her robe. The bell clanged again, and she ran to the stairway. Between her door and the first floor, it dawned on her that the noise came from Ramón's room.

Frightened, she hurried to his room. As she opened the door, his hand raised, ready to swing the bell again. He sat up in bed, showing no distress.

"What's the matter?" She yanked the cowbell from his hand and placed it on a table across the room. "This could be heard halfway across the ranch."

Ramón's teeth were shining through a broad smile, his eyes wide with delight. "It works. Lupe told me to ring the bell and you'd be right down."

"Did she tell you I might kill you when I got here?"

"No, she didn't. You've already failed at that once, you know."

Cara eased onto a chair near the desk. "I'm sorry, Ramón, that I haven't apologized for what happened that night. It's true, if I hadn't interfered you wouldn't have been shot. It's hard to forgive myself for that."

"Cara, I was just kidding. It wasn't your fault. Things happen when everybody's shooting in all directions. I just happened to be in the way of a bullet."

"I shot the tires out on the truck. It could have been one of my bullets. Thank goodness you're healing."

"No, not your bullets. The doctor said I was shot from the back. You can stop feeling guilty. However, if you're thinking of doing it again . . . that's a different question."

Cara smiled. "Why did you call me?"

"I couldn't sleep. I heard you walking." Ramón pointed his index finger, waving it from one side of the room to the other. "I thought we could worry together."

Cara stood. "Did Lupe show you how to use the TV?" She handed him the remote control. "When you can't sleep, you watch TV or read."

He laid the TV control beside him. "TV is not good when you can't sleep. All those nude girls. When do they sleep?" he asked.

"Not all the stations have naked girls. You should try *The Catholic Hour*." She moved to the door. Perhaps she had been harsher than was necessary. Her voice became conciliatory. "I'll be having breakfast on the portal in the morning. Lupe makes great coffee, and she'll fix whatever you're hungry for. If you'd like to join me, you're welcome. I'll bring the sugar bowl."

"I wouldn't miss it." He watched as she started to the door. "My mother used to turn off the light and kiss me good night."

"So did mine. I'm not your mother." She left the room and wandered up the stairs, puzzling over the strange emotion this man created in her. Why had her anger at him dissolved so easily following the rustler incident and his injury? Why couldn't she dismiss Lupe's assertion that he was in love with her? Maybe she shouldn't have suggested that he recuperate here. She couldn't deny there was an emotional spark between them, but she equated that spark to a silly high-school crush or a teenager's impossible dreams of loving a movie star. She had no intention of adding a love triangle to her life.

On Tuesday morning, she spread a woven Mexican cloth on the front porch table while she hummed, a little off-key. She plugged in the coffee pot and the toaster oven before going to get the newspaper from the box at the end of the driveway. Her humming ceased as she stopped to watch a herd of antelope grazing across the road. They lifted their heads to inspect her, their mouths full of grass as they stared, their bodies set like triggers, ready to spring into action. She moved toward the mailbox, while the animals closest to her pushed the herd farther from the fence.

The door to the porch slammed and the antelope scampered away, leaping like ballerinas over the tall grass, their long legs scattering seed pods into the air, making a path of sparkles in the reflected sunlight. Cara watched until they disappeared over the hill. She pulled the paper from the mailbox and hurried back to the porch, where Ramón was maneuvering his way to the table.

"Let me do that," she said as he struggled to pull a chair out with one hand.

"Thanks."

"¡De nada!" She was concerned that Ramón's demeanor seemed sad, and he moved as if in pain. She brought coffee, then returned to the kitchen to collect the bagels Lupe was toasting in the oven.

"Did you get back to sleep okay?" she asked as she laid the food on the table.

He nodded.

She smeared cream cheese on the bagels and set one in front of Ramón while he dipped two spoonfuls of sugar into his cup. She handed him the front section of the paper and sat down, hidden behind the editorial section. Most people didn't like to talk over their morning coffee and newspaper. Ramón's silence convinced her he was one of those.

Twenty minutes later, she dropped the editorials with a sigh and rose to refill her coffee cup. Ramón's gaze followed her. He was smiling.

"You found amusing news on the front page of the paper?" she asked.

"No. I confess I didn't get much of it read. Instead I listened to you read."

"You listened to me read? I didn't read aloud."

"You did. I never heard anyone read the paper before with so many sound effects. You groan, you mutter, you laugh, you snort. It's like a head puzzle, trying to guess what you're reading with each sound you make."

"I'm sorry. My groans and snorts were efforts to restrain myself from telling you what was in the news before you'd had the opportunity to read it yourself."

"You shouldn't have. I'd like to discuss the news with you. I value your insights so that I can understand what makes you tick. I assume I'm free to disagree with you the way your father did."

"Understood." Cara slapped the back of her hand on the photo of a conservative columnist. "Look at this, for example," and off she went, as if she were arguing with her father.

They talked for an hour, Ramón often asking her to explain or clarify her ranting. He offered alternative or compromising positions. She began to feel as if she were in a classroom, being challenged by a teacher who knew all the answers. She no longer felt the sexual tension that had dominated their relationship. Today she was discussing politics with a person who could challenge her intellectually, even better than her father, who refused to consider both sides. The conversation was reminiscent of her Sunday mornings with her dad, before he invited Clay to take her place.

18

Playing with Fire

Cara hesitated to call the sheriff about the rustling investigation, but she felt sure he would not call her.

"Not much going on," he said. "We're figuring whoever tipped them off won't dare to return to the ranch. Can you check the list to see if one of your wetbacks disappeared after the rustling took place?"

"We don't have wetbacks, Sheriff. But we've already checked our workers. Tony says we have a full roster."

"Did Pablo come back?"

"No, but he wasn't with us before this happened. He was working for the Martins."

"He's still our prime suspect, but Larry says he's not on his ranch. Do you know where he's working?"

Cara paused. "I'm afraid I don't know."

"I'll contact Clay Thompson. He may have shown up in town. Let me know if you hear anything." The telephone clicked in her ear.

She reached to pull the employee records from her file. Keeping track of the foreign workers was comparable to capturing mercury. Point to a worker and he moved off the chart, only to reappear where you least expected him. They moved from ranch to ranch as friendships changed, better wages were promised, or for no discernible reason. Cara searched the list of employees signing in before the July 4th bear attack. She compared them with the work schedule from yesterday. There were two names missing: Ramón and Pablo.

She leaned back in her chair. Maybe she shouldn't have dismissed Ramón from suspicion. What did she know about him? His claim that he was an undercover agent could be a clever way to hide his true reason for coming to the ranch. What did Tony know about him? Maybe he was using Tony. That he was well educated could mean many things. Among criminals, he would rate a position on the planning committee. Deciding to steal cattle and move migrants at the same time required smart planning. It included letting the rustlers know when and where to strike. And Pablo. Why had he gotten back on the van when the migrants arrived instead of staying with María and her child? How had he wound up on the Martin ranch unless he had met them through former connections? His green card would protect him from arrest as an undocumented worker. Could he be dealing drugs?

Cara laid aside her papers and wandered down the hall to find Ramón. He was her source for information about Pablo, but she questioned how much he knew and how honest his answers were. The covers on his bed were smoothed in place. His pajamas were folded on the pillow. She searched the closet and noted his cotton pants and sandals were missing. Had he also disappeared? If so, she had let the two suspects slip right thorough her fingers. She headed for the kitchen. "Lupe, where's Ramón?"

"He's on the front porch, reading."

Cara relaxed. Lupe concentrated on the pie crust she was rolling. She cut a small round design in the center of the crust and, with a fork, stabbed air holes into the dough. The work of art completed, Lupe placed the pie in the oven.

"Your pies are always beautiful," Cara said and left to find Ramón. Rain was falling, running off the roof and splattering onto the porch. Ramón rose and pushed back his chair to avoid the splashing.

"Buenos días, professor."

Ramón leaned back and closed his eyes. "Thank you, but it's difficult to have a good day when the sun is not shining." He turned her way and smiled. "However, I like it when you speak to me in Spanish, even if it doesn't make sense."

"Well, I have things to say to you in plain English."

"I like that too. Come around so that I can see you."

Cara moved to the chair beside him. "I'm sorry the rain didn't hold off. Can't brand today."

"That's too bad. We could have finished before the rain started if I had been well."

"Tony said he's all set. Migrants from the cattle truck wound up over here."

"Good. Is branding what you came to talk about?"

"No. I want to discuss your relationship with Pablo and what your real purpose is in working on my ranch."

"I told you why I'm here. I'm working for the INS. They are very pleased that we uncovered the tie between cattle rustlers and the human smuggling."

"I'll have to take your word for that. How can I be sure you weren't the one who tipped them off about our unprotected fences?"

Ramón stared toward the far pastures. "Trust is a very slippery concept."

Cara shrugged the comment aside. Beyond asking to talk to the INS, she had no way to prove or disprove his statements. And what proof would she have that friends at INS weren't in cahoots with him?

"What about Pablo?"

"He was hired by a *coyote* to recruit migrants. I was one of them, and he appreciated my protecting María from a predator. I also held Rosita when he got tired, which won his trust."

"You didn't know him before?"

"No."

"Could he have tipped the rustlers?"

"Could have. It is distressing to think Pablo is a traitor to the people who are taking care of his sister, but he's nineteen years old. Let me find him. I may be able to pull strings for him if he has information that will lead us to the gang bosses."

Cara eyed Ramón. "Where did you learn about plea bargaining, Ramón?"

"My father is an attorney. He had clients who traded information for lesser prison terms. The irony is that my father could not bring himself to rat on his friends, so he went to prison for their crimes."

Cara drew a deep breath. Tony's revelation of his relationship to Ramón had not included information about his brother. She had guessed that Ramón came from the upper classes, which explained his education, but the news of his father's criminal history surprised her.

"I'm sorry," she said.

"Politics."

"Is that why you were schooled in America?"

"Yes. My parents wanted to protect me from my father's politics. I stayed for college. After the Mexican government sent my dad to prison, I decided to change my citizenship."

"And you began working on ranches?"

Ramón did not answer. She waited. He sighed. "I didn't come to New Mexico as a vaquero. I've been working for years on immigration policies between Mexico and the United States. I wrote a book about my research while I was teaching at the University of Arizona, which led the INS to think I knew more about the problem than I do. I have a good friend in the Immigration Department who knew my uncle worked on a ranch not far from Quail Creek, so he suggested that I come here, undercover, to investigate the smuggler problem. You know the rest of the story."

"No I don't. What have you learned?"

"The same thing you did. The gangs are using cattle trucks instead of vans to transport migrants. They travel free from inspection by the state police on the highway and pay off the employees at weigh-in stations." Ramón lowered his eyes, uncomfortable with the conversation. "I'm sorry if I've made life more difficult for you."

"I can't say you have. Tell me what the INS is doing to stop the smuggling."

"They've expanded inspections both at the river and on the ranches where they suspect there are stash houses. But so far the problem has proven more difficult than we thought it would be. Cartels making twenty-five hundred dollars per person with up to twenty men on each load have a lot at stake, and they won't be stopped without a battle."

"So where does Pablo fit into this mess?"

"I hope he doesn't, permanently. We know he assisted with one load brought over by Raphael Cruz, but that was to get María and her daughter out of Juárez and not a full-time job."

Cara rose and faced him with a frustrated wave of her arm. "You keep defending Pablo when, to me, he seems suspect. We've found ties between him and the passage of information about our reduced surveillance, which we think led to the cattle rustling. Now we know those rustlers are the same people who are smuggling the migrants across the country. How does this all fit together?"

"I don't have any information that links Pablo to the smuggling, but I have sent a report to the Feds describing what happened. I'm assuming they are following up on that. They're understaffed."

Cara returned to her chair. "I'm sorry. It would make me feel better to know that someone, somewhere is on top of this mess."

"I'm not at liberty to reveal what's going on with other agents. I can say that they expect to make arrests soon, if that eases your mind."

"So, will you be leaving shortly?"

"Yes. I have to finish my report to my boss. Then I've had an offer from Senator Rodriguez to work with him, doing research on immigration laws. My interest in politics makes his office a good place to start."

Cara sighed. "If my dad were alive, he could have supported your ambitions. He was on speaking terms with everyone, including governors and congressmen."

"I'm sorry I missed knowing him."

"You would have enjoyed knowing my mother more—Consuelo Villa."

Ramón's eyes narrowed. "Yes. Reports I read before I came here stated your mother was Mexican. Your father was Anglo? How did they meet?"

"In Mexico. My father was rebellious when he was young. He left for Mexico right after he graduated from high school . . . set out to see the world. He became a vaquero herding corrientes to ranches in America. He stopped off here, and grandfather talked him into staying. He eventually took over the ranch. My mother was the daughter of Manuel Villa, who owned the Mexican grant below the border, from which they purchased the cattle. Pancho Villa was her great-uncle. You can understand why my father felt a connection to him. Dad commissioned that painting hanging behind his desk of our ranch. He insisted that the painting show Pancho and his gang looking down on the ranch, envying the riches Dad and his bride had accumulated." She laughed. "I imagine Pancho would have been flattered to know he was in the painting. In real life, he'd have stolen those thoroughbred horses in the corral."

Ramón leaned back and sighed. "Now I understand," he said.

"What?"

"Why you and I are comrades in spirit. Our blood is co-mingled."

Cara felt goose bumps rise on her arms. "You're kin to the Villas?"

"No. But their blood is our blood. We're bound by mutual heritage."

Cara searched his face. Surely he understood that having Mexican blood was not a matter Anglos bragged about in this part of the country. They shunned her mother despite their respect for her Anglo father. While she reigned as queen in his home, she was not invited to the women's gatherings in the community. That shunning had had a profound effect on the Morgan children, who took the easy way out by downplaying their own connection to Hispanics.

"When will you talk to Pablo?" Cara asked, changing the subject.

"Sunday. The church in town is sending a bus to pick up the migrants for special Sunday services. Pablo will show up, I'm sure."

"Isn't that flirting with danger—taking the migrants into town? It may require another rescue mission."

Ramón smiled. "I don't think so. One of your policemen belongs to the church, and he looks the other way when migrants show up. They don't have jail space to arrest them, anyway. Plus they understand how important the workers are to the county's economy, which pays their salary."

"Ah, politics and religion: a strange marriage. By the way," she added, "a pile of school supplies are on my desk. I purchased them while you were in the hospital, assuaging my guilt. If you want to look at them while you're bedridden, let me know." She left the porch and headed inside the house.

The telephone rang as she entered the office.

"Good news," Clay said.

"Great. I could use good news."

"Frank talked to Bette's attorney, and they've agreed to file for the divorce decree now and do the property and custody settlement later. They're submitting a motion for the decree today."

"That's wonderful. What does it mean time-wise?"

"If the judge signs the decree, I'll be a free man within days. I'll call you the minute I get the decree. We can celebrate together."

"No kidding." She had hoped to find the right time and place to discuss her fears of intimacy before Clay came face to face, chest to breast, with her scars. It didn't seem fair to surprise a man with her secret, but no appropriate time had presented itself. Since meeting Clay, long-neglected parts of her body had come to life and were demanding attention.

"I'll plan a special dinner to celebrate. Lupe can bake a cake! We'll have champagne." She paused. "Oh, I haven't told you . . . Ramón is still here." There was a long pause before she added, "I guess we should invite him."

Clay laughed. "That's not exactly the celebration I envisioned. I thought we were on the same track."

"What did you have in mind?" she asked, flirtatiously.

"Let's meet at my house. I don't have guests. I'd like you to spend the night."

Cara moved the phone to her other ear. "Oh. Of course. What I suggested was silly. I just thought since Ramón's a guest in my home, I couldn't . . . well, it would be impolite not to have him join us for dinner."

"You're right. That's why we should meet at my house." He paused. "If I'm off base, you need to tell me now."

Cara's breath caught and she forced herself to relax. "No, I'd like to come to your place."

"Great. I'll call you the minute I get the decree."

"Good." Clay hung up and Cara sat holding the phone to her cheek, relishing a fantasy of a night with Clay. Outside the door she could hear receding steps.

"Lupe?" she called.

As she stood and came from behind the desk, Ramón appeared at the door of the office. "I'm sorry. I came to collect the books. I didn't know you were on the telephone." He appeared pale, his eyes sad.

Cara waved him into the office and pointed toward the pile of school supplies. "I hope I found what you need. I got workbooks for the next level of difficulty from where you started."

Ramón smiled as he sorted through the books and pencils. "Perfect," he said. "It's a shame that I've gotten so far behind with the classes."

"All students need an occasional vacation. Don't worry about it."

Ramón looked at the telephone and then at Cara. "I feel I'm ready to go back to the camp if Tony will give me a ride."

"You've only been here a day!"

"I should go."

"You have a doctor's appointment on Thursday. At least wait until then, and let him decide whether you're strong enough to get by without Lupe's good food and pampering."

Ramón glanced at the telephone again. "I'm sure I'm imposing."

"Why do you say that?"

"My staying here is causing trouble for you."

They both stared at the telephone. "I'm sorry. Clay's just teasing me," she said. "You're an easy target. I don't mind. It's sort of fun."

"Why should he be jealous of me?"

"Who knows?" Cara smiled, evasive, almost coquettishly.

Ramón moved beside her and sat down on the edge of the desk, never releasing his hypnotic connection to her eyes. "You like playing with fire, Cara?"

"Is that what I'm doing?"

"Yes. That's what you're doing. Let me show you."

He pulled her toward him, careful of the bandages around his chest. He cupped her chin on his palm, his long fingers reaching to the curve of her jaw. His touch was slow, deliberate, ready to desist if Cara objected. She lowered her eyes to his mouth, his upper lip almost hidden by his heavy mustache. Though keenly aroused, she felt as if she were standing aside, watching, not wanting to stop what she felt was coming.

Ramón rubbed his face against her cheek, and she breathed in the essence she remembered from their wild ride down by the river. She closed her eyes, too engrossed to pull away. He kissed her lips, moving his mouth to the side, returning to touch her tongue. He pressed harder and she relaxed, moving her hands behind his head, returning his kiss.

With her response, his hands moved to her waist, then down to the softness of her hips. After a long moment, he lifted his lips and looked into her eyes. "That feels like fire to me."

Cara gasped and buried her face beneath his jaw, not wanting to pull away. Dear God, what am I doing? What would Clay think? She stiffened and pushed out of his arms, moving backward to sit down behind the safety of her desk.

"That shouldn't have happened." She faced upward, staring into his eyes. "It's been plain from the time we met that you and I cannot be regular friends."

"Because of the fire?"

"No." She searched her mind. There must be a better reason, one he would understand. She rose and walked to the window, her back to him, rubbing her hands over her chest, pulling at her shirt. She turned to face him. "Whatever it is, you're wrong. I don't like playing with fire."

"We could put it out—or douse the flames for the moment."

"No. That isn't true." Cara's voice broke. "Fire consumes a person. It scars you for life."

Ramón stacked the books, arranging them according to size. He steadied them against his hip. "Love consumes the lucky ones."

Cara's eyes were large, filled with fear, lost in an unfamiliar world. She watched as he gathered the books into his arms, torn between wanting him to leave and hoping he would stay.

At the door, he stopped. "Please forgive me if I have upset you. We Hispanics have a lot to learn about how to treat women. I very much respect you. I'll move out on Thursday."

He left and Cara stood staring at her shaking hands. This was my fault. I wanted his kiss. He's right about the fire, but Clay is the one I want to put it out.

She pulled her desk calendar to the center of her desk and glared at the notes she'd scribbled for tomorrow. She had to concentrate on business. Tomorrow she'd go to see her lawyer. Fighting with Howard would clear her mind.

19

The María Factor

The door squeaked as María let herself in the back door of Clay's home on El Paso Street at five-thirty a.m. Wednesday. Clay usually fixed his own breakfast and was gone by the time she came to clean at eight. But today she woke early with an even deeper longing than the one that had plagued her since she became his housekeeper. After he placed his arm around her shoulder last evening, thanking her for cleaning the supper dishes, she had gone home and was unable to sleep.

María loved living in the guesthouse with her brother Pablo. But Pablo had left for Mexico yesterday, and Rosita was still in the care of a foster home. Cleaning house for Clay and babysitting the children after school seemed like playing house. As María worked, she pretended this was her home, that Clay was her husband. All she needed to be happy was another baby. Rosita was the first thing she'd ever had to call her own, and now she needed another baby to cuddle and play with. It made sense that Clay would go along. He loved children so much, and he had plenty of money, so it would be no burden for him to support María and his child. His embrace and pat on the shoulder had given her hope that he felt the same.

The steps creaked as she crept up the stairs. In the bedroom, she watched as he snored softly, his arm thrown over his head. She slipped her dress over her head and threw it on a chair, then dropped her undies and kicked them under the bed.

Lifting the covers, she moved over to touch the warmth of Clay's body. Her own body was hot from rushing up the hill and climbing the stairs. She didn't hurry to touch him, but breathed near the brush of hair under his arm. She laid her hand on his chest, and he sighed but did not move. Her hand slid down his stomach and rested on the softness between his thighs. He moaned and rolled on his side, throwing his arm over the cool coverlet above her. His head rolled onto her long hair. She was trapped.

She massaged lightly, hoping that when he woke he would be too far along to stop. His hardness expanded inside her hand, and he groaned, searching for it with his hand. She smiled, raised on her elbow, and pulled her hair from beneath his face. He stopped snoring. His hand made an effort to push the covers aside. His eyes were moving beneath his closed eyelids. María lifted the covers and swung over him, resting on her knees, hiding her face in the pillow beside his shoulder. He breathed deeply, relaxed, and mumbled someone's name. His arms pulled her close as he struggled to wake.

On the ranch, Cara stalked into the kitchen. She was making no progress tracing telephone calls.

Lupe sat at the table, mending Tony's shirt. "Clay called," she said.

Cara tried to hide her smile. This must mean his divorce was finalized. She wanted to run upstairs to call him, but first she hoped Lupe had information about the latest actions of Ramón and Pablo.

"Lupe, does Ramón make telephone calls that you know of, or does he get telephone calls?"

Lupe shrugged. "He makes a lot of calls on his cell phone, and he goes into the office when you're not here. I don't know who he talks to. Only person I know who's called him is Pablo."

"When does Pablo call?"

"Every day."

"What do they talk about?"

"I don't know. He takes the calls in the office."

"How about letters? Has Ramón gotten letters? Does he mail letters?"

"No letters in our box. It's hard to send letters from Mexico, but he writes almost every day. He has family in Mexico."

Cara stood. "Thanks, Lupe. Don't tell him I asked."
Lupe frowned and resumed her mending.

Upstairs at 909 El Paso Street, María yanked the sheets from Clay's bed and piled them with other dirty linen on the floor. Her long black lashes were wet and mussed. Her eyes teared as she spread clean sheets on the mattress. She should have known her dreams of having Clay's baby were not realistic, but it didn't seem fair that she had to take all the blame. Most men she met would have welcomed her to their bed. Clay's rage when he woke shocked her. Not only had he knocked her off the bed, he had ordered her to call Pablo to come and get her. "And change these sheets," he ordered before leaving the house.

New tears ran down her cheeks as she recalled Pablo's voice when she told him she had to leave. He cursed and accused her of ruining their chances to live in America. "It was all Clay's fault," she wept. "He invited me to come to his bed." Pablo cursed again and told her to call Ramón and ask him to take her to the ranch. María relaxed. Ramón was a handsome Hispanic who should have a woman. María was sure she could make him happy, if she had the chance.

Her foot became entangled underneath the edge of the bed. She bent down and recovered her panties, thought about putting them on, then laid them on the pile of dirty laundry. She would wash them with the soiled sheets. She finished changing the bed, gathered everything in a roll, and carried it downstairs to the laundry room.

At the ranch, Cara went upstairs to call Clay. His secretary Tammy answered the telephone, and Cara took the opportunity to ask her to fax a copy of the business telephone records. "Clay said he paid the telephone bills for the guesthouse thorough his office, and that's what I need. He gave me permission to see them for the past two months."

Tammy said she could send them by tomorrow, and then she transferred Cara through to Clay's office.

"I'm holding the divorce decree in my hand, right now. The champagne has been chilling for days. Can you get here for dinner? I'm pretty good at grilling."

"Sounds wonderful. Around seven?"

"Perfect. I'll leave the garage door open. Park inside."

"I can do that. Are we hiding from the neighbors?"

"Nah. Mostly my kids. They're in and out all the time. I'll lock the doors."

Cara chuckled. "I'm pleased that I rate so high on the scale of preferred company."

"I'll bet your parents locked their bedroom door at times. You've just forgotten."

"You're right. They did. And I don't recall feeling neglected at all."

"So I don't get demerits for wanting to spend the night with you instead of my kids?"

"No way. I'll see you at seven."

Her hands were shaking as she stopped in front of the full-length mirror in her room. She lifted the tail of her blouse and hesitated as the scars began appearing below the hem. She pushed the blouse up to her chin and grimaced as she stared at long, lumpy scars running from her breastbone to her belt. There was no sign of breasts, nor indications of where they should have developed as she grew older. The doctor had warned they would never develop. He recommended that she return after puberty and have implants. Her mother and Emily urged her to do that, but her anger was so deep, she refused. Now she regretted her decision. She tucked her shirt in and hurried down the stairs to inform Lupe not to save dinner for her.

20

The Decree and Dirty Laundry

Changing from a deep broccoli color to a somber gray-green, the second cutting of alfalfa lay drying under the blazing August sun, the odor rising on heat waves from the grass as it changed from fresh-cut ripe to dry and dusty. At this stage in haying, ranchers watched the southern and western skies with furrowed brows. Wet August monsoons could soak the blanketed fields, rotting the hay before the balers arrived. Even the clouds without moisture were a problem, because they shielded the sun's burning rays that were needed to suck the juices from the alfalfa stems before the baling began.

Cara rode with Tony to check the status of the hay. They dismounted, and Tony took a handful of the straw, bending the stems and throwing them into the breeze.

Frowning at the afternoon clouds, Tony mumbled that the hay needed another full day of sun. Maybe a day and a half, in places where it lay thick and heavy. "Larry finishes with the balers tomorrow. He'll move them here and be ready to begin on ours by Friday at the latest. We can start on those thin ridges that are already dry."

"Looks like we'll have more feed than we need this winter, since we have to sell part of the herd. Maybe we can sell hay to make up for lost cattle." They headed back to the corrals.

"How did the branding go?" Cara asked. "Were the numbers as low as we feared?"

"Worse, I'm afraid. Looks like they rustled up to three loads. Fifty to sixty cows with calves."

"Damn, by the time I sell enough cattle to pay the taxes and bank notes, our herd will be way too small to cover the pastures next year. We'd better order a bigger lot of corrientes in the spring."

Tony nodded. "Unless the sheriff finds the cows that were stolen. Sure looks like a professional job, though. They're probably on the other side of the border by now."

"I'll keep pressure on the sheriff. You can't move that many cattle without someone knowing where they went. And I talked to Ramón," she said. "He's agreed to check on whether one of the vaqueros passed on information. The only person we can pinpoint right now is Pablo, and he's working for Clay. Ramón expects to see him this weekend."

Cara arrived at Clay's home at seven, parked inside the garage, then watched as the door closed behind her. Clay stood smiling at the kitchen door and reached out to take her bag. She walked into his arms, trying to sort out the intoxicating smell of masculine cologne from the charcoal smoke clinging to Clay's checkered shirt. He dropped the bag and put both arms around her. She buried her face under his chin. They stood there, rocking together until crackling from the grill reached them.

"Gotta check this," Clay said and pulled away, picked up the bag, and dropped it near the stairs. He led her through the dining room to the outside patio on the south side of the house.

Cara watched as he strung giant shrimp on a spit and placed it on the grill.

"Are you ecstatic?" she asked as he removed the champagne bottle from a bucket of ice and worked at removing the cork.

"I'm glad the nightmare's over. This is the first time I've failed so miserably at something important in my life, so I can't say I'm happy about it. I'm sad for the kids." He poured her drink. "Having you here makes me happy."

"Congratulations." They touched glasses and kissed.

The round table was set for two, with a white starched tablecloth, tall candles, and a pot of violets. A plate of hors d'oeuvres, arranged by color and size, sat on a table to the side.

"Don't tell me you made these." Cara pointed to meats wrapped in sheaves of cheese and pastry.

"No. I ordered it from Food Prep. Those gals do everything, even divorce celebrations."

They touched glasses again as the back door flung open. Jason and Ashley came charging into the house.

"Dad, I smell shrimp," Jason yelled. He ran to the patio and searched the table and grill for finger food. Cara felt dizzy. She saw her brother Howard running into the kitchen, pointing to a pan of hot fried chicken. She closed her eyes and gasped for air. Ashley ran past her, but stopped when she noticed Cara. She sidled to her father's leg.

"What are you doing here, Jason?" Clay asked.

"Mother went out tonight, so she left us with María."

"You don't seem to be with María."

"She's watching television," Ashley said.

"Have you eaten?" Cara asked, trying to take control of her memories.

"No," they both said. Clay looked at her and frowned.

"María's going to order a pizza."

"Well, I suggest you go back and tell María you're hungry and to please order the pizza," Clay said, his jaw muscle jerking over his clinched teeth.

"She's already called, but it hasn't come."

"I'd rather eat with you, Dad," Ashley said.

"Me too," Jason said.

Clay's face reddened underneath his tan.

"I have an idea," Cara said. "Why don't we have a party just for the four of us and share this beautiful plate of munchies?" She spread her hands to show the problem was solved. "By the time we've finished with the fun food, the pizza will be delivered, and," she looked at Jason, "you and Ashley can go eat with María." She looked at Clay. "How's that for compromising?"

He sighed and nodded. The children ran to find extra chairs to put around the table.

"You may have saved my ex-wife from being murdered, not to mention I won't be arrested for child abuse." Clay said.

"It's not that big a deal." Cara rubbed his back. "We have all night to make up for lost time."

A few minutes later the hors d'oeuvres were demolished. When Jason spilled shrimp cocktail down his shirt, Cara used her napkin to wipe the goop away, hoping to lessen Clay's impatience with the children.

The pizza delivery man drove past the house and stopped near the garages, setting off a race between the children. Clay followed them to the door, and Cara heard the lock snap shut. A chain clinked against the door.

"Where shall I put this soiled napkin?" Cara held the cloth stained with ketchup in front of her. He pointed through the kitchen. "Leave it in the laundry room, please."

Cara pushed the door to the laundry room aside and reached out to drop the napkin on the washer. A pile of dirty laundry lay there, a woman's pair of dingy cotton panties on top. Cara stood looking at them, puzzled. They were similar to the ones Lupe had washed for María while she stayed at the hospital with Rosita. Cara picked them up. The smell of feminine body secretions was so strong she gasped and dropped them. There were no other items of laundry for María. Cara suspected that María had her own laundry room at the carriage house. How strange that a pair of her panties lay with Clay's bed sheets.

She went back to the patio and sat down, confused. She stared at the warm, loveable man who expected her to spend the night. How much did she know about him? Frank had said he had other girlfriends, which he denied. Howard had accused him of having an interest only in her money. She found that laughable, since he was well-to-do himself. Yet, what proof did she have that both accusations were false? What if she was a naive sucker? Everyone would believe she was an old maid, desperate to fall for any man who sweet-talked her. However, public opinion wasn't what bothered her most. She knew who she was. She had lived as she chose, and she had never believed that a lover or husband was a necessary addition to her life—though she acknowledged Clay had added an exciting, wonderful improvement to what she already had.

She watched as he moved around the grill, confident, no doubt, in his next conquest. She remembered the smell of María's panties, an odor so strong it transported her imagination to the beautiful bedroom upstairs. Had he undressed her in the light of the full moon shining through those windows, while he sat on the windowsill pressing her between his legs? How often had he left the ranch and gone to María? Her hand missed the table where she sought to set her glass, and it fell at her feet, shattering into a million pieces, splashing wine across her feet and legs.

Clay laid aside his tools and hurried over. "What happened?"

Cara's voice teetered on hysteria. "You're sleeping with María, aren't you?"

Clay froze, unprepared to respond to such an unexpected charge.

"Her panties are in the laundry with your sheets, so don't deny it." Weeping, Cara grabbed her purse and ran to the garage. She slammed the car door, turned the key, then remembered she was locked inside.

Clay approached as she rolled up her window. "Can't we talk?" he asked. Cara shook her head and gunned the motor as he pushed the button to open the door. She spun out of the driveway onto El Paso Street.

Back on the patio, Clay stared at the shattered glass. Food was burning on the grill.

21

Mind over Heart

Cara's fury at the night's disclosure was stronger than she ever remembered suffering, even when her father died. It was similar to the anger Howard generated in her when they were children, often precipitating a fistfight. Once she threw a rock that left a scar on his forehead. It was the last time she remembered being so enraged.

By the time she arrived home, she realized it would be impossible to sleep, with her mind churning like boiling water. She went inside and changed to her riding clothes. The full moon poured a soft light over the ranch, like early dawn. Buck came running to the fence, eager to leave the corral. She rubbed his forelock but shook her head. She would ride Gus up to the lake.

At first Gus fought the bit, insisting on running up the trail while she concentrated on staying in the saddle, but the steep incline soon slowed him to a fast, strong walk. By the time they reached the lake, he was sweating, eager to drink and stomp in the cool water. Cara dismounted, loosened the saddle straps, and staked him near the water. Numb with fatigue, she lifted a blanket from behind her saddle and collapsed under the aspen trees. She stared at the moon's reflection streaking across the lake. Never had she felt so empty, so betrayed, so stupid, and so alone. She fell back on the thick mulch of leaves and pine needles, pulled her hat over her face and sobbed. Exhausted, she curled into a fetal position and went to sleep.

Gus's snorts woke her as the moon disappeared and the eastern horizon prepared for a sunrise that would come before she could get home. Damn. She'd come up here to think, to try to make sense of what had happened. Maybe her falling asleep meant there was no way to understand the craziness of her life. At least her rage was gone. Her blood pressure might be normal. The world was no longer in danger of her flying fists or thrown rocks. Her mind now ruled her heart.

She stood, swaying a little before getting her balance. The lake was dark, lapping over the rocks around its edge. To be fair to herself, she conceded that falling in love with Clay had not been stupid. Not what she expected of herself, but not illogical. And what of her anger, or was it jealousy, toward María? The image of María lying with her full breasts in Clay's bed swept all reason from her mind. Understand it, yes. Accept and forgive it, no.

Clay was a different matter, dammit. She tightened the saddle and Gus groaned in protest. "That was meant for Clay," she assured the horse, "although we both know he has no breakable parts."

Cara gave Gus his head. Maybe she could get home and clean up before Lupe appeared and started asking questions. She hadn't had time to decide what the answers were.

On the kitchen table, she found a note Lupe had left saying she and Tony had gone to town to shop before it got too hot. They'd have lunch in town. Cara was pleased she didn't have to face Lupe's questions. The note rested on the morning's mail, which included a large brown envelope with Clay's office address. That would be his telephone records, and if Cara were lucky, she'd find out if Pablo or María had made calls to Mexico or to neighboring states. If they had, she could turn those records over to the sheriff, who might find a link between them and smugglers or rustlers in the area. She'd like to finish that job and get on with her life.

Cara carried the mail to the office, sat down, and scanned the telephone records. The first ones were from the telephone Clay shared with Bette. Those were irrelevant, but on the next page, the guesthouse number showed three calls to Denver, Colorado, and two to Tucson, Arizona. There were also calls to a local number she found familiar. Wasn't that the Martins' number? She took a yellow marker and highlighted the telephone numbers that seemed suspicious. She was tempted to call the long distance numbers, but that might scare the person who answered, or let them know they were being traced. She wondered why Pablo had contacted the Martins after he moved to town. Maybe he'd left possessions on their ranch. The next step was to call the sheriff. Knowing she'd wait several minutes to reach him, Cara propped her feet on the desk.

"Cara," he said. "Good to hear from you. What's up? No more bear raids, I hope."

"No, Sheriff. I'm following up on your suggestion that one of our workers at the migrant camp tipped the rustlers to the information that we were shorthanded. You remember that?"

"Oh, sure. What you got?"

"Maybe nothing, but I discovered a few long-distance calls were made to Denver, both before the rustling happened and afterward. Other calls went to Tucson the next week, probably made by Pablo. He turned up at the Martin ranch for a few days, then went to town, working construction."

"Well, that's interesting. You got those numbers?" Cara read off the long-distance numbers for the sheriff. "How did you get these? Where'd he call from?"

"He's the uncle of the little girl who was attacked by the bear. He called from her mother's telephone."

"We'll need her name and address too."

"María Mendoza. She's living in the guesthouse at 909 El Paso Street. That's behind Clay Thompson's home. She's cleaning house and babysitting for him now." Cara felt her jaws locking. It was not her fault that María and Rosita were in danger of deportation. Nor was she any longer worried that Clay might get pulled into the migrant controversy.

"Well, that's an easy address to find."

"Sheriff, you mentioned this looked like an interstate operation. Is the FBI or Immigration Department working on it?"

"Yes, ma'am. We're not making it public, but they're on the case. They want this information and will trace it pronto."

"Good. Let me know if you hear anything." So. Ramón was in the middle of whatever was happening, on one side or the other. Was he squealing on Pablo or had he warned him to leave?

Cara laid down the telephone and tuned her ear toward the office door. She could have sworn she heard a bump into one of the dining room chairs, but all of them were in order as she passed through to the kitchen. She went out to the back porch in time to see Ramón walk from the north side of the house to the shed where the garden tools were kept. The noise she'd heard in the office could have come from outside the open window. She followed him to the garden.

"Are you sure you're well enough to do this?" she asked.

Ramón glanced her way, surprised at her presence.

"Still a little sore, but the exercise will do me good." He placed a long-handled garden fork near a potato plant and pushed the tines deep into the soft soil. He pulled down on the handle and dumped the plant over, uncovering several small new potatoes clinging to the roots. The soil was rich, with the pungent odor of compost. Ramón bent down and collected the potatoes, placing them in Lupe's basket.

"Were you able to get in touch with Pablo?" Cara asked.

She watched his long fingers rubbing the soil from each potato. His hands were beautiful, and she could imagine them moving along her jaw. She felt anger constricting her chest. Why had she been so quick to forgive him for what happened at the river? How was he any different from Clay? He'd no doubt slept with María too.

He interrupted her thoughts. "Pablo called me. He left for Mexico." He rose and pushed the fork into the soil again, lifting more potatoes to the surface.

"Why is he going to Mexico?"

"Business."

"Another job for Rafael?"

Ramón stopped digging. "Does it matter?"

"I thought you were working for the INS on border control. Do you get to pick and choose who you report as *coyotes* and smugglers? Pablo is the logical choice for who tipped the rustlers. I suspect he's going underground to escape the sheriff. Why can't you recognize this?"

Ramón shook his head. "You're wrong about the rustling. That was a Mafia operation. He's gone back to take care of family business in Juárez. He'll come back."

"He also made phone calls to the Martin home after he moved to town. What business would he have had with them?"

"The Martins live on the other side of the river, right?"

Cara nodded.

"I don't know. He stayed there a couple nights after the bear attack."

"About the same time the rustling started. Is there a connection?"

"How do you figure?"

"An informer let the rustlers know we didn't have enough riders to cover our fences. The Martins had that information and could have mentioned it in front of Pablo, accidentally or on purpose. He could have passed it on to the smugglers."

"What would the Martins gain from passing on that information? And everybody in the county knew you were shorthanded. Why focus on Pablo or the Martins?"

"It's a long story, and I don't want to accuse them unjustly, but it's my belief the Martins want the Los Lobos Ranch to go up for sale. They've wanted to buy portions of it for years, and Dad refused to sell. I can assure you they weren't happy to hear he left it all to me and that it wouldn't be divided as long as I was successful in keeping it above water. If my cattle are not recovered, I may be forced to sell the bottomland bordering their ranch."

"That's pretty wild guessing on your part."

"Maybe, but I'm trying to put all the puzzle pieces together. Despite your faith in Pablo, my gut tells me he isn't innocent. I find it strange he'd leave María here by herself."

"She's in a safe place." Ramón's voice softened as if he weren't all that sure of his information. He continued upending the plants, digging deeper and dumping them over, ignoring Cara.

"Maybe she's safe, but can she live on what she's making without support from Pablo?"

Ramón stood, using the fork to balance himself. "Pablo did what he could to protect her before he left. He knew if she married an American it would give her a better chance of avoiding deportation, so he asked me to marry María. I agreed. Her age is a problem, but it can be changed on her papers. I don't know how long it will take."

Cara felt her heartbeat skitter. She waited for it to return to the steady throbbing that often sounded in her ears. "You agreed to that?"

"I can't very well stand by and see her returned to Juárez. It would be signing her death certificate . . . and the child's too, if she is allowed to go. The alternative is leaving the child in foster care until she's an adult or is adopted."

Cara knelt in front of Ramón to lift the basket of potatoes. Did he know Clay was sleeping with María? Did Pablo know? Did it matter to either of them?

"Also," Ramón said, "it's a move that will keep me in close touch with Pablo and Raphael. Finding the connection between Mexico and the American Mafia was my reason for coming here." He pushed the garden fork into the soil beside another plant, and Cara set down the basket, and gathered another handful of potatoes. She rubbed away the dirt and dropped them into Lupe's basket. Without speaking, she rose and carried them to the faucet outside the shed and held them beneath the splashing water to loosen the soil. Tiny black eyes speckled the potatoes, little imperfections. Lupe would cut them out.

Cara went to the office, wondering whether to pass the information about Pablo to the sheriff. There was no way she could point a finger at the Martins without more evidence. She felt sure tracing the telephone calls would not get her cattle back, but it might lead to Rafael's trail of migrants crossing the Rio Grande, which might lead to María's deportation. Was she in favor of having the INS capture people like María and Rosita, whose lives were in danger every day in Juárez? She must talk to Tony.

She found him and a handful of vaqueros separating the older cows and yearlings into a pasture where their limited activity and diet of enriched grains would fatten them for sale. Tony saw her coming and rode out to meet her.

"Morning," he said. "Weather's coming in." He pointed to the sky, dappled with cumulus clouds, darkening, threatening to become thunderheads.

"Let's hope it holds off until tomorrow night. We bale tomorrow."

"Yeah, let it wait a while."

They pulled their horses to a standstill and watched the animals greet each other with nose rubs. Tony's bigger and older horse nipped Buck to put him in his place, and Cara pulled her horse away, circling and coming back to stand within easy speaking distance. "How many head do we have here?"

"Eighty-five, but I figure we'll reach a hundred. I keep hoping the sheriff will find our stolen herd. If he doesn't we'll have to round up a number of the corrientes and sell them early."

"Tony, I found telephone numbers that Pablo used the day after the vaqueros left. Three calls to Denver and two to Tucson. Would you know who he called?"

Tony shook his head. He sucked in his cheeks and pursed his lips. "No," he said. "Long-distance calls are costly. The vaqueros can't afford them."

"Well, Pablo found a way around that. He used María's telephone, which Clay is paying for."

"Oh." Tony released his breath, whistling through his teeth.

"Ramón said Pablo is headed for Mexico but will return in a few days. If you hear the migrants talking about him, please let me know what they say, will you?"

"You bet." Tony touched his hat and nodded.

Cara pulled Buck's reins, heading him back to the ranch house.

"Oh, Cara," Tony called. "I meant to ask you. The migrants are hoping to have their annual celebration on Mexico's Independence Day. The town church people agreed to bring food and music. Can I tell them it's okay?"

"Of course. What day is that?"

"September 16. It falls on Thursday this year."

Cara smiled. "I suppose they'll celebrate all weekend."

"Most likely."

"Fine. Check with Lupe and see what we can contribute in the way of food. Keep me posted." She urged Buck to a gentle lope toward the barns. The ranch had sanctioned the holiday celebration by the employees since she was a child. It had gotten bigger each year, with people from town coming for the music, dancing, games, and food. This year it would allow the employees to forget immigration problems for a few days, at least.

Inside the stable, Ramón sat on the ladder, boots resting on the ground. He held two kittens and three more chased each other around his feet. For the first time since his accident, he was dressed in blue jeans, his Mexican shirt, and the leather vest that Lupe had repaired by embroidering around the bullet hole. Cara paused, surprised at his presence. "You finished digging potatoes? You must be feeling stronger."

He pushed his hat off his forehead and smiled. "I came to say goodbye to my friends." One of the kittens crawled to his shoulder and licked his ear. Laughing, he shook his head to dislodge the kitten and pulled her claws from his shirt collar.

"Does that include me?"

The smile disappeared. He nodded.

Buck pushed his way into the stable and sniffed at Ramón's jacket. Ducking his head, Ramón fished an apple from his pocket, and Buck grabbed it with his lips and tongue, chomped it, and trotted from the stable, juice dripping from his mouth.

"Men have no sense of honor, do they? Buck is my horse. Why do you keep trying to come between us?"

"I'm sorry, but there's no way I can come between you. My intention was to pay back for our meeting at the river."

"An apple won't do it for me."

"You forgot the moment in the office." The silence in the barn vibrated with memories that sparked against each other like exposed electrical wiring. Cara's jaw hurt from the pressure of clamped teeth. In retrospect, it was too bad she hadn't allowed it to happen. She could have offered Clay used goods, comparable to his own. Another of her bad decisions. If she were going to live in a man's world, she should adopt their ways. Give in to her erotic needs any time she chose. She returned Ramón's questioning gaze and shivered. What if she had given in to the passion Ramón generated? Would it have lessened the pain of Clay's betrayal?

"Take one of the kittens with you," she said. "Rosita needs a pet."

"That's true. Thank you. You are kind."

Cara's gaze bounced off his face in angry sparks. "Don't say nice things about me, Ramón. I know myself well, and unlike you, my feelings for María are not kind."

"You know this plan is not of my choosing. I'm doing a favor for our people."

"They are not my people. And your concern is linked to a sexy teenager and her child. What of your school for the migrants? You'll just drop your work with them while you go off to live with María?"

Ramón set the kittens on the stable floor and watched them scamper to their mother, before staring at Cara. "Are you angry at María or me?"

Cara pinched her lip between her teeth.

"What is it you're trying to tell me?"

"Nothing. What you do is none of my business."

"We know that's not true. Everything I've done since I've been on the ranch is your business. At least that's what I've been led to believe." He stood as if to leave. "Perhaps you can't admit you're attracted to a Hispanic."

"That is a stupid accusation. Believe it, if it makes you feel better."

"You're right. I have nothing to base it on, but it gives me consolation to think your hatred isn't personal."

Cara turned to open the stall gate. "Don't you find it a little strange that you pretend to care for me, while at the same time telling me you plan to marry María?"

"I agreed to take care of María and her child. I didn't promise to love her. I won't be sleeping with her."

"Huh. I don't believe that, but it isn't any of my business." She turned to leave the stables.

"Cara, I want it to be your business. I care deeply about you, and if you care who I sleep with, it could mean you share those feelings."

Cara continued walking. She had cared who Clay slept with because he'd given her the impression he loved her. Last night she had discovered monogamy had nothing to do with his idea of love. It seemed clear that love and sex were separate, unrelated conditions for men. Why wouldn't that include Ramón?

22

The School Bus

Each day melded into the next, with few distinguishing markers to make Cara forget that her life consisted of rising, eating, working from daylight to dark, eating dinner alone, and falling into bed, muscles sore, mind numb, unable to think beyond the chores that existed to keep her moving from point A to point B. No calls came from Clay following the night she ruined the celebration of his divorce; at least, not calls to her. Tony reported that he was searching for new boarding arrangements for his horses and that Pepito would continue to care for them as long as they remained on her ranch.

Cara struggled to suppress the intensity of her anger, boiling like bile in her throat each time she questioned the reasons her relationship with Clay failed. At first she laid the blame where it seemed most rational. Women could not trust men. Even if she accepted her share of the responsibility for the failure, she could not accept his statement that he found her alluring, reacting to her the way men did to Emily. Common sense convinced her that no man wasted time pursuing a reluctant, older woman when a young, willing girl like María was available. She concluded that his attraction to her equaled lust, which he could satisfy elsewhere. Or maybe he did have his eye on acquiring an interest in the ranch. She fought against believing this debacle was caused by the scars on her psyche. That would place the blame on her, and she believed her responses to love were no different from those of the unmarked citizens of the world. Since Clay had not seen her body, that would leave her mind to blame. It was easier not to think of Clay at all.

She found it harder to avoid remembering Ramón. He had left the ranch to live with María, but when she caught sight of schoolbooks stacked unused in the guest room, or watched kittens skitter away from the hooves of the horses in the stables, or when she inhaled the sweetness of fresh vegetables from the garden, the image of his smile, his eyes, his voice invaded her mind. She suffered the most when she glanced at empty spaces on the library shelves, where she could not bring herself to replace the books he'd borrowed.

She worried about the occasions when memory of him invaded her thoughts. Perhaps Ramón was right. They did have a blood connection, and she was reluctant to fall in love with a man of Mexican birth because her mother's Mexican heritage had subjected her to shunning. Her children had tried to avoid the same fate by pretending that heritage didn't exist. Ramón refused to let her forget.

On the Saturday after Ramón left the ranch, Luisa appeared at the back door, shifting books and tablets from one arm to the other. Cara hurried to the door. "Luisa, what are you doing here?"

"I brought the books. We can't use them without Ramón." Tears blurred her eyes.

Cara bent forward and took several of the books. "Come on in." Luisa pointed to her dust-covered huaraches and shook her head.

"Oh, come on in," Cara said and held the door open, waiting for her to move. In the kitchen, she pulled out a chair, poured coffee, and set biscuits and honey in front of her guest. They sat untouched as Luisa wiped her apron across her cheeks.

"Maybe Ramón will come back on the weekend and continue the lessons," Cara said. "He could bring María and her child."

Luisa shook her head. "It is too little. He worked every night while he was here, and we still cannot fill out the forms. I tried to read the books after he left, but I do not understand them. The new hombres wanted to take the tests next month, so that they can get green cards and become citizens. We are so afraid of being sent back!"

She dropped her head into her apron. Her sobs became howls, rising from the apron through her hands, encircling Cara in a fog of memories and fears of the wolf pack. She jumped up from the table and hurried to the window over the sink. The sun was setting over the horizon, leaving the ranch in an orange glow, like that of a lamp just before it is extinguished. Standing near the corrals, migrant workers stared toward the house, not talking, standing like stumps or squatting, making small marks in the dust with fingers or sticks.

"Why are they here?" Cara asked.

"Who, señorita?"

"Los hombres."

"They carried the books."

"It took all of them to carry the books?" Cara was ashamed of the pressure that pushed her words toward Luisa, whom she knew was innocent, but she worried at the sight of the migrant pack. Ramón was no longer on the ranch to control them.

"They want you to teach them." Luisa's imploring eyes were wide and frightened.

Cara crossed her arms, holding on to her elbows, and leaned against the kitchen sink, her weight on one leg, the other crossed over to rest on the sharp tip of her boot. She wanted to snort loudly at the idea, but she knew Luisa would not understand the irony of the situation. While Tony had fired the ring leaders, a few of the men who stood by cheering when they thought Ramón was raping her remained on the ranch. These were men whom even Ramón admitted had no respect for women. They were asking her to become their teacher.

Cara gritted her teeth. At the table she shuffled through the papers the students had continued writing after Ramón left. Immigration forms he had given them were mixed with drawings, printing exercises, and signatures. His classwork was far from finished.

Ramón had accused her of denying her lineage, and she knew he was right. She refused to associate with a nation of men who raped, killed, or otherwise disrespected women. She didn't identify with women who allowed it to happen. Perhaps this was a way to address that problem. Also, if she continued the schooling, it should prove she was not prejudiced against the migrants, and it would assuage her guilt for occupying the privileged position of United States citizen. She looked out the window at the rag-tag group of migrants. There, but for the grace of God, go I, she acknowledged.

Continuing the school was possible, but she could not do it alone. Perhaps Father Angus would have ideas. Many in his church were qualified to work as tutors.

"Luisa, tell the men I will make a deal with them. I will see that the school is opened, and they will learn to fill out the immigration forms, but they must also attend citizenship classes. They must learn respect for women. They must promise never to abuse their wives and daughters or other women. I believe Father Angus will teach the classes if he sees the men are willing to change. They cannot attend the school unless they change. Can you convince them of that?"

Luisa let out a deep, victorious laugh. She jumped from her chair and clapped her hands. "Sí, señorita. Wait till I tell them the rules. They will turn pale. But they will agree." She headed for the door. "If they don't, the women will beat them over the head. When will the classes start?"

Cara smiled at Luisa's happiness. "Give me a few days. I'll let you know."

The classes began a week later. Father Angus needed Cara's promise to get the migrants to church services. He organized volunteers to tutor the migrants but confided that church members were complaining that the church resources were being wasted on the "foreigners." Lucille Martin led the parade of complainers, and this knowledge spurred Cara to complete the project. She asked Tony to make sure the men who wanted to attend the school were excused from work early each Wednesday, and he was to assign one of them the job of driving the tractor that pulled the flatbed hay trailer from the barns down County Road 84 to the church. Quickly, the trip became an old-fashioned hay ride, with the migrants singing on the way to school and back. When she could find time, Cara joined them to confirm Luisa's happy reports of their progress.

Opossum Hunting

Cara jumped from the flatbed trailer that carried the migrant students as it pulled into the driveway beside the ranch house. The timing was lousy. Clay's truck pulled off the highway and stopped in the driveway as the trailer rumbled over the cattle guard, headed for the camp. Cara turned her back to Clay's pickup and waved goodbye to the students.

"What's going on?" Clay asked, standing near her shoulder.

"It may not look like it," she said, "but that's a school bus."

Clay frowned. He leaned against the truck, one foot propped on the high front bumper.

"Could have fooled me," he said, shaking his head. "I'm surprised you don't think you're too old to ride a school bus."

Cara's eyes narrowed. He hadn't come to make peace, which was good. She wasn't in the mood for concessions. "What are you doing here?"

"I came to pay another month's boarding fee for the horses. Still haven't found a new place for them. Thought I'd go riding. Will you join me?"

Cara mused for only a moment. Time was not the deciding factor. The question was whether she wished to spend time with a philanderer, and he had not asked that. The answer was *no. Hell, no.*

"Sorry," she said. "I have other things to do."

Clay nodded and headed for the stables. Later she watched from the kitchen window, angry and uptight, as he rode off toward the lake. She would have loved to ride out to watch the sunset, but how could she do it without letting him think she approved of the way he had treated her? She couldn't go alone, for fear they would meet.

As time passed, Clay continued to arrive at the ranch in time to intercept the departure of the school bus. If Cara had not ridden with them, she came to the backyard fence to wave goodbye, at the same time acknowledging Clay's presence with a polite but cool nod. He then saddled one of his horses and rode off to find Tony or he packed his fishing gear and headed for the lake. Cara, simmering at home, came to the conclusion she was allowing him to corral her movement on the ranch on those days when he rode into her territory. Late one Saturday afternoon, when he'd left for night fishing on the lake, she determined to reclaim her freedom to move on the ranch as she wished. She saddled Gus and headed in the opposite direction. She dismounted at the river, contemplating a skinny-dip in the swimming hole. The day was hot and the cool water inviting. Gus whinnied toward the steady clip-clop of horse's hooves coming their way. She grabbed her rifle from the scabbard. The sun was setting and it wasn't safe to face a stranger in the dark, unarmed. Clay rode into view and she relaxed.

"I hope you don't plan to use that on me," he said, as he reined in beside Gus.

She replaced the gun in the scabbard and looked at him without responding. Sunrays filtered through the trees bordering the river, covering the area with a reflection of pink and mauve watercolors.

"May I join you?"

"There aren't any fish here."

Clay swung from his saddle and staked his horse in the meadow. Cara moved to sit on a large rock bordering the pool.

"I saw you ride this way, and it came to me that the fish might not be biting at the lake either." He stopped near the huge tree bound by a long rope swing. "We need to talk."

She didn't respond.

"It wasn't fair of you to leave that night without allowing me to explain."

"Explain?" She laughed. "Tell me. What sort of story could you have manufactured to excuse sleeping with a fifteen-year-old girl?"

"That's very simple. I didn't sleep with her."

Cara thought she must have misunderstood what he said, but no—he was denying the act ever happened. "That makes a good story," she said. "Tell it to someone naive enough to believe it."

"Cara, I didn't sleep with her. I'm not sleeping with her. I'm not sleeping with anyone." His voice was angry and firm.

Cara stood with her arms crossed, shielding herself from the urge to believe him, confident he was lying. The sounds around the pool were the gentle sighing of the horses as they stood facing each other, muzzles touching, tails swishing flies and mosquitoes.

"I almost slept with her." Clay's voice was conciliatory.

Cara's breath caught. He was getting closer to the truth. She let the air escape through tight nostrils.

"She came to my room that morning, the day you and I were supposed to celebrate my divorce. You know how I sleep like the dead. That's how I was sleeping. She crawled into bed with me, put her hand . . ." He slapped his thigh, heaved a deep sigh. "I swear I was dreaming of you and me on the couch. When she rolled on top of me, I woke up and discovered what was real, and it wasn't you. I knocked her off the bed. That's as far as it went." His voice was belligerent.

"So that's how you got semen all over the sheets. It looked like planned birth control."

Clay flushed and his eyes narrowed to slits. "It wasn't planned, but that's what it was. After I pushed her away, she kept crying that all she wanted was another baby. I was scared as hell I'd given her one."

Imagining the scene as Clay described it—far different from the seductive interplay her own mind had created—Cara's body shook with silent laughter. She kicked at the small rocks beneath her boots. "You expect me to believe you didn't seduce or rape her?"

"I didn't seduce or rape her. I'm offended that you even ask that question."

Obviously, he couldn't understand the pain she'd suffered from the imaginary scene that had resonated in her mind after she viewed the evidence. "You didn't undress her near the window where we stood. You didn't caress . . .?" Tears slipped down her cheeks and she turned away.

"Cara, she's a child. I'd kill a man who did that to my daughter. How can you think I'd do it?" He walked over to the edge of the pool. "Besides, I went wild when I discovered what had happened. I was afraid I'd lose my kids. Plus I could see myself set up for criminal rape charges." Distraught, he paced back and forth near the river.

Cara shook her head, not convinced she should believe his story. However, he was not presenting himself as a hero. The story didn't seem created to win her back by showing what a sweet, good guy he was. And she remembered the night she was unable to wake him while he slept with his head on her lap.

"I ordered her to move out," Clay said. "She was all packed, ready to go, when Ramón showed up and moved in with her." He heaved a deep sigh. "By then I had calmed down. The police hadn't shown up, so I decided to let her stay, figuring Ramón could control her. He could also give her the baby she wanted."

Cara's tears turned to silent sobs.

"She's still babysitting the kids for Bette, but she's not allowed in my house." He paused, drained of emotion. "Sounds like a soap opera, doesn't it?"

Cara breathed deeply. "Yes, it does, and I'm too old to believe in fairytales."

"You could at least display a sense of fairness. If a woman had been trapped in a similar situation, you'd say she was sexually assaulted."

Cara smiled as she wiped away her tears. Could she have done what he says María did on the night he slept on her couch? Maybe. Now she had spent a month hating this man, making up all sorts of stories to wreak revenge on him for a sin he says he didn't commit. She tended to believe him but questioned whether there was any way to undo the damage to their relationship.

"I'm trying to sell my horses so I'll have no excuse to come here. After that, I'll stop bothering you, but first I want you to know the truth. I can't go on like this."

Cara wiped her lashes. "Nor can I. We seem to be playing games without rules. I feel like you're waiting for me to fall into a trap. It's scary."

"There is no trap. Although to me, you've acted like a possum that falls out of the tree and lies there pretending he's dead. Then when I'm not looking, you scoot off into the underbrush, grinning like hell, ready for the next hunt. I'm not good at reading your signals."

"Maybe you should hunt something besides opossums."

"Maybe you should quit acting like one. We've been dancing around the sleeping together issue for months. I thought it was resolved when you came to my house. Then, wham, you pull another possum act on me."

Cara sighed. "If what you're telling me about María is true, I owe you an apology."

"I appreciate that, but I'm not sure it will fix things between us." The sun was gone. The moon and stars promised to replace the light on the water that splashed over the rocks, waking the frogs and crickets.

"You're right. I don't think things can get better if you ask me to sleep in the same bed where you sleep with other women. I know it's old-fashioned, but I grew up with parents who were faithful to each other. I know it works."

"That's no problem on my end, Cara. I told you a long time ago that I hadn't slept with a woman since I separated from Bette. Do I get the same promise from you? I'd like to know how you balance what you call my indiscretions against you inviting Ramón to live in your house. You knew it would drive me crazy, but you did it anyway. You want to have things both ways."

"You don't really believe Ramón and I were sleeping together do you? I assumed you were teasing." Cara felt her body flush at the memory of Ramón's hardness that day in the office. He'd begged her to douse the flames, but she had backed away even though her body wanted it. Clay might be right that Ramón's fire didn't differ all that much from María's plan to have a baby.

"To some degree, I was teasing. I didn't want to believe you would sleep with another guy after you'd refused to sleep with me. But I'm aware I have no claim on you, and if you want to sleep with Ramón or anybody else, that's your business."

Cara found herself searching among the tiny river rocks at her feet. She began flipping them into the water, watching the concentric circles spread out and disappear. An owl hooted in a tree top. She turned to Clay. "I told you once that I'm not apt to sleep with anybody. There is a reason."

A deep frown revealed Clay's puzzlement. "I didn't believe you. You never told me why."

Cara let her arm drop, and the other rocks dribbled from her fingers. "Dad didn't tell you anything personal about me, did he?"

"No. You keep alluding to it. Why can't you tell me?"

Cara sat, elbows resting on her knees, looking at the moon and its reflection in the pool. The light cast shadows through the tree branches, splattering moonlight on her shoulders, the side of her face, and reflecting lights from her hair. She knew how to put an end to Clay's pursuit of her and to make his attraction to other women irrelevant. She began unbuttoning her shirt, starting with the top button, down to her waist, then to the three buttons down each cuff.

The wind rustled tree leaves, and a twig, loosened by the squirrels during the day, dropped to the carpet of grass below. Cara glanced at the twig, then stood and pulled her shirt tail out of her pants. She opened the buttonholes beneath her belt and threw the shirt toward the rock, where it hung for a moment before falling to the ground.

She faced Clay, her back to the moonlight. She crossed her arms in front, pulling on the opposite sides of her undershirt, up her rib cage, her arms rising over her head. She flipped the garment toward the rock. She was nude from the waist up. She looked at Clay, hesitating a moment, then turned to let the moon shine on the hills and valleys of her scars—letting them speak for themselves.

Clay stood stunned, heaving air from his chest. He leaned forward, searching in the pale light for an answer to the puzzle of Cara's reticence. He moved toward her, stumbling as he clasped her arms and seated her on the rock. He bent down on one knee. With his finger, he traced the largest scar from her collar bone to where it disappeared beneath the belt of her jeans. He reached out and pulled her body toward his and hugged it to him, then pushing her away, he began kissing her jaw, down her neck, moving to her chest, where her breasts should have been, pressing against the smooth ridges, his tongue following the trail of scars, tasting his tears against the sweetness of her skin. He sought her lips, his mouth wet and salty.

"How did it happen?" he asked, his voice muffled through his lips on the corner of her mouth.

She rubbed her cheek against his face, speaking near his ear. "I was six years old. I went to the stove and reached up to see what Lupe was fixing for supper. I pulled on the handle of the frying pan, and it spilled hot grease all down my front."

"My God." Clay's voice choked. "I'm so sorry. It's a miracle you lived."

"I've wanted to die so many times. In the hospital, I begged the nurses to unhook the machines that kept me alive. In high school, I fantasized about dying and having people weep and wail at my funeral mass. By college, I'd gotten over making up death fantasies and spent my time being tough, making sure no one knew about the scars. Since Dad died, I've reverted to wishing I were dead when bad things happen."

"Don't say that." He tilted her chin and he was smiling. "What made you think I'd care that you have scars? We all have imperfections. We learn to live with them."

Cara examined her chest, still damp from the wetness of his touching. She ran her hand over the scars, looking at them with new awareness. "I've assumed it would make a difference to anyone who saw them—like the difference they've made to me."

"You're a very special person, Cara, and those scars are an important part of your history. Give them credit for making you tough and resilient. You're not like other women I've known. You've taken over this ranch just the way your father said you could, and, believe me, there aren't many men in this world who could have done as well."

"I hadn't thought of it that way." Cara began sobbing. "Maybe you're right. But what about that other person?" she asked between breaths. "The one who might have been. What would she have been like? She was taken away from me. It makes me angry just to think about it."

"Don't you think you've punished yourself enough for what happened to her?" He smiled. "If you're worried about not being sexy, forget it. You're turning me on right now." He ran his finger down the largest scar on her chest, letting it slip beneath her belt. "Sexy isn't all about breasts. You're perfect the way you are." He pulled a handkerchief from his hip pocket and wiped the tears from her face.

Cara looked down at her chest, then lifted his fingers to her lips. "You're not just telling me this to make me feel good? The scars don't repel you?" She stared through the pale moonlight to read his face.

"Do I act like I'm repelled?" He leaned forward and kissed her lips again, this time wet and promising. He let her pull away.

She stood before him, shy, embarrassed. His eyes moved over her body, stopping at her eyes. He didn't flinch at what he saw, and she relaxed.

"The water's cold," she said. "I'll bet I can stay in longer than you can." She pulled off her boots and slipped out of her jeans in one movement. Clay stood captured by the unexpected openness of her actions. She moved past him and grabbed the rope hanging from a large cottonwood tree, then sailed like a bird-of-prey out to the center of the pool. She dropped from the rope, held her nose, and disappeared into the blackness. Clay began unbuttoning his shirt.

Okay, sucker, he said to himself. Hurry up or she'll disappear into the underbrush again.

24

Breakfast in Bed

Cara woke the following morning and sighed, throwing her arm across the pillow beside her. She opened her eyes, wondering how to separate dreams from reality. From the kitchen the smell of coffee taunted her. Real coffee. She heard pans rattling. Real rattles. She rose on one elbow, and amid the rumpled sheets and pillows, she breathed in the strong masculine odor that Clay had left behind. She eased onto his pillow, closed her eyes, and smiled, remembering the wild and unexpected storm he had triggered in her body during the night. He had lifted her from the icy pool, wrapped them both in the woolen blanket she carried behind her saddle, and changed her life forever. She hardly remembered their return to the ranch house but would never forget the hours that followed.

She heard footsteps on the stairs, not Lupe's. It was Sunday.

Clay walked through the door, carrying a breakfast tray and the morning newspaper. "Breakfast in bed."

Cara started to protest.

"Don't ask what you did to deserve it."

She smiled, pulling the covers aside to let him slip in beside her. He wore no shirt to cover the hair on his chest reaching downward to the heavy cord that held his pants around his hips.

"Did you walk to the mailbox looking like that?"

He nodded. "I figured it was too early for traffic. The antelope were only mildly aroused."

Cara stirred a stick of celery in her tall glass of Bloody Mary. She lifted the glass to click against Clay's. "Thank you for last night."

"My pleasure. It was a first for me too, you know."

"You expect me to believe that when you have two children?"

"It's the first time I've been enticed to jump into a pool of ice water by a wild and beautiful river nymph."

"In your dreams."

"Yeah. There, too."

Clay hesitated then positioned the breakfast tray in front of her. They clicked glasses again. "To the beginning of a beautiful relationship."

"Didn't Humphrey Bogart say that?"

"If you're talking about *Casablanca*, that relationship didn't end so happily. Think of a better toast."

"To happy endings," Cara said. They clicked glasses and she picked up the unopened Sunday paper.

"What's the news?" Clay asked, while he continued eating.

"Same old, same old." She threw the paper aside and laid her hand on his thigh. "Did I tell you we moved the migrant school down to the Catholic church?"

"No, but I assumed the wagon you were riding came from somewhere called school." He eyed her hand. "Watch what you're doing. I'm drinking hot coffee."

Cara laughed and rolled back to her side of the bed. "The migrants were so upset when Ramón left. They asked me to teach them. I couldn't devote full time to such a project, so I asked Father Angus to sponsor classes through the church. He took it over. I'm buying the supplies. There was only one hitch. Lucille Martin complained that the foreigners were using the church property without tithing."

"But she wasn't able to scuttle the school?"

"No. There are more good people in the world than bad."

"You've counted them?"

"Yes, as a matter of fact I have. Our neighbors for the most part are wonderful. Even Larry is nice."

"It's a given that you always see the best in people. Even in Ramón. I was surprised when he left the ranch. He has no experience in construction."

Cara stirred cream into her coffee, pausing too long to answer. "Pablo asked him to marry María so that she and Rosita could stay in the States. It happened just when you threatened to throw her out of the guesthouse. This isn't information you should spread around, but Ramón is an undercover agent for the INS. He came to the ranch because Immigration wanted to know if the sheriff's suspicions about my having a stash house were correct. Now that he knows that isn't true, he's leaving. Maybe going to work for Senator Rodriguez."

Clay frowned and raised an eyebrow. "Is he taking María with him?"

"I don't think the marriage has taken place. But I don't keep up with his life anymore."

"I'm pleased to hear that." He pushed the bangs from her forehead. "I've thought his advantage over me was unfair. Sexy guy living in the house with you. Drove me crazy."

He laid his hand on her stomach, massaging muscles that tightened at his touch. She remembered Clay's story about María's touching. Now she understood how it was possible and pushed her body close to his. This was a world she'd never dreamed of. Was it what marriage was all about? Was it what her father and mother shared, almost oblivious to the rest of the world? It must have been, and if so, it was true—neither the age difference nor her scars mattered.

25

The Big Question

Following hours of consultation with her attorney the next day, Cara drove past Clay's house on El Paso Street. She felt tempted to stop and ask María whether Pablo had called, but the thought of knocking on María's door and perhaps meeting Ramón deterred her. She was not ready to face him. She felt like a different person than the one he'd held in his arms in the office. The passion she'd felt that day had since been concentrated and fulfilled in the arms of another man. She was no longer confused about whom she loved, and Ramón's charge that she was afraid to love a Hispanic did not bother her. It was her inability to prove that Ramón had nothing to do with the cattle rustling that made her leery of him. She drove past, determined to make a phone call instead.

At the ranch, Cara slowed as she came to the driveway leading from County Road 84. Cattle were milling around in the driveway, spreading out to the barns and stables, bawling in confusion, searching for their calves. What in heck was going on? Tony and half a dozen vaqueros were rounding up the cattle, pushing them toward the pasture behind the barns. The Kelpies were having a ball, snagging the strays, nipping their heels, and ordering the cows to move.

Tony saw the Dodge and spurred his horse toward Cara. He slid off his horse, a grin covering his face.

"The sheriff found most of the cows," he said. "They'd been dumped on the far reaches of the Maxwell land grant, where they thought no one would find them. The sheriff loaded them up and brought them back.

Just dumped them. We're having a heck of a time getting them started toward the pastures. Need a bell cow . . . or a lead bull." He couldn't stop smiling and Cara found herself laughing at the melee.

"How many?" she asked.

"Fifty-two. The calves were branded, but we can mend that."

"How did the sheriff find them?" Cara asked.

"The rustlers talked. The cows were be taken to a Texas ranch this fall and the calves to a sale barn. We're just lucky they found them before they got out of state."

"Did you find out who told them the fence was unprotected?"

Tony pulled off his hat and wiped his sleeve across his brow. "One of the men said it was Pablo. But I don't trust them. Ramón thinks Pablo wouldn't do that."

One of the cows came running toward the road. "Wup," Tony said and sped off to bring the stray back toward the barns.

Cara sat in the idling truck, not believing her good luck. Bless the sheriff's heart. She'd invite him out to fish at the lake for sure. Had her suspicions about Pablo been on target? These reports seemed to confirm them.

She pulled into the driveway and parked, then saddled Buck to join the cattle drive. Her depression, caused by working on the lawsuit, lifted. Life had taken one step forward, two steps back since she'd been in charge of the ranch. Today, she took two steps forward.

By the time she joined the roundup, the cattle were well on their way to the back pastures. They knew where they were going and ran, bawling to greet the herd they'd left behind. The vaqueros tried to slow their progress, to avoid running off more weight than was necessary, but it was a hopeless effort. The cattle were glad to be home.

Tony rode ahead to lower gates to the alfalfa field already stripped of its last cutting of the year. The grass was dry, digestible, and would not cause bloating and gas. He waved the herd into the field, their home until he and Cara determined which ones to sell. The drive completed, Cara rode back to the barns with Tony.

"I'll need a court order allowing me to sell the cattle."

"How come?"

"Howard's lawsuit requires me to get permission before I get rid of any of the ranch assets."

"How long will that take? Prices could go down tomorrow."

"My lawyer has applied for a general order that gives me leeway. I'll have it by next week."

Tony nodded. "We may want to get rid of a few of these cows we just got back and keep an equal number of those we planned to sell."

Cara nodded. They rode in silence until the barns came in view. "Have you heard from Ramón?"

Tony shook his head.

"Are you sure he isn't in cahoots with Pablo?"

"Sheriff didn't mention either one of them." He turned away, unwilling to discuss it further.

It was dark, with no moonlight, when Cara returned to the stables. Buck was sweaty, and when she pulled off the saddle and blanket he trotted away to roll in the dirt of the corral floor. Happy, he shook off the dirt and walked back to Cara to enjoy the water brush that cleaned and massaged his body.

Grooming finished, Cara headed for the house, where she saw Clay's truck pulling into the driveway.

"Hey," she called.

"Hey, yourself. What are you doing working so late?"

"You won't believe it. We got the stolen cattle back."

"No kidding? How did that happen?"

They sat on the steps where Cara banged the dust from her hat and explained the good news. When she rolled her shoulder to straighten the kinks in her muscles, Clay moved a step behind her and maneuvered Cara between his knees.

"You need a massage," he said, pressing his thumbs between her shoulders, working the muscles from her ribs to her neck.

Cara moaned her appreciation. "What I need is a shower. I'm sticky with sweat and dust."

"Just so happens a shower comes with the massage. Follow me." He pulled Cara to her feet and led her to the shower in the garage.

Then it was morning, and the sun was shining in the east window of her bedroom. They had spent most of the night in the apartment, coming back to the house to find food and drink around midnight and slipping up to Cara's bedroom to fall into an exhausted sleep.

Clay pushed strands of hair away from her eyes. "Cara, I hope you don't think I'm rushing things, but I wonder how you feel about getting married? The kids are asking questions about why I'm spending my nights out here. They think they should get to come too. I don't like to lie to them, but my excuses are getting weak."

Cara moaned. It wasn't as if she were surprised. They were in love and marriage was the natural next step. But the speed with which this affair was flying left her speechless. Lots of relationships went on for years before the decision to marry was made—if ever. But he was right. The children made a difference.

"I'm tempted to say yes, but it's so sudden; it scares me. There are so many things to consider." His proposal of marriage was unexpected, and Cara needed time to think of the consequences. She loved the changes in her relationship with Clay and was afraid to alter what she thought was perfect.

"If we stop to consider everything that might get in the way of marriage, we'll never make it. I say let's get married first, and let the considerations take care of themselves." He smothered her in kisses, covering her mouth so she couldn't object.

He pulled away. "Is it a deal?"

Cara's laugh was deep and happy. "You sound like a car salesman. I suppose if we don't close the deal today, the price will go up."

"Sounds about right. But I'm not selling cars. Just me—and my kids, of course." He frowned. "You don't mind if I throw in the kids as a bonus, do you?"

"No, I insist."

"Good. We're a package deal."

"Are you sure you know what you're doing, Clay?" Cara felt her resistance lowering and needed to know that Clay had thought this matter through.

"I just told you. I love you. I wouldn't ask you to marry me if I didn't love you. It's important that you love me too, though."

"I do love you. And just as important, you've taught me how to love myself." It was the first time she had put her feelings about that night at the river into words, and it surprised even her. It was true. Clay had proved to her that her body was loveable, not grotesque. The wild responses he triggered with his lovemaking were things of beauty. They had freed her soul.

"It makes me sad that we didn't meet a long time ago. I'd like to have known you when you were in high school and college," he said.

Cara shook her head. "No way. You were in grade school when I graduated."

"My mom always worried that I was an early bloomer. She's lucky I didn't meet you at that time."

"Seriously, Clay, are you sure the age difference doesn't matter?" It was a question she'd raised the first time he'd approached her, that day by the lake, before the bear attack. She still feared the answer.

"You know what? The age difference may be what makes this work. There's no way you're going to let a snotty-nosed kid boss you around, so my age shouldn't create a problem for you. I'm tired of taking care of helpless females, so you fit my needs. We couldn't find a better pairing."

"What if I'm too old to adjust to marriage?" Cara imagined herself in a rocking chair, knitting sweaters while Clay rode off on Gus, followed by a beautiful young woman on a white steed. She hated the picture and forced it out of her mind. She never sat in a rocking chair. She didn't knit. She couldn't imagine the day would come when she couldn't ride. She planned never to grow old.

"I don't know that adjusting is necessary. Why can't we go on the way we are? However, you'll have to get used to 'Mrs. Thompson.' How does that sound to you?"

Cara paused. "I don't know. I've been Cara Morgan for thirty-six years."

"Well, you can stay Morgan if you want to. These days women do. That's not a deal breaker."

She laughed and hit him playfully on the chin with her fist. "You know, it's a good thing you're such a good salesman. No other man has gotten this far with me."

"A good salesman knows to close the deal while it's hot. Can we shake on it?"

"I would prefer a kiss." Cara was tired of thinking of reasons to say no. Getting married would make her life with Clay better than it was now. They kissed, long and tenderly. The contract was sealed.

Clay left for work, leaving Cara dizzy. She'd gone from an exhausting legal meeting yesterday to a bedtime session with Clay, where she feared she was guilty of influencing him to propose marriage to her, to a sudden engagement. She jumped out of bed, unable to contain her joy. She was no longer jogging in place. This day she'd taken several steps forward. She stayed in her room, moving from one familiar object to another, unable to concentrate. What seemed so natural and positive in Clay's presence now frightened her beyond belief. She couldn't imagine herself married.

She heard Lupe talking to Clay in the yard as he went to his truck. The screen door slammed, and she came inside, making noises in the kitchen. Was she upset that Clay had spent the night? What had he told her?

Cara recalled her conversation with Tony. Love is when two people want to take care of each other. She knew she wanted to care for Clay. She couldn't imagine how to let him take care of her.

She picked up the telephone and dialed Emily's home in Taos. "Emily?"

"Yes. Where are you?"

"At home. What are you doing?"

"Getting ready for work. Oh, honey. I've worried so much about you. How is the lawsuit going?"

"It's fine. I have a good lawyer. She says we won't have to have a jury trial."

"Why not?"

Cara explained the process of out-of-court arbitration.

"Oh." Emily seemed relieved. "Well, how are you doing otherwise?" she asked.

Cara had trouble finding words to tell Emily her good news.

"What's wrong?" Emily asked.

"Nothing. Everything's great. That's what I called to tell you."

"Well, tell me."

"I'm getting married." The only sound was Emily's scream. "Did you just say you're getting married?"

"Yes."

"I thought I was hallucinating."

"No. It's Clay. The man who's been living in the servants' quarters. You saw him at Dad's mass."

"Oh, sure. The cute one. He's, uh, he's the young one?"

"He's very young."

"Well, good for you. He won't wear out before you do!"

"Emily, you're impossible. Do you think I'm crazy?"

"I hope so—crazy in love."

"I am in love."

"When is this big event taking place?"

"No big event is planned. We'll just go before a judge."

"Oh, this man has children, doesn't he? They'll want to share the excitement. I want to be a part of it."

"You do?"

"Sure. You can't just show up on his pillow some morning like a baby from the cabbage patch. The kids won't understand."

"Yeah. He says they are already confused about his trips out here without them. I hadn't thought of that. We just decided to get married this morning, so there are a lot of things we haven't discussed."

"Like—are you moving to town?"

Cara felt as if she had been hit with a body punch. "I don't think so," she said. "He can drive to work from here. Doesn't that make sense?" Her voice was tense.

"It does to me. I'm sure he won't mind. But it's one of those decisions you'll have to talk about."

"Of course. Of course." Cara found her breath coming in short gasps. "Emily," she said, "maybe I shouldn't tell anyone else I'm getting married. What if it all falls apart?"

"Oh, I'm so sorry. I didn't mean to throw monkey wrenches into your happiness. Of course it will work out. I'm delighted for you."

An hour later, Cara hung up the phone, feeling grounded and mature. Emily had that effect on her. They had never acted like girlfriends, telling each other secrets or double-dating. Emily was older and had taken on a mature role when their mother died. Cara was twelve. Conversations they had were reports from Emily on what was going on in the teenage world. Cara learned what she had to do to survive those years with her scars. Today she'd listened while Emily chatted about her own failed marriage, telling Cara what not to do to screw up this wonderful opportunity to have a family. Cara believed she could do a better job than Emily had. Her fears went away, and she bounced down the stairs to tell Lupe her good news.

26

An Arrest

Clay pulled into the driveway at 6:00 p.m. as Tony and Cara stepped off the porch steps, headed for the barns. Cara hung back, not understanding why she felt shy in the presence of these men who meant so much to her, in different ways.

Tony stopped, with his hands on his hips, and smiled man-to-man at Clay. "I hear you're gonna be the new boss."

Clay looked at Cara, puzzled. She laughed and ran her hand beneath his arm. "Don't worry. These damned Mexican men believe that a woman's property becomes her husband's when they marry, and the woman becomes his slave."

Clay dropped her hand, crossed his arms, and leaned against the truck. "Hey, I like that. So, do I need it in writing?" he asked Tony.

Tony slapped his hat against his knee, pleased with Clay's reaction to his joke.

Cara tried to pretend she was offended.

Tony stopped smiling as he pointed to her. "I've known this little lady since she was in diapers. She was the youngest in the family, but I swear she's been the boss from the day she was born."

Cara ducked her head, peeking up to see Clay's reaction. He was smiling.

Tony started toward the barns, talking over his shoulder to Clay. "You're sure gonna have your hands full, partner. Good luck." Cara noticed he was limping more than before. He refused to go to the doctor. She'd have to talk to Lupe.

The following week was a blur for Cara. Trace sent an order allowing the ranch to sell enough cattle to pay the inheritance taxes and refinance the bank notes. Cara confirmed with Tony that the trucks would be at the ranch Tuesday morning to take the cattle to the sale barn. Ramón called from town to discuss details of the Mexican Independence Day fiesta. And Emily insisted on coming for the weekend to supervise plans for the wedding.

By the time Emily arrived, Cara was exhausted. She hugged her sister with a vehemence that left them gasping for breath. They unloaded the car, packed with gifts and a few changes of clothes for the weekend.

"Clay and I have decided to do a very small wedding." Cara said. "We think it's too soon after Dad's death to have a big celebration. And besides, that's not our style."

"Okay. When?"

"I left a message with my attorney, but she hasn't called back. One of the issues, of course, is that my marriage will cut off your and Howard's chance of inheriting in case I die. So it might impact the outcome of an arbitration. The judge might see that as an end run around the lawsuit."

"Well, it just gives us more time to plan."

"I'll have time to shop. Nothing I own would be appropriate for a wedding."

"How about Mother's wedding dress? You'd fit into that, and it's still on a shelf somewhere."

"What a great idea. I'll look for it."

"Of course you have to have a trousseau, and shopping for that will be fun. Let me help. We'll go to Albuquerque."

When Ramón reached the carriage house after work, the door was unlocked and slightly ajar. There was no sign of María. He read her note saying the police were taking her to jail. A copy of the subpoena allowing them to search the house lay beside it. In a rage, Ramón threw the documents to the floor. What were they looking for? He hurried to his bedroom in the attic and found papers scattered everywhere. The box holding the finished pages of his report lay up-ended and on the table.

A small suitcase remained on the floor near the window, the top open, leaning against the wall. Ramón always left it open on purpose, with underwear and socks dumped inside, to give it the appearance of serving as a drawer. Those socks and underwear were thrown to the floor, but the case had remained upright. Ramón picked it up and smiled. They had not found the secret compartment in the bottom, holding his small laptop and cell phone.

He checked the time. Six o'clock. It was too late to find an attorney for María. He'd have to call Cara. He regretted dumping the news on her but knew of no alternative.

"This is Ramón. María's in trouble," he said. There was a long pause. "She's in jail. Can you give me the name of a lawyer?"

"When did this happen?"

"I don't know. She was gone when I got home from work. She left a note."

"And Rosita?"

"She's still in foster care."

"That's probably good. She won't have to go through this trauma. You should call Trace Leader. Let me get her number. Tell her you got her name from me."

For the next hour, Ramón made calls on the cell phone. Leader impressed him with her knowledge of criminal and immigration statutes. She agreed to visit the jail and to represent María at her arraignment on Tuesday.

He called Pablo in Mexico to let him know of María's arrest and to urge him to return and care for her.

"You promised you'd marry her. What happened?"

"What happened is I got shot during the rustling, and it's taken a long time to get well. We've had no chance to get married. When are you coming back?"

"Tell María I'll be back in a couple of days. If you can get her out of jail, I'll take her down to Texas and find a safe place for her there."

At the ranch, Cara found a voice message from her attorney. Arbitration of Howard's law suit was scheduled for October 15. The parties had agreed to place all the evidence before a judge in a conference room rather than in court. That judge, instead of a jury, would decide whether the will was valid. Trace felt their chances were good that the judge would dismiss the lawsuit, and if not, that he would find for Cara on all counts.

She also mentioned that she had received a call from Cara's friend, Ramón, concerning María. She would take care of that matter.

Cara relaxed. Two more steps forward.

27

The Mexican Fiesta

Cara was not sure how she survived a week of following Emily around while planning the wedding and shopping in Albuquerque. It was impossible to remain her usually sober self in the presence of the excitement the wedding was creating.

Emily used her practiced eye to suggest the colors of a trousseau, plus dresses for the bridesmaid and flower girl. They had already solved the choice of a wedding dress by delving into Consuelo's closet and finding that the loose-fitting style popular in their mother's day slipped perfectly over Cara's slim body. After hours in the shoe and lingerie departments, the women returned to the ranch, where Clay and Cara agreed with Emily that a wedding under the gazebo in Clay's backyard would be perfect—unless it rained, in which case, they would go indoors before the fireplace. Afterward, guests would nibble at a catered buffet, eat cake, and drink champagne. Clay and Cara would return to the ranch alone. Then they would fly to Barcelona for two weeks of touring Spain and France by car.

"This is all a fairytale, right?" Cara asked Emily, as they rested.

"Yes, and you are Cinderella. Keep those glass slippers wrapped in lots of tissue paper, baby, under lock and key. We don't have time for disasters."

Cara laughed. "Emily, please don't expect me to do this for you the next time you get hitched."

"Are you kidding? You're getting special treatment because this is your first—and last."

Cara shivered. Of course it was her last.

Only one thing stood between her and total happiness. The arbitration of Howard's lawsuit loomed in the distance. Cara felt a certain amount of comfort in knowing that this was the last step in securing her ownership of the ranch. Trace seemed sure she would win the lawsuit. She was delighted Clay had asked to attend the hearings with her. He seemed to understand she did not want to face Howard alone. She pondered the weird changes that the planned marriage had made. She was no longer a separate entity. She marveled that Clay seemed to require her presence, calling her during the day to satisfy his need to make contact. They had become one.

The Independence Day celebration began early on the 16th, with heavy traffic bringing Hispanics from town and nearby ranches to join the Los Lobos residents in the annual party. Cars parked on the highway, in the driveway, and near the barns, where a hike began to the lake. Tony drove the school bus, filled with older celebrants and children, over the jeep trail to the migrant camp. Straw padded the trailer bed. Bales of hay formed seats for las madres and abuelitas, who clung to the smallest children, worried they would fall off the trailer as they bumped over the rocky road. Older children jumped off and ran along the path, keeping up with the slow-moving vehicle. Fathers followed, herding the older children.

Everyone wore traditional Mexican dress, the women carrying umbrellas to ward off the burning sun, men and children sporting broad-brimmed hats. Blouses, skirts, and shirts were white with bright red, white, and green embroidery decorating the collars, cuffs, and hems.

Mexican band members insisted on driving their bus up the road. It arrived to cheers from the crowd, who shared the excitement of carrying the instruments into the dining hall, which had been emptied of tables and chairs, leaving the floor cleared for dancing. The band set up at one end. Children crowded around them, were shooed away, and were soon hopping and whirling on the floor to the noise of the instruments as the players warmed up and tuned the strings.

Other children joined the young men and women playing softball in the meadow. The older padres yelled in triumph when the horseshoes they threw clanged like loud bells against the stakes.

Huge pots of beans and chili con carne, roasting poblanos, and slabs of pork and chicken for tacos cooked on the grills, sending waves of spicy odors over the campground. A pot of tortilla soup bubbled over coals in a fire pit. Large boxes of sopapillas, cakes, and jalapeño cornbread, cooked the day before, sat ready to accompany the soup.

Children vied for a chance to rotate the spits, heavy with the cleanly butchered beef donated from the Los Lobos herd. Their fathers took the handles from the children after a turn or two convinced them it was work, not play. Men stood guard beside pits where they had buried goat meat over hot coals the night before. Others stored boxes of fireworks in one of the cabins, latched the windows shut, and locked the door against the children, who could hardly wait for the display promised after dark.

At the ranch house, Lupe found herself in charge of Jason and Ashley. The children played in the backyard, waving to the parade of visitors headed for the celebration site near the lake, while Lupe ironed the costumes Cara had ordered from Mexico. There were new clothes for Lupe and Tony also, and she could hardly wait to see Tony in the gayly embroidered shirt and a Mexican sombrero. She pressed the last pleat, unplugged the iron, and gathered Tony's and her own outfits to take home.

By four o'clock, Clay lifted the children to seats on the hay trailer, one on each side of Lupe. Cara sat sidesaddle on Buck, her voluminous skirts spreading from flank to shoulder. Clay had insisted that she use her mother's sidesaddle to complete the look of a real Mexican princesa. She knew that people would ooh and aah when they saw her, bringing a blush to her cheeks just thinking about the attention she was not used to. She had agreed to ride sidesaddle to complement Clay, riding Gus, who pranced under the weight of Dave's silver-laden saddle. There would be gossip about Clay taking over her new position as head of the family.

Dinner was being served when they arrived at the campground. Clay lifted her from the saddle. "Are you okay?"

She laughed. "There's a real art to riding sidesaddle. I kept wanting to use my spurs."

Tony arrived and swept them away through the crowd toward the tables made with planks on sawhorses, weighted with food. Cara worried that Jason and Ashley would get lost as they ran to join a crowd of children playing on the hillside. For a moment she relived the bear attack on Rosita, then laughed at herself as she watched Jason pull out his red handkerchief and instruct one of the boys to charge like a bull. The boy came straight for Jason, and the bull won. The boy jumped up, whipping out a pretend knife to cut off Jason's ear, all of them confused about whose ear was at stake. As the boys piled on top of Jason, Cara turned from the scene, shaking her head. Maybe fighting bulls wasn't Jason's strong point, but he would learn.

Clay wandered off with Tony to join many of the men gathered in a separate area of the campground to talk and to play horseshoes. Most of the women were serving food or caring for children. Those carrying infants gathered around a table, dipping their fingers into plates piled high with food and wiping their fingers into the wide baby mouths, open like chicks in a bird nest.

As she listened to the chatter, Cara saw Ramón standing at the dessert table, where a beautiful, young Hispanic girl filled his plate. She wondered if María was still in jail. Ramón looked handsome dressed in black, with tall Mexican boots and a black hat. She searched the crowd and found Clay standing with the men playing horseshoes. The stakes were driven into the soil far beyond the tables to avoid the flurry of dust that puffed after each throw. Cara glanced back at the babies. The one across the table from her had finished nursing, and now the mother laid him across her shoulder, patting his back. A loud rumble of air belched from his tummy. The mother put him back to her soft breast, but he pushed it away, satiated. He began fussing and the mother rocked him, eager to return her attention to her chattering friends.

"Let me hold him." Cara was surprised at her sudden needs. She leaned over and gathered a blanket around the infant and carried him several steps from the table, searching for a separate world with just the two of them, the mothers' chatter like soft music in the background. She breathed into the baby's thick hair as she kissed him. The odors were new to her: oil rubbed into the scalp, sweet and heavy; baby powder, she recognized, but not the mother's milk crusted on his lips, smelling of the burp he smacked away. No baby of mine will smell of mother's milk. A sharp pain thrust through her chest, and she blinked tears away.

The child's eyes opened wide and his small fingers dug into her cheek. Cara laughed at his investigation of the strange face above him.

She rubbed her nose against his. He cooed and grabbed at her hair as she sat down at the table.

"Señorita," Ramón said. "You'll make a lovely mother."

Cara raised her head, shaken from a dream world of motherhood. She had not talked to Ramón since María's arrest. He set a plate filled with sopapillas and honey on the table and invited the women to share.

"How nice," she said, looking at the dessert. "But I have my arms full of baby. His mother would not appreciate my getting honey all over his new clothing."

The mother hurried over to take the fussy child, while the other young women hid smiles behind their hands as they pretended not to notice Ramón.

"Have a seat," Cara said and reached for a corner of the pastry. "How are María and Rosita doing?"

The smile left Ramón's face. "Not well. María left town after Ms. Leader got her out of jail. She's in Texas with Pablo. She may be back in Juárez before long."

"But you said she could die there—I thought if you married her she'd have a better chance of staying here."

Ramón looked away.

"You did get married?"

"No. Things got too complicated. The D.A. threatened to charge María with child abuse because of the bear incident. She was so frightened she took off with Pablo as soon as she got out of jail. Now, of course, there's a warrant for her arrest."

"What happened to Rosita?"

"She's still with the foster family. She doesn't have full use of her arm, and the scars . . . María wouldn't be able to pay for those operations."

"I told her I would pay for them." A chill shivered through Cara's body. It would be devastating for Rosita to go through life with those scars. Cara knew that first hand.

"There isn't much you could do to keep María out of jail or to keep her from being deported. She left Rosita here so she wouldn't be sent back with her."

"Did anyone contact Trace or Frank Wallace about the D.A.'s charges? Maybe they could have reasoned with him."

"Yes. I talked to both of them, but their hands are tied. The courts are being blamed for being too easy on the migrants. There's lots of pressure put on them from taxpayers who want all foreigners sent back home. María's is a high-profile case because of the bear incident, so it won't be passed over just because a lawyer knows the judge."

Cara sighed. "And where does your work with INS stand?"

"I'm finishing my last report to them. I came to the ranch to find out whether the Mafia was setting up a stash house in this area. I did determine that Rafael was the primary *coyote* funneling migrants through New Mexico to stash houses in other states. That's a major breakthrough and should slow the crossings at El Paso."

"So your work here is finished?"

"Yes. I'm resigning from the INS and have decided not to go back to teaching. Senator Rodríguez offered to hire me in his Santa Fe office. He's pushing for new legislation regarding immigration, which will be a win-or-lose proposition in the next election. He thinks I can help with those issues."

"That's good. You wanted to get into politics, didn't you?"

"Yes."

"It seems to me if you are so close to the senator, you could pull strings to keep María here."

"I have tried. But like most congressmen, he can't afford to take a stand. Votes are more important than migrants."

"I'm surprised you'd compromise your principles to work for a man who advocates closing the borders."

"I'm looking at it as a good place to influence changes."

"Now who is the dreamer?"

"I'm guilty."

"Well, I wish you luck. It's good to see you." She pointed toward a group of women. "I must speak to Luisa." As she stood to leave, Lucille Martin arrived and seated herself beside Ramón.

"Cara, how are you? And Ramón? I haven't seen either of you since Dave's funeral."

Ramón nodded. "I'm living in Santa Fe now."

"Why did you leave the ranch? Tony is so proud of you." Her eyes scanned his features. "I can understand why." Without waiting for an answer, she looked at Cara. "Tony's getting quite old, isn't he? Arthritis is a terrible disease."

Cara stood dumbfounded. She had never cared for Lucille Martin but had wasted no energy naming a reason for her dislike, only remembering that Lucille was one of the women who had shunned her mother. More recently, she had struggled to overcome her prejudice against the woman who, for whatever reason, seemed to have undue interest in the unguarded fences on Los Lobos Ranch. She felt sure Lucille had let Pablo know that stealing their cattle would be an easy task and that she had expected him to pass on the information—but there was no proof.

Lucille's silky voice continued. "It's too bad you may have to sell the ranch, my dear. Do you have plans to move to town, now that your father's gone?" She smiled at Ramón, as if there were a connection in her mind.

A rush of hot acid rose in Cara's throat. The honeyed sopapillas were creating havoc in her stomach. "The ranch is not for sale," she said. "Why would I move to town?"

"Oh, well, the Los Lobos is quite a big ranch for a woman to run by herself. Perhaps you have plans to marry?"

Cara was too angry to respond.

"Well, if you change your mind, let us know before you look for a public offer. Larry Jr. plans to marry next spring, and he's looking to expand our holdings." She rose and patted Ramón on the shoulder. "Neighborhood gossip had it that Cara would follow her father's example and marry a Hispanic. We all assumed you were in the running when you moved into her home." She glided over to an adjoining table, where her shrill laughter sent chills in their direction.

Cara felt nauseated. She looked to Ramón for strength, but the anger sparking from his eyes made her forget her own problems. "That woman has mental problems. Don't let her get to you," she said.

"Don't worry about me. You're the one who should watch her closely." He paused as if reluctant to go on. "I saw no profit in revealing this information because it can cause dissention in the neighborhood, but you deserve to know. The INS believes Lucille Martin and her son are the informants who revealed to the smugglers that your fences were unprotected. We just can't prove it was deliberate. Pablo was in the van with Rafael when they dropped a load of migrants at the Martin ranch. Mrs. Martin came out to greet them and remarked that she'd heard the bear scare had caused vaqueros to leave the Los Lobos Ranch, leaving no one to ride their fences for the next few days. Rafael asked if he should take this load of migrants to your ranch, and she said no. She was sure you'd manage with a reduced crew. Pablo said Rafael laughed, thanked her, and said, "A phone call is in order."

"So it wasn't Pablo who revealed that our fences were vulnerable?"

"No. We couldn't believe one of your neighbors would deliberately think up such a scheme. At first we saw no motivation for such an action, but it's now obvious her son hoped to acquire the ranch when your father died. Like a good mother, she hoped your bad luck would force you to sell."

Cara was stunned. She stared at the woman holding court at the next table. How could she look so sweet and yet exude so much evil? Did motherhood do that to a woman? She hated to think so. But Cara could not imagine what she had done to initiate such venom in a neighbor. She flushed at the thought that having Ramón in her home during his recuperation was the subject of neighborhood gossip. What would the Martins have done under the same circumstances? Sent him up the rocky road to perhaps die in the camp?

She turned to Ramón. "Are you saying the INS has determined that the Martins were in cahoots with Rafael in the rustling on my ranch?"

"The report isn't official yet, but I expect they'll determine that. It's unlikely the Martins will be named because there's no solid evidence. Rafael, on the other hand, is in deeper than just acting as a *coyote*. He's directing gang activities."

"Has Pablo been cleared?"

"I'm not sure. He definitely worked as an assistant to Rafael in the load that María and I were on. The government may decide to discipline him—send him back to Mexico."

"Where does that leave María and her child?"

"As I said, she's likely to be deported. Rosita will be safe until she finishes her rehabilitation. Maybe she'll be adopted here."

"And your marriage?"

"It's too late for that."

"What a mess."

Clay waved from where he was playing horseshoes. "I have to go," she said. "Let me know what happens to María. I'll keep in touch with Rosita."

"Save a dance for me, Cara."

She pretended not to hear.

The sun dipped to the horizon, sitting there like a large burnt-orange ball. The band was loud now, accompanied by voices singing Mexican love songs. Cara moved to watch the children playing across the meadow near the forest, where the bears had hung on the low branches of a tree. She shivered and searched for Clay. He was washing his hands under a faucet, wiping them on a paper towel, laughing at something one of the partygoers said.

As she started toward him, she bumped into Sheriff Placer and stopped. "Why, Sheriff, I'm surprised to see you here. Was trouble reported?"

"Oh, no. Just checking out the crowd. This being the end of your season, it's my duty to check up on where the wetbacks are goin'."

Cara felt her heart sink. What a dirty deal if the sheriff stood aside and watched them work all summer—to the county's advantage—and then arrested them when they were ready to leave for new jobs. It was doubly dirty to do it on the happiest day of their year.

Cara took his arm. "Have you eaten, Sheriff?" She motioned for the deputies to follow them. The women from the Guadalupe Church began appearing behind the tables, taking the place of undocumented migrants who'd slipped away. The women piled plates high with beef, pork, and roasted goat meat, along with mounds of beans and chili sauce. A strange tranquility spread over the camp. Cara caught Clay's attention as he watched from the edge of the crowd.

She led the sheriff and deputies to a table. The Hispanics who had lived there for years crowded around and cut off the vision of the sheriff and his men from the rest of the camp. The band began playing, louder than they had played all night.

"That's a hot band you got there," the sheriff shouted.

"They came out from town."

"I thought I'd heard them suckers before."

"You'll have to stay for the fireworks." Cara hoped to lead the sheriff and his men away from the center of the camp to the edge of the lake. That would give the undocumented migrants time to leave if they wanted to. She knew how quickly they could disappear and where they might go.

Clay walked up to the table, all smiles. He shook hands with the sheriff and deputies.

"You won't find any better food than this in the county, will you?" Clay asked the sheriff.

"Nope. Too bad we're on duty. That barrel of beer sure looks good."

"Oh, I thought this was a social call, Matt. Who you looking for?"

"Is Ramón here?" the sheriff asked while he chewed.

There was shuffling at the edge of the crowd and Ramón appeared. He stopped next to Clay and put one boot on the bench across from the sheriff. He leaned over and propped his elbow on the raised knee and nodded to the sheriff. "Did I hear my name?"

"Yes, sir," the sheriff said. "That's you, all right." A low snicker echoed through the ranks.

"What can I do for you?"

The sheriff sopped up the juices on his plate with tortillas and stuffed his mouth. He chewed while he glared at Ramón. His mouth emptied, he spoke, looking over the crowd.

"I hear you been keeping a journal with information about the migrants."

"That's right."

"I'm here to confiscate that information. Just need to make sure there ain't any bad-mouthing about the way we handle migrants in this county."

"Sorry, Sheriff. You're too late. The police raided my room in town and took it." Eyes shifted from Ramón to the disgruntled sheriff, who concentrated on his plate.

"Guess I can get it from them, then." Laying his fork down, he said, "Well, I got one more request." He handed Ramón an arrest warrant. "I'm looking for this young lady." María's name was on the warrant.

"The police beat you to that one, too, Sheriff. She was jailed last week."

The sheriff reached for the cake a woman was pushing in his direction. "I know that, but she's not there anymore."

"You're right. She was released and she's on her way back to Mexico," Ramón said.

The sheriff rubbed his tongue over this front teeth. "I told the judge that bail bond was too low. Makes you think the government wants 'em to pay their own way home." He chuckled.

The crowd waited in stony silence as the sheriff stood. "Let's go see them fireworks." The crowd followed him to the lake, cutting off his view of the escape trail.

Cara reached for Clay's hand and led him to the dessert table. "I talked to Ramón, and he said Pablo took María to Texas and probably on to Juárez."

"When did you talk to Ramón?" Clay asked, as he concentrated on selecting a dessert.

"While you were playing horseshoes. He said he was going to work for Senator Rodríguez after he leaves here."

"No kidding. Well, he should do well. I'd like to see his report."

Cara smiled deep inside. She lifted a fork of pecan pie to his lips and he took it, in lieu of a kiss. She loved this man more than she could have dreamed possible and so wished they were already married.

"We'd better go find the kids," Clay said and led her toward the meadow, where they were playing ball. The four of them, holding hands, found a place to sit on the side of the hill to watch the fireworks.

Afterward, they doubled up on the horses, Ashley riding with her father, falling asleep against his chest, and Jason, embarrassed at riding behind the princesa's side saddle, not knowing where to put his hands. At home, the fiesta over, they fell into bed exhausted.

28

Arbitration

On October 14, arbitration of the will dispute was held in a conference room in the district courthouse, where a roaming judge from northern New Mexico explained that he had reviewed the evidence presented. He would hear witnesses, listen to the attorneys' arguments, and make a decision whether David Morgan had been mentally capable of independently forming the intent to give the ranch, the livestock, and his personal property to his daughter, Cara Rose Morgan, or whether Cara had used undue influence to convince him to leave Howard and Emily out of his will.

Howard breezed into the conference room, ignoring Cara, who sat at a table beside Trace. He walked past Clay without acknowledging him. Wendy moved to the chair behind Howard and twisted her hands in her lap. Emily was a witness and, therefore, not allowed to hear the other testimony.

Throughout the hearing, Howard sat immobile, neither smiling nor frowning. Has he lost all feeling for family? Cara wondered. When did it happen, and why?

The arbitration ended two days later after numerous friends, cohorts, political allies, and his doctor testified that Dave Morgan at the time of his death was the same spirited, mentally alert, and active man he had been all his life. They testified to being shocked at his death and even more so that charges of mental incapacity were being made about a man whose opinion they respected and relied upon to the very end. In contrast, the petitioners based their charges on testimony from witnesses who pointed out that Cara had failed to pursue an outside career after she graduated from college, suggesting that she had returned to the ranch with the undisguised purpose of taking over the ownership. They pointed out that she ran the office without consulting her father on the financial aspects such as banking, payroll, purchasing cattle, and paying taxes. These were duties he had enjoyed handling until she pushed him out, telling him he made too many mistakes. No longer needed, they pointed out that he declined in health and mental capacity. They stated that they were shocked at how quickly his mental capacity declined.

At the close of testimony, the parties were told they would receive a written decision within the week. Trace squeezed Cara's hand beneath the table; it had gone well.

In the hallway, Emily left Cara's side and hurried toward Howard as he walked between his attorneys toward the door.

"Howard!"

He paused and looked in her direction.

Emily held out her arms. "Howard, can't we remain friends? No matter what the decision is, we love you," she said. "You're part of our family."

Cara stopped beside her, eyes averted.

Emily dropped her arms. "Please?"

Howard looked away as if searching for a way out of this situation. Stepping back, he pointed a finger at a small scar on his forehead and spoke to Cara. "Remember when you hit me right here with a rock?"

Cara nodded and smiled at the memory. "One of the few times I won a fight after you got bigger than I was."

"Well, I think you've done it again, with Dad's help this time. I have to say, this hearing has changed my mind about the will. The testimony I've heard convinces me that it was all about him—not you, not me, not Emily. It wasn't what Mother would have done. It sounds like he was obsessed with the idea of keeping his name alive; of having the Los Lobos named in history books as an example of how agriculture helped to create this state. He was savvy enough to know that wouldn't happen if he allowed it to be divided at his death. History covers a long period. He had to keep the ranch intact, and you were his key to accomplishing that. This lawsuit is not about money, Cara. It's something bigger.

It's about why Dad would choose his public image over being fair to his children, and I have to agree that you had nothing to do with his decision. We could argue about it forever, but frankly, I'm ready to give up." He held one hand flat in front of him, waiting for her to slap it, the way they had ended their fights as children. "Whoever wins, wins, and we'll bury the hatchet."

Cara slapped his hand, flipped hers over, and he matched the whack, closing his hand over hers. Without changing expressions, he held out his hand to Clay. "Congratulations. I understand you're joining the family." Without waiting for a reply, he turned and found Wendy standing alone. They walked out of the building, trailing their attorneys.

Cara stood, disbelieving what she'd heard. Howard's analysis of their father's state of mind shocked her. She had never heard him speak of securing a place in history through the ownership of the ranch. It was true the Los Lobos began as a grant from the State of Texas and was a part of settlement history in New Mexico, but had her father set out on an ambitious path to gain a place in history? She doubted it.

Clay stood by, wondering who had told Howard of the marriage plans. Trace came from the arbitration room and, seeing him alone, shook his hand. He congratulated her and nodded toward Cara and Emily.

"Howard declared a family truce—no matter who wins."

Trace's mouth fell open. "You've got to be kidding. That's not how these cases usually end. I've seen families continue the fight as long as they lived."

"Well, it seems Howard has decided to blame his father instead of Cara for what happened."

The lawyer nodded. "He's right, of course."

On October 21, Trace called with the good news that the judge had ruled her father was competent to write his will, and declared it valid. The ranch was Cara's.

"It's over," Cara called to Clay. "Can you believe it? I guess my only duty now is to see that the ranch survives as long as I do—and to have some children worthy of inheriting it when I die."

29

Big Events

The weather gods smiled down on Clay's backyard as the wedding party walked to the gazebo. A retired judge, who had been a long-time friend of Dave Morgan, stood ready to greet them. Ashley scattered rose petals along the path, stopping only once to pick up a bird's egg that had fallen from the towering trees. After the wedding party paused to admire her find, she continued to the steps of the gazebo, where Jason waited to stand by his father as best man. Tony, solemn but proud, escorted Cara to the gazebo, and Emily followed as maid of honor, beautiful in a pale blue dress that matched her eyes.

Clay's parents from Florida, plus his scattered sister's and brother's families, were all present for the weekend celebration.

Cara held tightly to Clay's arm as the judge informed the guests that God gave his blessing on this ceremony that bound the couple together as husband and wife. While the bride and groom kissed, Jason hurried to inspect the basket, empty now of rose petals but still harboring the bird's egg. Ashley refused to let him carry the treasure, and he pretended he didn't care.

Following the ceremony, Jason and Ashley begged to stay with their cousins overnight before returning to their mother's home, while their father "honeymooned," whatever that was.

"Two weeks of heaven" is the way the bride and groom described it when they arrived home from a trip through Spain and France.

Lupe and Tony waited on the back porch steps to welcome everybody home.

"I smell cookies," Jason said to Lupe as he submitted to a hug.

"Put your things in your room and come back for cookies," Lupe told him.

"Can't I have one now?" Ashley asked.

"Nope," Clay said. "Good try, though, girl. Put your stuff away."

"Did you have any problems while we were gone?" Cara asked Tony.

"Nope. Not a one," Tony said. "Well, that dumb mustang fell through a cattle guard, but we hauled him out with only scratches."

"No broken legs?"

"No. Lucky he fell on his knees. He was sore for a week or so, but he's healing okay."

"How was the soybean crop?" Clay asked.

"Good. Sent 'em to market last week, before it was flooded." Tony turned to Cara. "You'll make a killing on that crop."

She smiled and laid her hand over Tony's fist lying on the table. "Thank you, Tony. Next to my husband, I love you most."

Tony blushed, looking at his wife.

"Huh," Lupe said to Cara. "You'll give him a big head."

"I love you too, Lupe," she said. "You two are the grandma and grandpa in this family now."

Tony stood. "I'm going to the barn. After you kids put your things away, come on out and help me catch some kittens. Ramón is taking them to town to share with the church members." He looked at Lupe. "Can you find me a box big enough for six?"

When they left, Cara took Clay's hand. "Why don't we go empty suitcases while the kids are occupied?"

He followed her to the bedroom, guessing it wasn't unpacking on her mind. She sat on the bed, a mysterious smile on her face. "Clay, do you remember saying you thought I'd make a good mother?"

"I do, and you will. Why ask?"

"Do you think it's too soon?" Cara pulled him to sit beside her.

"No way."

"Okay. Mission accomplished."

"You're kidding."

"No. Does that make you unhappy?"

"Me? Unhappy? You know better. The question is how do you feel?"

"I'm surprised and excited. It's a good thing we got married right away. People will be counting on their fingers."

"Who cares? This is a wonderful way to start our life together."

"Wait until I tell Emily!"

"Hey, nobody could be more thrilled than I am." He wrapped her in his arms and they stretched out on the bed together.

"Don't plan anything out of town for the middle of July," Cara mumbled in his ear. "I should be dropping your offspring."

Clay shook his head. "Do you know how crass that sounds?" He rubbed her head with his knuckles, encouraging her to fight back.

"Crass? Why is it crass?" She elbowed him.

"You make it sound like you're a cow out in the pasture, just serviced by a stray bull." He stopped, embarrassed.

Cara stroked his cheek. "No. The guy who knocked me up is definitely purebred."

Clay pulled her head onto his shoulder. "Please listen to me. You and this baby are the most wonderful things that have happened to me since Ashley was born. Please don't take it so casually."

Cara nodded but rolled on top of him, covering his mouth with her lips.

He waited until she tired of her delaying tactic. "You're not listening."

"Honey, having babies is what females do. It's no big deal. If you'd grown up on a ranch, you'd know that."

"Thank you, Ms. Never-Done-It-Before. I'll repeat those words to you every morning when you start vomiting your head off."

"Vomiting?" She rose on her elbows, looking at him.

"I believe it's called morning sickness. Bette had it for three months with both babies."

"I guess I've heard of that, though I've never seen a pregnant cow vomit."

"My point exactly. You aren't a cow."

"You know, it's embarrassing to be married to a man who knows more about having babies than I do."

"I promise to check my credentials at the door as soon as you find an obstetrician. Okay?"

"Okay."

"Just one last thing. You should stop riding Buck until after the baby's born."

"I can't stop riding my horse, Clay."

"Of course you can."

"How am I supposed to get around the ranch?"

"You have me and Tony."

"But I've always ridden a horse."

Clay kissed her. "Well, at least agree that you won't ride until you get your doctor's approval."

There was a long silence.

"Clay, you remember when we got married?"

"Umm, vaguely." He raised an arm to counter her blow.

She rolled over beside him. "Well, I discovered this week that I've become a different person. I'm just half me now. The other half is you."

"No kidding?"

"Yes, and you just told me that with this baby, I'll now be divided into thirds. It's disconcerting. One part you, one part the baby, and one part me."

"Are you sorry?"

"No. But you may have to be patient with me. I'm trying to figure out which third is in charge each time I say something."

"I'm the most patient man in the world. And you're not the only one divided. I have five parts. You'll have to be patient with me too."

"It's an amazing phenomenon," she said. "We should go drink to our success."

"Sorry, honey. You shouldn't drink alcohol for the next nine months."

Cara rolled out of bed. "I'm going to call an obstetrician. I have the distinct feeling that modern science has overcome a lot of the restrictions you're saddling me with." Her voice trailed off as she headed for her office. "I'll bet they even let cows have alcohol."

She searched through the yellow pages to find obstetricians. She dialed and the telephone rang several times. The message said if it were an emergency, go to the hospital. Otherwise, call tomorrow for an appointment.

"That figures," she muttered. "By then I'll be having morning sickness."

And she did. Otherwise her pregnancy was uneventful. She finally gave up riding when it became uncomfortable—and risky when snow began falling on the golden aspen leaves that shivered in the woods; winter had arrived early in the mountains of northern New Mexico.

Cara was ready: Los Lobos cattle were herded to winter pastures before the vaqueros left in September. Checks were mailed to pay the taxes. The purebred bulls were herded into the barns, where year-round employees supervised the servicing of heifers and cows, both those that belonged to the ranch and others delivered from surrounding ranches for breeding. Cara suppressed a desire to call Lucille and chortle that she would not be selling her forty-acre bottomland.

Winter was a calmer time for both the ranch and construction work. The crops were harvested. Clay's business slowed to account for snow days and below-zero weather, when it was impossible to complete outside construction. Most often he stayed on the ranch, fussing over Cara and trying to keep her occupied around the ranch house. By May she was definitely restless and somewhat rebellious against Clay's attempts to keep her from the spring calving and planting regimens.

On May 30, she sat at the kitchen table watching Lupe and Ashley concoct a beef casserole for dinner. Lupe was in one of her quiet moods, half listening to Ashley, frowning as she looked toward the barns where an inch of spring snowflakes covered the ground. It was not unusual for New Mexico to get an unwelcome late-winter blast that froze the fruit tree blossoms. Lupe knew better than to plant her garden before the 30th.

The rich smell of braised meat and onions made Cara's mouth water. She was hungry all the time—feeding three, she told Clay, after they discovered she carried twins. Today she felt especially good. She ran her hand over her stomach. Almost eight months, she thought, and the babies are kicking and elbowing, fighting for territory. Outside, the snow storm whirled past the windows, piling ridges along the garden fence rows. Cara was happy that Clay had stayed home from work. Winter driving was always risky, because blizzards came without warning in this country. While he was confident of his driving and made fun of her worries, her pregnancy had made him cautious. He often stayed home without her nagging.

Clouds hid the sun, but no moisture was falling when Clay agreed to take Jason along with Tony up the canyon trail above Junction Creek to look for a mother cow who had escaped from the drive back from winter pastures. She likely would be hiding with her yearling in the rabbitbrush along the waterway, not too far from the barns. Shortly after they left the barns, snow began falling.

Cara looked at the clock. The trio should have been home. She closed her book, fiddling with the bookmark, moving it back and forth, trying not to worry. She laid it aside and listened to Ashley's chatter.

"I told mother you were teaching me to cook," she was saying to Lupe, "but she won't let me in the kitchen. She thinks I make too much mess. Even if I promise to clean it up, she says no."

Cara smiled. Thanks to Lupe and Tony, the children had taken to the new family situation as if they had been born on the ranch. Tony took great pride in developing Jason's riding skills. The eight-year-old rode a quarter horse and roped young calves with promising skill. Ashley was happy to stand at Lupe's elbow, cooking, setting table, or handing her wet clothes from the basket to hang on the line when the sun shone. At night, she curled up in Cara's or Clay's arms while the family read aloud.

Cara glanced at the telephone, wondering if Clay's cell phone would pick up a signal in the canyon. She sighed, pushing herself back from the table. She tried to smother a tiny gasp when one of the babies kicked against her hand. She massaged the spot until it quieted.

Despite the multiple conception—a boy and a girl, the doctor said— Cara's pregnancy had been as she predicted, commonplace, nothing spectacular, normal in every way. She had spent the winter mostly inside the house, surrounded by loved ones, exercising routinely to a television program for pregnant women. Clay told her she was more beautiful than before her pregnancy, but what did he know? She felt like a bean pod carrying a watermelon in a middle pocket. However, the pregnancy had brought a special peace that she had not known before. Memories of her own happy family, when she and Howard were the ages of Jason and Ashley, drifted like snowflakes alighting on the bushes outside the window. The bad times faded, replaced by daily activities with her new family. She liked being married and was glad she had waited until she met Clay, who spoiled her, bringing a handful of flowers, pickles, ice cream, nail polish for the toenails she couldn't see, any trinket he saw.

She loved that Clay sat for hours touching her while he read, stopping to lay his head against her stomach, listening for the babies' heartbeats. When an elbow or foot moved beneath his hand, she pretended not to notice the tears in his eyes. This was the man she married, not a skirt chaser, as people had described him.

She stood at the window watching the stables. Through the thick snow, she saw Tony riding like mad toward the house. Good, they're back, she thought, but she frowned, biting her lower lip. Clay and Jason were not with him. They must be putting their horses in the stables. Why was he riding to the house?

He burst in the door and collapsed in a chair, his face brick red. Ice hung from his mustache.

"Call Mountain Rescue," he whispered hoarsely. "We got a disaster in the canyon. The phone won't work down there."

"What happened?" Cara asked as she hurried to the telephone and dialed 911.

"Buck slipped and fell." He shouted to Lupe, "Put soup in a thermos!" and ran to the coatrack on the back porch, where he collected wool coats and scarves.

Lupe put soup in the microwave oven, zapped it for a minute, and filled a thermos. She handed it to Tony and grabbed her own coat. "I'll go get Jason," she said.

"No," Tony ordered. "Call Larry and have him round up as many men as he can." He ran out the door.

Cara stood at the telephone in shock. "This is Cara Morgan," she said. "We need an ambulance quickly at the ranch. There's been an accident. Let me talk to the sheriff."

"All our ambulances are out on call right now, ma'am," the lady said. "Hold on. You're on County Road 84, aren't you? Maybe I can divert the guys from a wreck we have out there. And we can send the medics in the fire department. Hold on. I'll transfer you to the sheriff."

Cara's voice cracked and she hiccupped as she tried to make the sheriff understand the emergency. "Hurry. Hurry," she said and laid down the phone.

She turned to Lupe. "He said Buck fell. Who could have been riding Buck?" She pressed the telephone into Lupe's hand. "Here. Call the neighbors." She ran to the back porch and pulled on boots, her heavy woolen coat, and a cap. She lumbered out the door, with Lupe screaming for her to stop.

At the stable, she found Pepito sleeping in the hay. He jumped up, dazed, when she screamed, "Get the sidesaddle." She hurried to Gus's stall and led him to a bale of hay. Together they lifted the saddle and placed it over the blanket Pepito had thrown on the horse's back. "Hand me the first-aid kit," she ordered as she pulled herself into the saddle. She had not ridden for months.

The snow was not deep, but it was slick. Gus fought to keep his footing, and Cara leaned forward, her hands glued to the saddle horn, following Tony's trail that rose along the canyon wall, away from the river. A blanket of snow hid the scrub oak and rabbitbrush down to the river.

In front of her, Cara saw Tony's and Jason's horses standing beside the trail. She looked down the embankment, and the noise of the world went away. Buck was lying immobile on the ground. Tony was spreading a wool blanket over Jason, who sat bent over, cradling his father's head, sheltering him from the snow.

Cara urged Gus down the bank. Although he screamed in fear, his strong legs held steady as he slid to the bottom. He shied away from the blood on the fallen horse. Cara slid from his back into Tony's arms. "You shouldn't have come, child," Tony said. She pulled away and dropped beside Jason. Tony reached down and lifted the boy, allowing her to wrap her arms over Clay's body. Then he sat down on a fallen tree trunk, rocking the boy back and forth as he moaned.

That's how the sheriff and neighbors found them half an hour later—Cara curled beside her dead husband; Jason weeping in Tony's arms.

The rescuers pulled Cara away from Clay and placed his body on Gus's back. They led him beside the river to the meadow where the trail down the canyon began. Cara clung to the ropes tied to Gus's saddle, her head leaning on the horse's flank, as she held Clay's cold hand. This was the end of her world. She would die with him. There was no way she could go on alone.

She felt a baby kick, and she cried out in pain. Why was God doing this to her? As a child, she had begged to die after the burning accident, when even the doctors had said she could not live. But God had his own way, paying no attention to her suffering. Fate had given her Clay's love as a reward for living, but now fate had taken it away. This accident was more than she could bear. She didn't want to live through it. How could the children survive? They'd be scarred.

When they arrived at the edge of the canyon, Tony explained to the rescuers that Clay's horse had moved too close to the edge of the trail. One leg had slipped on the snow. Unable to recover his balance, the horse began sliding down the steep bank, rolling over and over, the saddle horn crushing his rider's chest. They rolled until the underbrush caught them. Clay lay with one leg under the screaming horse.

"Jason jumped off his horse, and we scooted down the embankment," Tony said. "I checked for a pulse, but I knew it was hopeless. I told the boy to get back on his horse and go home, but he wouldn't. I moved him out of the way and put the horse out of his pain. I told Jason we had to get help, but he wouldn't leave his dad."

Cara woke in the hospital, puzzled by the sight of Emily watering flowers on the sunlit window sill. The medicinal smell of the room made her dizzy, and she closed her eyes only to see vivid pictures of Clay pinned beneath Buck and to feel the chill of the winter snow freezing her body. Gasping for breath, she felt herself suffocating, unable to cry out. Emily rushed to her side, calling for Howard, who sat outside the door with Lupe and Tony. Cara heard Howard's voice telling the nurses what to do, just before she fainted.

When she woke, the room was shaded in an evening glimmer. She closed her eyes again and moved her hand over her stomach. Tears began rolling down her cheeks. The babies were gone. She hadn't allowed herself to think of the danger she was creating for the babies when she followed Tony to the canyon. Her presence had not saved Clay, and her plea to die with him had been denied. God had taken the babies instead.

"Are you awake?" She recognized Emily's voice and lifted her arms, clinging to her sister for support. They rocked, locked in each other's arms, until she heard Howard calling for warm soup. She struggled to sit up.

"Howard! Where are my babies?"

"The babies are fine." He folded her into his arms. "They're in incubators, but both are doing well. You'll be able to take them home in a few days. You should eat a little something while we're waiting for the doctor. You've been a very brave girl." His voice broke, and she found herself consoling him.

"How did you get here?" she whispered.

"I flew."

"In the snow?"

"We didn't get snow in Denver. It didn't last long here. Emily called me—and I almost beat her here." He was smiling and Cara's tears began again.

"Thank you for coming."

"I feel like a heel, Cara. I hope you'll forgive me for . . ."

"You know I do. We've both been acting like kids. I'm so happy to see you."

"Is Jason all right?" she asked Emily

Emily nodded. "He's with his mother."

"The babies?"

"They're both fine," Howard repeated and added, "We were afraid we were losing all of you. By the time you arrived at the hospital, you were having contractions. Because you were in shock, the doctor recommended a caesarian." Howard smiled. "I was here in time to assist him. The doctor tells us you'll recover better with the babies around you. We'll get all of you home as soon as we can. If you're up to it, we can wheel you down to the nursery now to see them."

"Let's go."

Peering through the window, Cara leaned over, shaking her head in wonder. A fat baby face, with a replica of Clay's nose and mouth, screwed up and smacked its lips. Cara closed her eyes, a little dizzy, feeling new pain for the loss of her breasts. Clay had loved her despite her body. Perhaps the children would also.

"This is the girl," another nurse said, and Cara was struck by the beautiful dark hair that reminded her of her mother's Mexican heritage. The boy's blond hair promised to mimic his father's, even with a budding cowlick.

Cara squeezed Emily's hand in an effort to feel grounded. The room seemed to disappear as she struggled to place herself in this new world. She was a mother of beautiful twins who had no father, somewhat like her father had been when he was left with three children to rear after her mother died. He did a good job, she thought. I will too.

Clay's body was cremated, and a week later a memorial service was held in a large church in town so that his friends and employees could attend. Afterward, at the ranch, his ashes lay in a rosewood container on a pedestal near the fireplace, beneath the paintings of him, standing beside Gus, and of Cara with Buck.

His ashes were taken to the aspen grove where he and Cara had gone fishing the day the bear attacked. He became a part of the rich loam beside the lake, beneath the pine needles and the aspen leaves. The site became Cara's favorite place for reading on lazy Sunday afternoons.

Epilogue

Three years after Clay's death, on a bright Sunday morning, Cara sat on the portal having breakfast with Clay Jr., Michelle, Rosita, and Solana, a teenager hired from the migrant camp to assist Lupe with the children. Rosita had become a part of the family when the court accepted Cara's sworn commitment to reunite her with María, as soon as she could be found.

Clay Jr., who sported his father's mischievous blue eyes and untamable cowlick, had also inherited his father's work and sleep habits. Lupe and Solana were on constant alert to keep up with his exploits. In contrast, Michelle reminded Cara of Emily. She was always singing or humming and spent a great deal of quiet time with crayons, puzzles, and books. Cara could not imagine that she would ever throw a rock at her brother—and she probably would not grow up with the rebel spirit that led Cara back into the saddle shortly after the children were born. She'd worked long hours with Tony to get through the seasons of planting and harvesting each year, while dealing with a stricter enforcement of laws related to hiring migrant workers.

Absently listening to the chatter of her children, she recalled the Sunday that she and Clay had gone on their first fishing trip and how it had been interrupted with gun shots, dead bears—and her father's death; things she'd rather forget. Too bad her father had not lived to enjoy his beautiful grandchildren.

Happier thoughts reminded her that her stolen cattle had been returned, allowing her to pay her taxes without selling the rich bottomland near the river. She was pleased to learn the INS had arrested Rafael Cruz for his part in delivering migrants to stash houses in New Mexico and Colorado, based upon Ramón's investigation, and that the Mafia connection near Chama had been broken before it became established. Cara no longer wondered about who informed the Mafia of the unguarded fences. Life was too short and unpredictable to spend time worrying about problems with no solution. Pablo had hightailed it to Texas, leaving his murky connection between Lucille and the *coyote* Rafael unresolved. María joined him there, leaving Rosita behind to continue her physical therapy. Cara fought with the court over whether it was in the child's best interest to be adopted into an Anglo family instead of staying in foster care with the Hispanic family that had kept her for two years. She won the argument after convincing the court that she would be better able to re-unite the child with her mother sometime in the future. As she watched the children playing together, she shuddered at the thought that María had not been found, nor had Pablo returned to the area.

These thoughts brought back bittersweet memories of Ramón. Today on the front page of the local paper, she had seen his picture: matured, appearing wiser, even more handsome. The article said that he would be entering the race for Congress from this district, hoping to replace the retiring Senator Rodriguez, for whom he worked. Cara wondered if he had married and was rearing a family similar to hers. She was delighted that his career dreams were coming true. She should write letters to her dad's friends on his behalf. Wouldn't he be surprised to hear that his dream of a school for the migrants had become a reality? Luckily, one of the vaqueros Tony hired was married to a teacher, and with Cara's approval, she had established classes to teach both the adults and children the English language. Cara did take credit for adding health insurance benefits to the workers' pay. While reviewing in her mind the accomplishments she had made since inheriting the ranch, she wondered whether her father was rolling over in his grave or whether he might be saying, "Go, girl!"

"Let's go," Clay Jr. said as he jumped up from the table and rushed to the sand pile that Tony had made for the children beneath the large cottonwood tree in the front yard. Michelle followed him, and Solana took the newspaper and seated herself near them in the sunshine, to work on an unneeded tan.

Cara was left alone on the portal, which resonated with memories both painful and comforting. She still could see and hear her father and Frank laughing when one of them topped the other in a domino game. She smiled at memories of Clay sitting here in his sexy pajamas on moonlit nights, turning her on before she was ready. Her heart ached when she thought of the time she'd wasted worrying about her scars. She suddenly needed to be near him.

"Solana," she called, "I'm going riding. I'll be back by the time the children get up from their naps."

At the corral, she put her arms around her mare's neck. After the accident, Buck had been buried in the pasture behind the barns, and a feisty mare named Trixie had taken his place in the stable. The mare moved around Cara toward the stable, eager to receive her saddle. Inside, she snorted and pushed her way toward the ladder leading to the loft. There, Ramón was seated, holding Mouser. Trixie nudged his shoulder, expecting a treat.

Cara felt dizzy, lost. So many things had happened since the time she'd come into the stable and chided Ramón for feeding apples to Buck. She was a different person. Buck was dead. Yet the circumstances seemed the same.

Ramón nodded a greeting and reached into his pocket for the horse's treat, cautious of Cara's reaction.

She frowned. "What are you doing here?"

"I thought it was time I confessed to you, Cara. Without your approval, I've been using Tony's address as my political home base. I've checked in occasionally, just to make it official."

Cara shrugged. "I have no objection to that. I did notice in the paper today that you're running for office from this district." She ran the plastic curry comb over Trixie's back, taking her time. She threw on the saddle blanket. "I'm glad for you. I hope you win."

"Thank you." He moved over and picked up her saddle, settling it over the blanket. Cara smiled, remembering the times he'd chided her for doing the heavy lifting. She was more careful these days. Her muscles weren't as strong as they had been before the children's birth, but Pepito had grown a full six inches and took pride in swinging the heavy saddle onto her horse. She tightened the cinch.

"Has Gus been exercised?" Ramón asked.

She couldn't respond, smothered by memories of the times Tony had ordered Ramón to ride beside her when she mounted the gelding. After her marriage, she had given the horse to Clay, making all the men happy. She wondered to this day why Clay had not been riding the bigger, stronger horse on the day he died. Gus might not have slipped on the icy slope.

"I should work to pay for my use of your address," Ramón explained. "If I can be of assistance."

"Ride him if you wish. I gave Gus to Clay when we married, and then to Tony. But he prefers the slower mares. He won't admit that he's getting old, but I notice he's turned Gus's care over to Pepito."

Ramón went to the stable door and whistled. Gus came running and slipped his head into the bridle.

"You do have a way with horses."

"I must confess that I have come here many times, when the congressional offices were closed. Gus and I have become friends."

Cara shook her head, puzzled, as she led Trixie out of the stable. "I know I haven't been as active in the pastures as I was before the children were born, but I'm surprised you could hide your visits from me." She watched as he saddled the gelding. "Or that you would come without greeting me."

"It was intentional, for sure. My presence didn't seem appropriate under the circumstances."

Cara blinked to avoid tears. "And why are you making yourself known today?"

They led the horses out of the corral. Ignoring her question, Ramón shut the gate while she mounted the mare. As she settled into the saddle, he swung up to Gus's back.

"Where to?" he asked.

Cara had intended to go up to the lake, where Clay's ashes were buried, riding past the migrant camp, not up the canyon where he died. But she couldn't go there with Ramón.

"To the waterfall."

The horses took their heads and raced, Gus stretching to a lead until Ramón pulled him in, allowing Trixie to feel good about passing her friend. At the creek, the horses stomped into the water, drinking in long gulps.

Cara pulled Trixie's reins and headed toward the waterfall. Ramón smiled. Marriage and motherhood had not diminished the lady's courage.

Seated on rocks around the pool, they fell into separate reveries. Cara pulled her light jacket closer, turning up the collar to cover her ears. The air was colder coming off the water, away from the sun.

Ramón stood and skipped small, flat rocks over the pool. A young man's game, intended to impress a woman. As the rocks flew over the water, she remembered her swing on the rope and her plunge into the water the night she and Clay consummated their love. The pain was unbearable. Would she never forget the good times they'd had together? She blinked away tears.

"You asked why I'm here," Ramón said, without looking her way. Cara nodded, happy to have her memories scattered.

"Tony has not wanted to complain, but he is going on eighty. He has arthritis. Riding and handling the cattle are very painful for him. He has to cut back on his riding duties."

Cara was astounded. Of course she knew of Tony's arthritis. But he never complained to her, and she avoided thinking of how she would make the changes his retirement would require. She nodded.

Ramón stopped throwing rocks and put his thumbs in his hip pockets, the way Clay used to stand. He faced her, frowning, almost belligerent. "He has suggested that I take over as manager."

"Of the ranch?"

"As manager of the ranch."

"Well, I . . . I suppose that would work. If that's what he wants."

"It is. You can be sure that I have put the past behind me. I have been very careful not to bother you even once. With this job, my duty would be to keep you, your family, and the ranch safe. I can do that. I believe Clay would have trusted me."

"But what about your career?"

"Many Western politicians live on ranches. The work sessions mesh nicely." Cara sighed, thinking there must be reasons it wouldn't work.

"I suppose Tony could guide you."

Ramón smiled. "Of course. He will remain head honcho as long as he lives."

Cara held her breath. His smile sent a rush of memories flooding through her mind, noisy like the waterfall, shaking the earth.

She cleared her throat. "We'll need to talk salary and housing. Sleeping on a couch at Tony's isn't appropriate for a manager."

"That's true. And you wouldn't want a tired, worn-out manager." His eyes were soft, teasing her.

Cara smiled for the first time. "Ramón, you haven't changed a bit. Why don't you move into the servants' quarters across the road from the ranch house? They've been empty for a long time. It would be comforting to have someone living there." She lost her train of thought. "I mean, you will be close enough I can call if I need you." Her voice became strong, managerial.

"We can hang the cow bell on the back porch."

Cara's eyes widened, and they each laughed at the memory of Lupe's solution to his need for a nighttime alarm. "Do so at your own risk, my friend. Please check the quarters, and let Lupe know if you need anything."

"Yes, ma'am."

"When can you start?"

"¿Mañana?"

Cara stood and held out her hand, pleased that the manager's position had been filled. "It's a deal. This solves a lot of my problems. Thank you so much."

Ramón lifted her hand to his lips. "Thank you, ma'am."

She pulled her hand away. "Come by the office, and we'll work out the details."

She sat on the rock overlooking the waterfall and pool, ignoring him. This was the most beautiful spot on the ranch. It was where she had learned to love herself and to love Clay. It was also where she had faced her greatest challenge in managing the migrant workers and where, in the long run, she had succeeded in preserving the family estate. Her father's dream had stayed intact, and with Ramón's help, the future of the ranch would be secure.

A breeze rustled the shining yellow aspen leaves above them, and the weight of Clay's death seemed to slip off her shoulders. It was a relief to share the heavy work of managing the ranch with capable hands.

She smiled. "One last thing, Ramón. Tony calls me Cara."

The End

Acknowledgements

Books are never published full-blown from the author's imagination. They hatch there, develop wings, and fly from the nest to visit talented friends and editors who read, critique, encourage and share the excitement of publication. I am indebted to the following—and many more—for having shared their time and talents in the making of *Rebel on Horseback*:

Dorothy Smoker, long time resident in New Mexico's northern ranch country and current docent at the New Mexico History Museum in Santa Fe. She guided me through this historical era and introduced me to local ranchers who shared their fascinating history. We traveled around the famous Mundy ranch near Chama and to the Hibner ranch in Cibolla. She shared the fascinating memoir of Violet Dawson Hager, Cibolla Canyon Memories.

The Reverend and Ms. Charlie Hibner, whose ranch in Cibolla is part of the former Hawkins land grant, shared a tour, sight of their prized Highland cattle, stories from the past, and a lovely lunch. Mr. and Mrs. Phillip Stermer guided us through the historic home on the ranch where they live.

Sylvia and Roy Rhodes shared stories from northern New Mexico's history, of which they were an important part.

Melanie and Marshall Faithful guided me over the famous Bell Ranch, south of Las Vegas, New Mexico, almost to Tucumcari.

LaVonne and Al Heaton of the Lone Pine Ranch near Dove Creek, Colorado, introduced me to the thrill of driving cattle many miles to the winter range up a steep, narrow trail above the Doris River.

Critique members and readers Kate Curry, Donah Grassman, Valerie Stasik, Bethany Baxter, Reverie Escobedo, Joyce Townsend, Bob Keeton, Jan Marquart, Sandi Wright, and Dorothy Smoker.

Editor and book designers Mary and Andrew Neighbour of www.MediaNeighbours.com.

About the Author

Maxine Neely Davenport's writing evokes the toughness and passion of Westerners born in the post-Steinbeck era and portrays the struggles today's ranchers have with such problems as illegal migrant employees and cattle rustlers. Davenport grew up riding horses in Oklahoma's Hereford Heaven territory. In college, she won national awards as editor of the East Central Journal. At Colorado State University she received a master's degree in literature, followed by  a law degree from Oklahoma University. Following a career in law, she began writing fiction, including a number of prize-winning short stories. This is Davenport's third published novel; a fourth, *Sierra's Passions*, is planned for 2015. Now living in Santa Fe, she keeps in touch with mountain climbing friends who shared her hikes up twenty-six of Colorado's fourteeners. Davenport is the mother of three children, seven grandchildren, and two great-grandchildren.

Please visit www.davenportstories.com to learn more about her and her books.

Book Club Questions and Topics for Discussion

1. Do you empathize with Cara Morgan's feelings about her body? How might you have reacted—as a child, teenager, and adult—to such scarring?

2. Do you believe that Dave Morgan, Cara's father, acted fairly in leaving the ranch to Cara in order to preserve the family heritage? Was there a better way to reach that goal?

3. If you had been left out of your parent's will, would you have reacted more like Emily or like Howard?

4. How do you feel about Clay? He and Cara had several important differences, including age, sexual experience, and marital status. How might you have reacted in a relationship to these differences?

5. How do you feel about Ramón? Did you doubt his motivations? Are you conflicted about the staged rape scene by the river? Could you have forgiven Ramón?

6. Compare Cara's reactions to Clay's and Ramón's declarations of love. Which, if either, would you have responded to?

7. Do you think Cara might have chosen Ramón if her mother had not been shunned socially by the community for being Mexican? Do you personally know of prejudicial incidents in our neighborhoods today? In our schools?

8. Cara's rebel nature was challenged a number of times: assuming management control over the ranch after her father's death; firing undocumented migrant workers who might be connected to the Mafia stash houses; paying burdensome estate taxes; confronting cattle rustlers; convincing the court that her father was mentally competent when he made his will; learning to love herself despite her bodily disfigurement; allowing herself to accept the love of men. Are you satisfied with the manner in which she addressed these problems? How would you have acted differently?

9. Does the migrant problem depicted in the novel conform to your knowledge of migrant workers in the early 2000s? Did you learn something new? How have these problems changed? Does Cara solve them to your satisfaction? To Howard's?

10. Does María's effort to become pregnant seem understandable? Sympathetic? Would you have left your child in America if you were in danger of being deported to Juárez?

11. Do you feel affectionately toward Tony and Lupe? Why or why not?

12. How do you feel about the attitudes of Sheriff Matt Placer regarding immigrants? Regarding women? How have attitudes in law enforcement changed or not changed?

13. What is your feeling about the snow storm and its consequences?

14. Does the ending leave you satisfied emotionally? Why or why not?

15. Would you say this novel's ending upheld Cara's strong personality throughout? Did her rebel spirit change throughout the story?

Praise

Davenport's *Rebel on Horseback* sets the reader firmly in northern New Mexico's beautiful ranching country, where the characters and the plot develop. The lifestyles, attitudes, troubles, and triumphs of ranch work are all captured with real-life events and driven by an intriguing love triangle. This book grabs your emotions on page one and doesn't let go, even when the last page is turned.

~Dorothy Smoker, researcher of New Mexico history
and ranch life, NMHM docent

Davenport creates a strong woman of substance in Cara Morgan and masterfully weaves her personal struggles with the struggles of the papered and illegal immigrants who work the ranches and farms of New Mexico.

~Val Stasik, author of *Incidental Daughter*

I found *Rebel on Horseback* to be an absorbing story of characters involved in New Mexico's ranching history. Their situations, including immigrant employment, are compelling, important, and relevant. I loved it—a 5-stars read.

~Bob Keeton, host of the *Living Successfully* national
radio talk show

Rebel on Horseback is a compelling story about the life of Cara Morgan, her beloved ranch, commitment to migrant workers, and the man who finally, unsuspectingly, steals her heart. Woven with drama, romance, heartbreak, and recovery, *Rebel on Horseback* is a fabulous read.

~Jan Marquart, CEO and Founder of About the Author
Network, author of *Kate's Way* and eleven other books

An intricate plot, rebellious heroine, and vivid New Mexico settings are the hallmarks of Davenport's latest page-turner.

~Donah Grassman, literary researcher and writer of
fiction and nonfiction

Rebel on Horseback enlightens, inspires, and educates us about the fears, feelings, and frustrations of immigrants. This is a timely and compassionate depiction of the trauma and risks these individuals take to have a better life—and gives us all a view of how we can live together.

~Sandi Wright, therapist, artist, and author of the
children's book *Santa Fe Sam*

47556628R00162

Made in the USA
Middletown, DE
29 August 2017